SWEET
PAYBACK

Connie Shelton

D1738416

Books by Connie Shelton

THE CHARLIE PARKER SERIES

THE SAMANTHA SWEET SERIES

SWEET

PAYBACK

The Eighth Samantha Sweet Mystery

Connie Shelton

Secret Staircase Books

Sweet Payback
Published by Secret Staircase Books, an imprint of
Columbine Publishing Group
PO Box 416, Angel Fire, NM 87710

Copyright © 2014 Connie Shelton
All rights reserved. No part of this book may be reproduced or
transmitted in any form or by any means, electronic or mechanical,
including photocopying, recording, or by an information storage and
retrieval system without permission in writing from the publisher.

Printed and bound in the United States of America
ISBN 1495953939
ISBN-13 978-1495953934

This book is a work of fiction. Names, characters, places and
incidents are either the product of the author's imagination or are
used fictitiously. Any resemblance to actual events or locales or
persons, living or dead, is entirely coincidental. Although the author
and publisher have made every effort to ensure the accuracy and
completeness of information contained in this book we assume
no responsibility for errors, inaccuracies, omissions, or any
inconsistency herein. Any slights of people, places or organizations
are unintentional.

Book layout and design by Secret Staircase Books
Cover illustration © Suto Norbert

First trade paperback edition: February, 2014

As always, my undying gratitude goes to those who have helped make my books and both of my series a reality: Dan Shelton, my partner in all adventures, who is always there for me, working to keep the place running efficiently while I am locked away at my keyboard. My fantastic editing team—Susan Slater, Shirley Shaw, and proofreader Kim Clark—each of you has suggested things that help me see something new in my writing. My daughter, Stephanie, you are a huge inspiration to me and I think we will do great things together. And especially to you, my readers—I cherish our connection through these stories.

Thank you, everyone!

Chapter 1

A bright pink bunny stared upward at Samantha Sweet with blank white eyes. She picked up her pastry bag of dark chocolate frosting and added pupils, giving the last of the two dozen Easter cupcakes its own little perky personality. A tray of the fluffy cottontails, in shades of pastel yellow, lavender, pink and green waited on Sam's worktable to be sold away to homes all over Taos county and devoured by sugar-hyped children. She picked up the tray and carried it to the showroom of Sweet's Sweets.

"Those are adorable!" exclaimed her slender assistant, Jennifer Baca, who turned from the cash register and slid open the glass door on their vintage display case. She made space between the half-empty tray of Sam's secret-recipe amaretto cheesecake and another of spring-chick cookies which the shop's decorator, Becky Harper, had finished only minutes before.

"Three days to go," Sam said. "I hate to say this, but I'm glad we don't have another complicated holiday for awhile."

Jen sent Sam a sideways glance. "I think you said the same thing after Christmas and again at Valentine's Day. But when each new season comes along you're right in there, coming up with fantastic new pastries." She gave her boss a wink. "You love this."

Sam had to admit it—she did love her work. Opening her own pastry shop had been a lifelong dream and eighteen months into the venture she was still thrilled with the results. Her location, just two blocks off the famed Taos Plaza, was ideal for attracting tourists as well as locals. The winter ski season had been good and the crowd of spring-breakers exceptional this year. Traditionally, the northern New Mexico ski areas closed right after Easter weekend and the locals took their own vacations, getting away from the bipolar moods of the weather, seeking out warmer climes along the Gulf Coast or Mexico. But this year the spring temperatures had risen earlier than normal; skiing was finished by the end of March and now in early April everyone was ready to toss aside heavy coats, break out pastel cottons and enjoy some time outdoors. Apparently the cakes, cookies and chocolates from Sweet's Sweets were to play a big part in the upcoming weekend festivities—Sam and crew couldn't seem to bake and decorate fast enough.

"I took two more orders for the Easter Basket cakes," Jen said, handing the forms over to Sam as soon as she had set down the cupcake tray.

"Woo. Maybe I'd better make up a few extras. I have a feeling people will be popping in for them right up to the last minute on Saturday."

"Think you created a monster?" Jen asked with a chuckle, pointing to the complicated display model in the front window.

Sam had come up with the idea of sculpting a large layer cake into the shape of a basket, frosting it a golden tan and piping it with a basket-weave pattern. She'd filled it with hand-crafted chocolates, decorated Easter egg petit fours, an assortment of their pastel cookies and cupcakes, and topped it with a handmade chocolate bunny. Crowning the whole thing was a curved handle formed of white modeling chocolate and tied with a huge fondant bow. The entire confection was edible and from the moment she'd placed one in the window display, the orders had come non-stop.

After attempting to bake, decorate and assemble each one herself Sam realized she had to streamline the process. Her head baker, Julio, could crank out cake layers, cookies and cupcakes by the dozens but Sam and her assistant decorator, Becky, were running ragged to keep up. They'd finally gotten a little ahead of the rush last week by devoting one entire day to making chocolates and cookies so they would have a supply on hand. But the cakes could only be done a day or two before delivery, so there was still a push to turn out a dozen or more each day—in addition to their normal flow of birthdays and weddings and other special occasions. Sam had shifted the kitchen duties a little, enlisting Julio's help in a few aspects of the decorating and bringing in a part-timer just to keep the dishwashing under control and provide that necessary extra pair of hands when there were heavy cakes to be moved around and delivered.

She surveyed the display case from the front, satisfied that there was enough stock to get them through the morning. Grabbing a cup of coffee and the order forms from Jen, she headed back to the kitchen.

"Sam, can you take a look at this?" Becky called out. "I don't think I'm getting the spray right."

On the worktable in front of her sat a small two-tier cake—a six-inch layer topped by a very small four-inch one—covered in smooth white fondant. A trail of tiny pink rosebuds cascaded down the side and Becky had done a nice job of arranging them so they appeared to pool at the base of the cake into an almost-liquid puddle of flowers.

"I wanted it to be similar to the one you made for yours and Beau's six-month anniversary. That's the occasion for this couple too. But that little spray of flowers you did on top of yours . . . I'm just not getting it."

Sam smiled and reached for a package of thin, nearly-invisible floral wire. A celebration for six months of marriage had seemed a little silly, but she'd wanted to mark the occasion with something nice. The girls in the shop had thought it the most romantic gesture ever and had begun selling their customers on the idea of having their own done.

"All you do," she told Becky, "is clip the wire to the length you want. Not too long or it will overwhelm the design. Then take your little bits of pink fondant, like so. Give a twist. Attach the petal to the wire . . ." She pinched the malleable sugar dough into petal shapes and stuck them to the thin wire. "When it's fairly full of petals, just bend it into the littlest bit of an arc. And don't put too many on the cake. Half a dozen should be plenty for the size of this piece."

Becky quickly mastered the technique and within a few minutes carried the finished cake to their big, walk-in fridge for storage until the customer came to pick it up. Sam told Julio about the extra layers they would need for the Easter Basket cakes and was pleased when he immediately began loading the ingredients for the batter into the big Hobart mixer. The tattooed biker had startled her a bit when he first applied for the job, but his expertise in a commercial kitchen quickly became evident and now she wasn't sure what she would do without him. He didn't much engage in the friendly chit-chat with the women, just quietly and efficiently did his work.

Sam surveyed the room. Her desk looked, for once, fairly organized. She picked up the stack of order sheets and was in the process of checking them against the contents of the fridge when the back door opened.

"Hey, Mom. Hi, everybody." Kelly walked in and dipped a finger into a smear of chocolate frosting that hadn't yet been wiped off the stainless steel worktable, popping it into her mouth. "Ooh, yum." She went back for a second swipe at it.

"What's up?" Sam was getting better about not jumping to conclusions, but since Kelly often showed up with an unsolved crisis she'd learned not to assume it was just a friendly visit.

"Oh, not much. Things are slow next door, so I thought I'd leave a little early and get a head start on dinner at home. *And*, I'm inviting you and Beau if you're not doing anything else."

"You want to cook for us? Wow—I'm impressed."

"It's kind of an experiment. I found a recipe in a magazine for this way to do pork tenderloin with a maple glaze and some kind of pecan crust. It looked so good in the picture . . ."

"Let me make sure Beau isn't going to be tied up." Sam picked up her phone and hit the number for her husband.

As sheriff of Taos County, Beau never knew what each day would bring and that always left Sam unsure what their dinner plans might be. More often than not, she either picked up something ready-made at the store or they ate out. It was far from a healthy lifestyle and she had vowed more than once to be more diligent. Now, with the offer of a home-cooked meal, even one labeled 'experimental' by her thirty-five-year-old daughter, she hoped he would have the evening free.

"I will be out of here by six," Beau said, "and you can tell Kelly that I am looking forward to her meal."

Sam turned to Kelly. "He can make it, and I don't have any houses to break into this week, so we'll be there. Want me to bring dessert?"

"Whatever you made that has this on it," Kelly said with a smile and another swipe at the chocolate frosting. She left as quickly as she'd arrived, saying she had to brush out a cocker spaniel's new haircut and then she was leaving for home.

"At least it's convenient that she got the job at Puppy Chic," Becky said.

"Sometimes more than others," Sam answered, scanning the room to see where those chocolate Kahlua cupcakes had gone.

She caught the expression from her part-time holiday employee. Whenever someone learned that Sam also broke into houses for a living, there were always raised eyebrows. The fact that Sam was under contract to the Department of Agriculture to get inside abandoned houses, clean them up, and maintain the property until it could be sold usually answered most of those questions. She quickly ran through all that once again.

"At the moment, I'm blissfully free of that obligation,"

she said. "Foreclosures are down a bit, and that's good news for everyone."

She boxed up a half-dozen Kahlua cupcakes as she talked, then checked with Jen out front to see if everything was ready so they could close for the night. A half-hour later she pulled up beside her old house, the home she'd bought more than thirty years ago and left in Kelly's care when she married Beau and moved out to his ranch property on the north end of town. His department cruiser drove in beside her bakery van before she had reached the back door.

"Hey you," he said, pulling off his Stetson and bending toward Sam for a kiss.

She balanced the bakery box on one hand, enjoying the kiss and marveling that this movie-star-handsome man had fallen in love with her. Good looking, romantic, kind and considerate, even law-abiding. And, he respected her opinions, sharing details from some of his cases and asking her ideas on them—what more could she have wished for? Maybe all new brides felt that way, but Sam never wanted to forget just how lucky she was.

A sound at the back door, and Kelly was standing there with a teasing look in her eye. "Newlyweds. You know I can only let this behavior slide for another few months. By the one-year mark you'll have to start acting like old, married folks."

"Have to?" Sam asked.

Beau just laughed. He took the bakery box and handed it over to Kelly.

Inside, Sam noticed more changes. Kelly had obviously been thrift-store shopping and added a shelving unit in the living room for the stereo that used to be in her bedroom.

Sam felt some pangs about leaving this home and its convenience to the plaza and her shop. But Beau's log home, with acreage, dogs and horses, was so spacious and nice that she'd been happy to let Kelly take over the little two-bedroom adobe near the center of town. New placemats at the kitchen table, some kind of potpourri and the house was scented with a new ambiance. She sniffed the air. Potpourri wasn't the only enticing fragrance; her stomach growled a little as she realized how appetizing the dinner smelled.

"Come on in," Kelly said, setting the cupcakes on the countertop. "I'm just finishing the salad, veggies are going into the steamer right now, and the meat will be out—" An oven timer dinged. "Right about now."

Sam offered to help and Kelly steered her toward an unopened bottle of wine and three stemmed glasses.

"Beau, if you want to escape the kitchen, someone left a Santa Fe newspaper in the shop today and I brought it home. I think I left it beside the big easy chair in the living room."

"Haven't seen one of those in ages," he said. "I'll leave you ladies to it if you don't need any help in the kitchen."

Sam filled wine glasses and the meal went together quickly. When she stepped into the living room to tell Beau it was ready, she caught an exclamation from him.

"Look at this," he said. "The Taos Sheriff's Department got a mention."

"Really? What's up?"

He held up the lower half of the front page for her to see. The headline read, "Two Taos County Men Get Early Prison Release." She took the paper and was about four words into the story when Kelly peered around the corner.

"Hey, guys? Dinner?"

Sam sensed that Beau wanted to discuss the story further, but it would be rude to keep Kelly's meal waiting. She folded the page and carried it to the kitchen, laying it beside her backpack so she would remember to take it home. Kelly handed Sam the bowl of steamed vegetables and Beau the platter of sliced tenderloin.

"So, Mom, you said you were fresh out of caretaking jobs at the moment?" Kelly posed the question while she swabbed a piece of the meat in the accompanying maple glaze. Minutes into the meal, they had all pronounced the new recipe a keeper.

"Delbert Crow hasn't called in weeks, and I'm hoping it stays that way."

"Ever since our honeymoon, those duties seem to have tapered off," Beau said.

"Well, I had asked him to cut back on my workload, offer more cases to his other contractors. I just didn't think he would really do it." She speared a tender-crisp carrot. "I'm not complaining."

Kelly entertained them with a story of a terrier who, determined not to have a bath this morning, had hidden himself behind one of the dog crates at Puppy Chic and how she and the owner, Erika Davis-Jones, had nearly gone into a panic that he might have gotten outside somehow in the crazy traffic near the plaza.

"I finally came up with the idea of giving all the other dogs a liver snack. The minute he smelled those he showed up for his and we nabbed him. He had the most forlorn look on his face when he figured it out."

"Maybe we should get Nellie and Ranger in for baths," Sam suggested to Beau. The two ranch dogs mainly stayed outdoors, and she suspected they might be allowed inside more often if they didn't smell quite so much like a horse corral.

He nodded agreement, but she could tell his attention was split. Shortly after their coffee and cupcake dessert she suggested they better make an early evening of it. Since they had come in separate vehicles they didn't get the chance to talk until they got home. He headed immediately for the corral to check on the two horses, while Sam went inside.

By the time he came in she had settled in the living room and picked up the newspaper to read the short article about the two prisoners.

"I only vaguely remember that case," he said. "I was still pretty new with the department back then, which meant Orlando Padilla assigned me traffic duty and domestic disturbances more than anything else. But this one, it was the abduction and murder of a young woman and it turned into a pretty big deal. Angela Cayne was her name, age twenty, lived with her parents as I recall."

Sam nodded, sliding over to make space on the couch. The names in the news article seemed vaguely familiar to her, too, but other than the facts that Lee Rodarte and Jessie Starkey had now left the state penitentiary, their convictions overturned, the article was surprisingly slim on details, and Sam was too weary to turn on the late television news to learn more.

"Padilla handled it himself, I suppose?" The former sheriff had left the department more than a year ago in disgrace, but before that he'd been a real glory-hog, taking the high-profile cases if and when he might get his picture in the paper. With friends in high political places, he'd hoped one day to run for a state senate position and eventually governor. Despite his affair with a married woman and covering up crucial evidence in a murder, who knew—in this state he still might make a comeback.

"He did," Beau said. "Now, if there's trouble over this, I suppose it will fall right into my lap."

Chapter 2

Sam's alarm clock went off at the usual hour—four-thirty—and she suppressed a groan. This part of it never got easier, although she had, before the Easter rush, begun sleeping in an extra hour so she could awaken when Beau got up. However, today she had a half-dozen Easter Basket cakes to assemble and decorate, and their Good Friday sales would probably go through the roof.

She rubbed at her grainy eyes as she stumbled toward the large master bath. A quick, hot shower before slipping into her standard bakery attire of black slacks and her white baker's jacket. She opened the lid of her jewelry box, poking through the contents for her favorite earrings. As she fastened the wires on the gold hoops, she caught herself staring at the oddly carved wooden box on the vanity. They had a history together, she and this box which had been a gift from an old woman who many claimed was a *bruja*. The box certainly had some kind of power, scary at times, but Sam still didn't know if the old woman had really been a witch.

Occasionally, the thought nagged at her that perhaps she could locate someone who'd known old Bertha Martinez, someone who might know more of the box's history. But there'd been no time to investigate that angle and there was certainly no time to do it this week. She snapped the lid of the box closed, turned out the bathroom light and tiptoed through the room so Beau's extra bit of sleep wouldn't be interrupted.

Downstairs, she paused at the kitchen doorway. Cereal and fruit would certainly be healthier choices for breakfast, but with the amount of work facing her she decided one or two more days of grabbing a pastry and coffee at the shop wouldn't mean the end of the world. She picked up her parka and backpack from the coat rack near the front door and walked out into the frosty morning. The calendar might say it was spring, but that meant nothing in the mountains at 7,000 feet. Her van made a little vapor cloud in the chilly air as she let it warm up and within minutes she was on the nearly empty road toward Taos.

True to form, Julio was already there when Sam arrived, and the scent of blueberry muffins filled the kitchen. His skills in the kitchen continued to impress her. The baker worked quickly and efficiently; without having to be assigned a task he simply knew what needed to be done. While Sam had been away on her honeymoon she'd entrusted him with a key to the shop, knowing he would get there early and have most of the breakfast pastries ready by opening time. Since she'd been home again—other than the holiday seasons when the workload seemed to quadruple—she'd left that arrangement in place. She greeted him with a thanks for being so vital to the business, then she picked up the first of her order forms.

An hour later the worktable was filled with shapely wicker-look frosted cakes and Sam had pulled out the chocolates and petit fours to fill them in assembly-line fashion. Jen appeared at the curtain which divided the sales area from the kitchen, exclaiming over the basket cakes.

"Will there be room on the back counter for these when I get them done?" Sam asked. "I'm running out of space here."

"I'll make it happen," Jen assured her. "Do I have time to start the coffee first?"

Sam smiled up at her assistant. "Sure. In fact, when it's ready I would love it if my mug were to show up, filled."

"You got it." Jen disappeared and Sam could hear her humming as she readied the sales room for the first customers of the day.

Cakes came and went, her coffee turned cold. At one point Sam stepped out front to check how things were going and saw that all the bistro tables were occupied and customers stood two-deep at the counter. She watched Jen for a moment but the young woman seemed to have everything under control; not a hair of her dark chignon strayed out of place.

Sam looked over the beverage bar—all the coffees and teas were there in adequate supply, so she refilled her mug and disappeared back into the kitchen. The next thing she knew someone said it was five p.m. and she had to stretch her aching shoulders to believe the day had ticked away so quickly. She walked out into a glowing afternoon that really did feel like spring. Tossing her coat onto the passenger seat of her delivery van, she started toward home.

When she pulled into the long driveway she saw that Beau was out at the corral fence, holding buckets of oats for the two horses. The dogs raced toward Sam and she ruffled Nellie's fur and rubbed at Ranger's ears for a moment before walking over to join her husband.

"You got home early," she said.

"Poor darlin', you didn't." He set the buckets down and pulled her close. When he held her at arm's length a minute later, she caught him studying her face. "You've got a little—" he said, rubbing his thumb along her jawline.

She laughed. The day she came home *without* a smear of sugar or chocolate or some brightly colored frosting, now *that* would surprise her.

"One more day of this craziness . . . then we're closed on Sunday . . . and *then* I'm taking a couple days to catch up on things here at home." She hoisted the backpack she always carried as a purse up to her shoulder. "Although I'll feel guilty that the rest of the crew isn't getting extra time off."

"Give 'em a bonus and that'll help make up for it." He glanced toward the barn. "I took some chicken out of the freezer. Let me finish up out here and I'll help you with dinner."

Sam walked to the house, dumped her coat and pack, and headed upstairs to change out of her sugary clothes. In the kitchen she found two chicken breasts on the counter, put them into a teriyaki marinade, then pulled ingredients for a salad from the fridge. When she went to the dining table to lay out the place settings she saw a thick brown file, the kind the sheriff's department used for each case. On the cover was a white label with the name Angela Cayne typed in capital letters.

Beau walked in just as she'd peered inside, unable to resist snooping.

"That story from yesterday's newspaper," he said. "This is the murder file. There's more on it in today's paper—I brought home a copy but haven't read it yet."

"I thought the case was solved." She set out the knives and forks, dodging Nellie who had followed Beau in.

"Two men went to prison and now they're out. We got a call from the Corrections Department to be alert for trouble in Sembramos. It's where the crime happened. Thought I'd review the case and see if I can brush up on the circumstances."

Sam recognized the name of the little town in the northern part of the county, but she'd never actually gone up there. It was a community of farmers, as she recalled, many known for the quality of their organic produce although a lot of them grew more utilitarian crops, such as alfalfa and Timothy hay. She asked Beau to light the grill on the back deck while she went back to put the finishing touches on the salad.

"So, why would the release of these two men from prison cause trouble?" she asked when they sat down to their meal. "They did their time, right?"

"*Part* of their original sentences, and now that's been overturned." He speared a chunk of lettuce and it hung at the tip of his fork while he spoke. "It's a small town, everybody knows everybody. Victim's friends, suspects' friends . . . According to Withers, my only deputy who was there at the time, tempers ran pretty high during the trial."

Sam could certainly see how that could happen. "So,

half the people were happy with the guilty verdict, half weren't. And now that the men are out, those roles are reversed. Won't people have to accept that? Move on?"

"In a perfect world, darlin', everyone would take responsibility for their actions and everyone else would be logical about it. But this is far from a perfect world."

She had to agree with that.

"Anyway, I'm not saying there *will* be trouble. If I'm extremely lucky, both Jessie Starkey and Lee Rodarte will move far, far away from here and their freedom will cause nothing more than a blip on the radar screen of my week."

They finished the grilled chicken by turning the topic to what might be for dessert, and Sam surprised Beau with his favorite. Despite the fact that he seemed willing to eat anything she brought home from the shop, there were times when she knew he really wanted nothing more than plain old vanilla ice cream. She dished it up and they carried their bowls to the sofa. Sam spotted the new paper Beau had brought home; she picked it up and read it aloud.

Today's reporter provided more background. The article about Starkey's and Rodarte's release from the state penitentiary in Santa Fe gave a quick recap of the circumstances of Angela Cayne's death and the subsequent confession that had put the men away. Angela's photo stared from the page, a beautiful strawberry blonde of nineteen with large, liquid eyes and a dimpled smile that would have charmed everyone she met. On the night of her death she'd been home while her parents went to a church function. She was missing when they came home and signs of a struggle inside the house led to the conclusion that she'd not left willingly. Two days later her body was found at the outskirts of Sembramos, beaten and strangled. Jessie Starkey had been picked up and, after a long interrogation by the Taos County Sheriff's Department, confessed and implicated his friend Lee Rodarte. The two men were put on trial together, and although Rodarte denied any involvement, Starkey's confession was enough to earn life sentences for both of them. A series of legal appeals overturned the shaky confession and brought in enough new facts that the verdict was overturned. Starkey and Rodarte walked out of the pen this week, free men.

Beau processed the information without comment then switched on the television to a program on how diesel engines were made, but Sam found her attention wandering to the death of Angela Cayne. How traumatic it must have been for her parents, coming home to find signs of a struggle and their daughter gone. How would she have handled it if something like that happened to Kelly? She couldn't imagine. No wonder emotions had run high during the subsequent events.

Sam reread the article, but it seemed like old history and she couldn't seem to concentrate. When she yawned for the third time Beau gave her hand a squeeze.

"It's been a long week, darlin'. Why don't you just go to bed? I'll be along as soon as this is over."

He was right. Waking six days a week before dawn didn't leave a lot of energy by evening. She seldom made it through an entire episode of even her favorite shows. She waited for the next commercial and then kissed him.

"See you upstairs," she murmured.

But she didn't. Despite the image of Angela Cayne's sweet face, and the reminder that Saturday at the bakery would be crazy, her body was just plain tired and she fell into an uneasy sleep before he ever came into the room.

When her alarm went off in the darkness of the early morning, Sam slapped it and dragged herself out of bed, thankful that this was her final workday of the week. She emerged from the shower to find Beau standing at the mirror, looking nearly as bleary as she felt.

"Why are you up?" she asked as she toweled off and reached for the fresh clothes she'd left on the vanity. "You could have slept another hour, at least."

"Phone rang. I put Rico on patrol last night and he spotted Jessie Starkey heading for Sembramos."

"Trouble?"

"Not yet."

"And Rico couldn't have waited until eight o'clock to tell you this?"

Beau shrugged and squirted toothpaste onto his brush. "I better drive up that direction and keep an eye on things. Warn Starkey not to start anything."

Wrapped in her towel, she combed out her short, graying hair. He caught her eyeing him as he dropped his robe to step into the shower.

"You can join me if you'd like," he said with a teasing gleam in his eye.

"Tempting. But we're both running late already." Disappointment showed on her face. "Tomorrow's a day off for both of us. Let's make it a romantic Sunday."

He gave her a kiss that almost changed her mind. Then he stepped into the steamy shower.

She ran through a list of things she could do to make the weekend more fun. Morning sex followed by eggs Benedict or strawberry waffles . . . maybe a walk in the woods or a picnic in a secluded spot . . . She would have to give it some thought. Right now, all she could concentrate on was the waiting stack of order sheets, the dozen or more pastries that would be picked up today. Where would she find the energy for all of it?

Her glance fell to the wooden jewelry box on the vanity. She reached out, tempted. No. She couldn't rely on its strange powers at every whim. She pulled her hand back and took a deep breath, turning her back on the odd artifact and walking into the bedroom to dress.

Determined to tackle the long day ahead, she picked up her baker's jacket from the bedroom chair and slipped it on. Grabbing her pack and keys, she went out into the chilly morning and drove toward Sweet's Sweets.

Long rays of golden sunlight were hitting the sidewalk in front of her shop by the time Sam stepped out of the kitchen to place four finished Easter Basket cakes on the back counter, the order forms attached to the boxes for easy identification. Eight o'clock and she'd accomplished a lot, even without supernatural help. A picture of the box flashed through her head. Julio was alert and sharp and he knew how long certain tasks took. She'd been able to bluff her way through several times when she'd used the wooden box's power to achieve Herculean amounts of work, but one day he would stop her and ask questions. Questions she wasn't ready to answer.

She still didn't know what was behind the power that the box conveyed, or why she had fallen heir to it. Bertha Martinez, the old woman who'd insisted that Sam was meant to own the box, hadn't lived long enough to tell her anything. And there was the startling fact that Sam's uncle had owned the twin to this box—but then he, too, had died before telling her about its history. The questions continued to nag as she went back into the kitchen and started putting cute little chick faces on cupcakes.

Perhaps she could locate some of Bertha's old friends here in Taos, see if any of them could tell her anything about the box and its origins. Later. For now, there were Easter egg cookies and more of those delectable petit fours to make. She turned her attention back to the work.

Beau called, midafternoon, to ask how things were going.

"I spent half the morning up in Sembramos," he said, after Sam had stepped out the back door because the clatter of pans in the kitchen, competing with the laughter and voices from the sales room, made conversation impossible. The outside air had warmed by twenty degrees.

"Problems?" she asked, turning her face to the sun.

"Not that I could see. I went to the Starkey house and talked to Jessie. Kept it friendly, let him know that I don't approach law enforcement in the same way that Orlando Padilla did, and that he could call on me if needed."

"And how did that go?"

"Jessie's older and wiser than when he went on trial. Prison toughened him but I think it also matured him. He doesn't say a lot, just seems glad to be out. Jessie's father, Joe, sat there in an old T-shirt, taking slow sips from a beer, staring at the TV set with this scowl on his face. Helen, Jessie's mother, now that's where I got an earful. She's still very resentful of how the system treated her son."

"Aren't all mothers like that?"

"Well, sure. I expected it. I guess all my talk about how I'm different from Padilla was more for her benefit than Jessie's anyway. It's an awkward position for me. I can't admit that the department made mistakes, but I certainly can't condone the work that was done on the case or the tactics Orlando used to get that confession out of Jessie. It's touchy. I'll just have to play it cool and hope that the Starkey family will, too."

A cloud obscured the sun, driving a chilly breeze down the alley; Sam hoped the spring weather wasn't about to take a turn. She wished Beau luck and told him that she would do her best to close up shop precisely at six and be home twenty minutes or so after that.

Back inside, the kitchen had quieted somewhat. The steady stream of new pastries went to the sales room all morning and early afternoon; by this time of day they simply needed to sell it all. Whatever didn't sell, Becky had offered to drop off at the battered women's shelter on her way home. Sam had held back a couple of boxes of cupcakes for that purpose anyway, something to brighten the lives of the frightened women and children who resided there.

Now, the bakeware was mostly washed. Julio was mixing dry ingredients for Monday's standard breakfast items, and the helper was drying pans and putting them away. Becky had taken the initiative to see what orders were due on Monday and Tuesday, and she was making sugar flowers for two birthday cakes. Sam gave herself a leisurely moment to take it in and make sure they hadn't overlooked some vital detail before she headed toward the noisy sales room.

Jen's normally unflustered face had a sheen of perspiration as she rushed back and forth to box up items the customers pointed out. When Sam stepped up to help, she gave a grateful smile. Together, they took care of those who'd made their decisions and rang up sales for the last of the large basket cakes. Sam checked with two ladies who were having cheesecake at one of the bistro tables to see if they needed refills on their coffee. It was five minutes to six when the last person walked out the door.

They'd judged their quantities pretty well. Only a couple dozen cookies remained in the case, five petit fours, and one of their stock layer cakes decorated in pastel flowers. Jen turned over the Closed sign and dimmed the lights while Becky came out to box up the leftover goodies and head out with them. Sam didn't even bother to count the register receipts—she could tell it had been a profitable day—she just jammed it all into a bank bag to take home with her.

She drove home, pulled her van to the side of the house, and walked in to find Beau pacing the living room floor with his cell phone at his ear.

"Do *not* tell them that," he said in a very firm voice. "Just say that we expect everyone to stay level-headed and that we will be keeping an eye on things. They'd better behave or arrests will be made. Then get two patrol cars up there to cruise the streets."

He clicked off the call and seemed startled when he saw Sam.

"Damn," he said. "It's always something. Lee Rodarte showed up in Sembramos this evening."

Chapter 3

Is everything under control?" Sam asked. Beau's face seemed flushed and she could tell he was agitated.

He blew out a breath. "Yeah. For now. It's just—" He paced the length of the room one more time. "Why did Rodarte think it was a great idea to go back to that town? Why did either of them?"

"Family ties?"

"Yeah, but now that both of them are in town we're getting calls. 'Jessie had words with a guy in the bar.' 'Rodarte walked past my house.' 'I don't like them being here,' " he mimicked. Beau ran his hands down the sides of his face. "I feel like the recess monitor at the elementary school, dealing with a lot of petty stuff. Jessie Starkey's family doesn't want Rodarte in town; Rodarte's friends are furious with Jessie for framing their buddy. It's like a bunch of five-year-olds squawking things like 'he looked at me.' "

"It goes a little deeper than that," she said.

"I know. I don't mean to be insensitive about their emotions. I just don't know what they expect that we can *do* about it."

"And there's no way to keep them apart." Sam had dropped her bank bag on an end table and headed now toward the kitchen. Beau followed.

"Exactly. We're talking a town of two hundred people. It's a one-gas station kind of place. The citizens mingle all the time." One of several little towns from which people drove to Taos for their major shopping, to get health care or attend high school.

Sam pulled a container of Beau's homemade chile from the fridge, poured it into a pan and turned on a burner.

He kept talking while he picked spoons out of the drawer. "Town government in Sembramos consists of a mayor and three-member council. Their law enforcement is me and my department. At least half of them are farmers—have been for generations—pretty gentle souls. They grow their corn and peppers and tomatoes and stuff and they drive down to Taos every weekend in the summer and fall to the farmer's market and chat amongst themselves while they make an outing of it. Half the families have intermarried over the decades, so everyone knows everyone and are related to most of the others. After the trial it was all we could do to prevent a war in the streets. Now, I'm afraid we may be facing the same thing all over again."

The hearty stew began to bubble so they carried steaming bowls and the conversation to the table.

"The two of them, Starkey and Rodarte, didn't work this out between them while they were in prison?" Sam asked.

"No way. They were kept in separate cell blocks and released on different days. Knowing that one man's confession put the other behind bars, the system did its best to keep them apart." Beau shook his head sadly. "I thought these two were friends, back before all this."

The murder of one innocent young woman had forever changed the lives of so many people, Sam thought.

They cleared the dishes and Beau loaded everything into the dishwasher while Sam located her calculator and carried her bank bag to the table. While she separated cash from credit card receipts and began adding it up, Beau settled into his recliner with the thick brown murder file on his lap. By the time they headed upstairs, both felt mentally spent.

Although they'd fallen into an exhausted sleep, Sam awoke to the pleasant sensation of Beau's kisses trailing across her shoulder and neck. Maybe their Easter Sunday would go the way they'd planned after all. She turned toward him, tucking her fingers into the waistband of his pajamas. It didn't take but a minute for all other thoughts to leave the room.

* * *

Beau pulled the first golden brown waffle off the iron. Sam stood beside him at the counter, de-stemming strawberries and slicing them into a bowl, occasionally taking a seductive bite from one, keeping with the morning's mood. Then his cell phone rang.

He poured the next ladle of batter onto the hot waffle iron and reached for the phone. Sam took the plate with the finished waffle and stuck it into the preheated oven to keep warm. Two seconds after Beau said hello, she could tell this wasn't good news.

His face lost a shade of color and he stared into the middle of the room as he listened. His responses consisted of "okay" "yeah" and ended with "great, just great." He concluded the call and his mouth pulled into a tight line.

"Trouble." Sam didn't exactly phrase it as a question.

"Jessie Starkey's been shot."

"He's dead?"

"Yeah. I need to call the OMI." He scrolled through the numbers on the phone and picked one.

Sam realized that the waffle iron was smoking and she grabbed the handle. This second waffle was a very dark brown and she pried it out with a fork.

Someone at the Office of the Medical Investigator picked up right away and Beau couldn't stand still as he talked. He outlined the situation in Sembramos. The incident had been reported as a hunting accident and the body moved. He gave an address and said he would be there to meet the investigator in an hour. Then he called his own office and told the dispatcher to get two men up to secure the scene.

So much for a full Sunday off.

They ate their waffles in silence, both of their minds whirling.

"Can I come with you?" Sam asked as she cleared the half-eaten breakfasts.

"Better not. I have no idea what we'll find up there." He'd gone upstairs and come back in uniform, complete with his holstered pistol and handcuffs and more—ten pounds of stuff around his waist. "If it truly was a hunting accident, things could be all right. But until I have the OMI's report I'm not ruling anything out. That town could be a tinderbox. I can't put you in danger, darlin'."

But what about yourself? Sam thought as she wrapped her arms around him and pressed her cheek against the badge on his chest. It never got easier, watching your lawman husband walk out of the house, not knowing what might happen.

* * *

Had he been on horseback, Beau would have felt like the sheriff in an old Western, riding into an eerily quiet town while atonal music played in his ear. A tumbleweed actually blew across the road, borne on the spring wind that had come up yesterday. He passed numbered cross-streets, the elementary school on his left, the gas station on the right. Both places seemed buttoned up tight. Same with the variety store and market. He cruised the entire mile-long stretch of two-lane highway, to where the farm supply store marked the end of town, without seeing a soul.

Yes, it was a holiday. That explained the closed businesses—but still . . . He U-turned, cut over on Third Street, the only other paved one in town, and cruised back down Cottonwood Lane. Four cars sat outside the church on the left, where closed double doors didn't especially make the place look all that welcoming. He powered his window down and barely caught the sound of organ music before it wafted away on the shifting wind. In the next block, the volunteer fire department showed where the action was. Both of the station's tall garage doors stood open, the town's very dated ambulance backed up to one of them. The local medical investigator's black vehicle had pulled up next to it, and two of Beau's deputies had strung yellow tape to keep out the dozen or so people who were milling around.

Leaving an exit path for the MI's vehicle, Beau pulled in and got out of his cruiser. All eyes of the townsfolk seemed to follow him as he ducked under the tape and approached the back of the ambulance.

"Hi Ben." He greeted the older man who'd served as Taos County's field deputy medical investigator, under the main office in Albuquerque, for as long as Beau could remember.

"Sheriff." Always a man of few words, Ben Alison went about his work quickly and efficiently. He climbed into the back of the ambulance, where Beau could see a pair of booted feet on a gurney.

He stepped over, took a quick look and saw that it was, indeed, Jessie Starkey. The stringy yellow hair and stubbled face were unmistakable; he was wearing the same clothes Beau remembered from his visit to their home yesterday. A commotion out at the driveway caught his attention. His deputy, Rico, was attempting to restrain a very agitated woman. Helen Starkey.

She had apparently recognized Beau when he drove up and now she wanted his attention. He walked over and started to speak but she overrode his words.

"This is your fault, the lot of you!" she shouted, the lines in her face fixed in anger and a deep furrow pinching her brows together. Her chin-length gray hair had probably been brushed this morning, but now it flew out in wild tangles and her flowered rayon dress wasn't nearly adequate in the chill air. She didn't seem to notice being cold.

"Mrs. Starkey, I—"

"I mean it! If you all hadn't let him out—"

"Ma'am! Hold on. Let's just talk a minute." It was a damned-if-you-do, damned-if-you-don't situation. She'd been furious when her son went to prison, now she was furious because something happened right after he got out.

"I'm sorry about your loss," Beau said quietly. "I truly am. No one could have foreseen this. We were told it was a hunting accident."

Helen Starkey settled down only marginally. She stared at Beau with flashing blue eyes.

He met her gaze evenly. "I need to know what happened, Mrs. Starkey. Did Jessie go hunting this morning?"

Joe Starkey had stepped up. He was dressed in camouflage pants, heavy boots and a flannel shirt. Beau made eye contact. "Mr. Starkey, maybe you can tell me what you know."

"I told 'em I didn't want 'em huntin' today," Helen said, pushing her way into Beau's line of sight once more. "I just wanted ever'body to stay home, have a nice day together . . . I made a roast."

Beau made eye contact with Rico and suggested that he take Mrs. Starkey home. She walked a few steps away but refused to get in the deputy's cruiser.

Beau turned again to Joe Starkey. "So, you and Jessie went hunting?"

Joe's eyes shifted left and right. Turkey season didn't open for another week, and he knew he was in trouble.

"I got me a permit," he said, a bit defensively. "Jessie and me used to go every spring. The boy had such a good time. Well, he just got home and we wanted to go. He was so eager. I didn't figure it'd do no harm. What's the difference I shoot the bird today or a week from today?"

"The difference is the law and you know that, Joe. But I'm not here to bust you for hunting out of season, even though I probably should. I need to know what chain of events put your son into that ambulance."

It sounded harsh, Beau realized, but he had a feeling he would get a huge runaround unless he kept the guy focused.

Starkey's gaze shifted again, as if he was having trouble concentrating, and Beau wondered whether he'd been into the liquor already this morning.

"You and Jessie got up early, I suppose?"

"Yeah, well, you gotta be out before daylight to find turkeys. So we did. We got up, dressed, headed out. Got out to the woods about six."

Beau looked toward the mountain, wondering if any of the forest near here was within the legal hunt area. He knew the Wild Rivers area and Taos Valley Overlook were not, but wasn't sure about others. Again, beside the point right now. He waited for Starkey to start talking again.

"So, anyways, we're walking around out there in the dark, decide on a place to sit, and then we just wait for sunrise. Figured we had about fifteen minutes before we could, uh, legally shoot."

Again, Beau had the feeling that *legally* didn't much factor into this man's way of doing things. Again, he stayed quiet.

"Anyways, Jessie says he gotta take a leak, so he lays his gun down beside me and he goes off around the bushes somewhere. I can hear him walking over there." He squeezed his eyes shut. "That's when I hear a shot."

He drew a deep breath. "I'm thinking somebody's starting at them turkeys a little too early, but then I hear a crash in the dry leaves on the ground. I give a shout and I hear Jessie groaning. With the flashlight I spot him lying on the ground. I run over there but, Sheriff, my boy's gone before I even get to his side." Starkey's voice broke.

Beau gave him a moment, then the medical investigator's wave caught his attention.

"Excuse me just a second," Beau told Starkey. "Wait right here."

Ben Alison had stepped down from the ambulance and now he pulled Beau into the fire station, out of sight of the crowd outside.

"If this was a hunting accident, it wasn't someone hunting turkeys," he said in a low voice. "I can't tell you caliber—Albuquerque will have to dig the bullet out and determine that."

"Bullet. Not bird shot."

"Exactly. By the size and shape of the wound, I would venture a guess that it was a high power rifle. It suggests someone followed them and was waiting to take his shot."

"A sniper did this?"

"That's what it looks like." His expression looked grim.

Chapter 4

Sam walked to the relief map that hung in the recess under the stairs. Sembramos was only fifteen miles away, probably twenty minutes by car, if Beau didn't turn on his siren. She paced. Worried. Realized how vital her work at the bakery was, keeping her busy and sane while he did this kind of thing every day. There was no way she could simply sit at home and wait for news.

She started to dial her best friend, Zoë, then remembered that she and Darryl had closed their B&B for a month and used the spring lull for a much-needed vacation. Rupert, her writer friend, had a rule about no phone calls before noon—mornings were the magic hours during which he became Victoria DeVane, bestselling romance author. Secretly, of course. But she had to respect his creative time, even on holidays.

She called her own phone number, Kelly's now. If she was home it probably meant she wasn't doing anything in particular. Sam couldn't honestly remember whether Kelly had mentioned Easter plans or not. She drummed her fingers on the countertop, realizing there would be no answer. What was she going to say anyway? I'm bored? I'm worried about Beau? It didn't seem fair to dump those things on her daughter. She hung up and wandered upstairs.

With nothing else to occupy her mind, she started a load of laundry and gathered cleaning supplies. Dusting furniture and scrubbing the bathroom would at least accomplish some needed tasks while she continued to wish she was with Beau. She had planned to take a few days off for spring cleaning—here was her big chance to get started. But it didn't feel like a satisfying way to spend the day.

She had finished the upstairs bathroom, her gaze lingering on that mysterious wooden box, when her cell phone rang. She yanked it out of her pocket, thrilled to see that the readout said it was Beau.

"Hey there, sorry I didn't touch base sooner."

"You don't owe me a minute-by-minute account," she said. "Just glad to know that you're safe."

"I'm fine. Not so sure about the town, though. But I'll fill you in on that when I get home. It shouldn't be too late. They've just loaded the body into the medical investigator's car and he'll be taking it to Albuquerque."

"So it wasn't clearly an accident?"

He chuckled. "You're learning a lot about this stuff. No, the MI didn't agree with that story. So, I've got a whole lot more questions to ask."

Someone started talking to him so he had to hang up, leaving Sam wondering how 'whole lot of questions' and 'won't be home late' went together. She ran the dust cloth over the deep grooves in her jewelry box, still thinking about her resolve to find out more answers about it.

She tossed her dust cloth down and decided it was now late enough in the day to call Rupert. He knew a lot of people in this town, and maybe she could distract herself from Beau's case.

"Afternoon tea? What a lovely idea," he said when she reached him.

Although tea and pastries weren't exactly an unusual thing for a bakery owner, she mainly wanted to spend a little time with a friend and see what she could learn. Rupert suggested a quaint place that only women or a gay man would know of, Miss Rose's Lovely Tea House. Despite her reservations over whether it would be open on a holiday afternoon, true to Rupert's prediction, it was. They walked past shelves displaying delicate English cups and saucers, tea spoons, tea balls, and finally a case full of delectable sweets. Sam studied them, as always, thinking of ideas she could 'borrow.' Their hostess arrived and showed them to a table. She eyed the delicate chair legs a little apprehensively as Rupert cast aside his flowing purple scarf and lowered his two-hundred-plus pounds onto the seat.

He recommended the Darjeeling so they ordered a pot of that and an assortment of miniature pastries and sandwiches. After some minutes of chit-chat, catching up on each others' lives, what their mutual friends were up to and pouring the tea, Sam brought up her true reason for the visit.

"You remember my jewelry box," she began, "the funky carved one with the little stones mounted on it?" She went into a short version of how she had discovered that her uncle in Ireland had one nearly identical, only a bit larger.

Rupert nodded as she talked, plucking a crustless sandwich triangle from the serving plate and finishing it off in two bites.

"Well, knowing there was another such box out there in the world has made me wonder where mine came from. And you are always doing research for your books . . . so I wondered if you might have some ideas where I might find out more."

"Honey, the Internet. It's where I look up historical data for my purposes. Have you tried that?"

Sam had to admit that she hadn't, but she had a feeling its place in history was only a small part of what made her box unique. She debated—Rupert had entrusted her with a major secret about his identity as a writer. Surely she could trust him with some of the unrevealed aspects of the box and its powers. On the other hand, he might very well turn around and use the information in a future story. She waited until he'd finished his third sandwich.

"What I'm looking for is more about where this one came from before I got it. I told you that an old woman named Bertha Martinez gave it to me?"

He nodded vaguely.

"Well, according to Beau, people here in town thought Bertha was a *bruja*. When I cleaned out her house I found some curious artifacts." *A dried up old snake and bunches of odd herbs and candles.* "I wonder if there's anyone else around who might have known her."

"Did you look for her relatives?"

"We checked that when she died. There were none that she had regular contact with."

Rupert reached for one of the small éclairs, his mouth

pursed in thought. After he'd chewed on it for a minute his expression brightened. "There's a reference librarian at the Harwood who has helped me out several times. Cora . . . Cora . . . Well, I can't think of her last name at the moment. It's probably in my address book at home. For *Shaman's Love* I had to do some rather specialized research on New Mexico traditions along those lines. This lady knew what books to point me to."

It didn't sound exactly like what Sam needed, but it was worth a try. She thanked him and picked up the last sandwich. With a bit of free time coming up, this could be the perfect time to pursue leads on the mysterious box.

She said goodbye in the parking lot and wished Rupert luck with his book, then started her truck. Her hand was on the gearshift when her phone rang. She shoved it back in Park and picked up. Delbert Crow's name showed on the readout. Darn.

Unfortunately, if she ignored it he would only call back so she answered.

"Got another job for you," he said. No greeting, no niceties, no Happy Easter.

"Hold on a second," she said. "I'm in my truck." She rummaged into her pack for paper and pen. "Okay. Give me the details."

Under her contract with the Department of Agriculture, Sam was obligated to break into houses that had been abandoned and were in foreclosure. She would clean them up, empty out whatever possessions the owners had left behind, and maintain the property until it went up for sale. As her contracting officer gave directions to the house, she heard children's voices laughing in the background. Although Delbert hadn't hesitated to call her on a holiday, it was a little reassuring that maybe he had relatives and some kind of a real life. Unfortunately, there went some of the time she had hoped to use for personal pursuits.

She repeated what Crow told her. The property was located somewhere in the unincorporated part of the county. She would have to look at the map.

A loud shriek came over the phone connection and the single word "Grandpa!" and Delbert Crow told Sam he needed to go but that she could call his office if she had further questions once she had checked out the property. In the years she had done this work she'd come across all types of scenarios—hoarder's dens, ordinary homes neat as a pin, creepy artifacts, and even a body buried in the yard at one place. Each new job always brought a moment of trepidation.

* * *

"I need you to show me where you and Jessie were this morning," Beau said to Joe Starkey. He almost regretted putting the man in the front seat of his cruiser. The flannel hunting shirt reeked of several days' sweat. And now, in close quarters, he would bet that at least a beer or two had been consumed this morning. He lowered his side window and put the SUV in gear.

Starkey directed him to a county road at the north end of Sembramos and he turned east into the foothills. Two more turns and they were on a two-track dirt lane. About a mile in, Beau could see where a vehicle had pulled off the crude road and made a hasty turn. The grasses were shredded and skid marks showed in the dirt. He glanced over at Joe.

"We parked right there," the older man said. "After they shot Jess, I dragged my boy to the truck and took him back. Hoped the EMTs in town could help him."

"So you were hunting close to here?" Beau stopped the cruiser. As they got out he scanned the ground for signs of any other vehicle but saw none.

Starkey headed into the forest.

"Hold up," Beau said. "I need to be watching for footprints." Not an expert tracker by any means, nevertheless he could see where two sets of prints led into the wooded area, and scuffs and drag marks came back out. At least that seemed to fit Starkey's version of the events.

He stayed side-by-side with the other man as they walked toward a small clearing ahead. No other tracks had shown up yet.

"Here we are," Joe Starkey said, pointing to a huge pine tree. "We was leaning up against the back side of it here."

Both men circled the tree. There against the side of the tree sat a shotgun, propped against the trunk. A second shotgun lay on the ground, apparently where Joe had flung it when he went looking for his son.

"Dang. Good thing we came back. I'd forgot all about leavin' these." Joe bent to pick up the guns.

"Leave them for a minute," Beau said. "We'll take them with us when we go."

Joe nodded.

"So you were sitting here at the base of this ponderosa. Which direction did the shot come from?"

Joe positioned himself with his back to the tree, closed his eyes for a few seconds and pointed over his right shoulder. "Somewhere over thataway."

Beau looked over the two shotguns. Normally with

a hunting accident they would both be bagged and taken back for tests and prints. But since the medical investigator had said Jessie's fatal wound came from a rifle there was no point. He picked up each gun, unloaded it, stuffed the shells in his pockets, and draped the guns—cracked open—over his arm. It was a bit of a burden but he certainly wasn't going to leave two weapons within reach of a man whose story he hadn't fully verified yet.

He stared off in the direction Joe Starkey had indicated. The trees were thick here, the ground littered with pine needles. A shooter had a thousand places to hide and a pretty safe bet that he could walk around without leaving tracks. Still . . . he had to check it out.

"Stay right here by this tree," he told Starkey. "Do not move."

The older man nodded and sat with his back to the tree.

Beau circled the tree, found the place where Jessie's blood stained the needles, the spot where the evidence that he'd been dragged out of the woods began. He stared off into the trees, trying to envision a straight path for a bullet. Walking slowly and turning frequently, he stayed on line, scanning the ground.

The shooter would have wanted some kind of cover; the sun hadn't risen but he could have been spotted in the early gray light of dawn. So he would have kept to the trees, ducked behind one until he had a line on Jessie and could step out to get the man in his sights. The problem was that the shooter couldn't get too far away. More than fifty yards or so and there would have been too many obstacles in the way. Beau kept turning, getting that picture in his head. He scanned the ground, hoping to find a brass casing. If the killer had gotten careless and left it behind, it could be the very thing that would convict him.

But—no such luck. He widened his search area. Joe could have been mistaken about the direction. Shots echo in the hills, way more than most people would imagine. Still, no brass and not a single footprint.

He made his way back to the tree where Joe Starkey sat. The man's eyes and nose were swollen and red, his face wet with tears. Beau cleared his throat and Starkey looked up.

"I didn't find anything," Beau said. "I'll get a team out here. Work a larger search area, more people . . . if there's evidence here we'll find it."

But down inside he didn't believe it. The shooter merely had to be careful to walk on the blanket of pine needles, and to pick up the one small piece of brass that would implicate him. As long as he did that he, or she, probably had gotten away with murder.

"Come on, Joe. Let's get going."

Joe wiped his shirt sleeve across his face and sniffed deeply as he stood up. Beau put the shotguns into the back of his SUV and they rode quietly back to Sembramos. Joe pointed out the turns to his house, apparently forgetting that Beau had visited there only yesterday.

The plain little blocky house sat two blocks off the main drag, on a dirt road with no sidewalks. Tan stucco, flat roof, a yard that might have once had a lawn but was now taken over by the wild grasses and a generous number of dandelions. The only thing that differentiated it from most of its neighbors was the shade of red on the peeling front door and the dozen or so people milling around outside. Some had angry expressions. Beau pulled to a stop and Joe opened his door.

"I'd better come in," Beau said. He checked his sidearm

and got out of the cruiser.

One of the men spotted the sheriff's vehicle and started toward him. The man stood at least a head taller than Joe Starkey, much closer to Beau's height, but otherwise Joe and this one came from the same mold. Thin limbs, lined faces, generous gray in the dark hair.

"Them Rodartes done this," the man said through clenched teeth that had a tan cast to them. "If not that Lee Rodarte hisself, then one of them others." Even the gnarled finger that shook when he spoke reminded Beau of Joe Starkey.

"Do you have some evidence of that, Mr. . . .?" Beau kept his voice quiet.

"This's my little brother. Bobby." Joe Starkey had watched the exchange.

Beau took in Bobby's size and nearly smiled at the description.

"Do you have evidence that he *didn't*?" Bobby said, his eyes flashing.

Beau wanted to glance around the crowd, judge the mood, but didn't dare break eye contact with Bobby. Finally the other man looked away first.

"We are just beginning our investigation, sir. Every bit of information is helpful. What can you tell me?" He relaxed his pose, took a minute to survey the gathering. Inquiring minds wanted to know what was going on, but so far no one else had stepped forward to challenge him.

"I can tell you that that Lee Rodarte showed up here in town. This mornin' early." A blonde woman stepped toward them, aligning herself near Bobby Starkey. The ragged ends of her hair hadn't seen a beautician's shears in a long time, and Beau guessed that her weathered face was as much the result of cigarettes—she dropped one to the ground as she approached—as from working some patch of nearby farmland.

"JoNell? You saw him?" Joe asked, his jaw clenching.

That didn't sound good. Beau glanced between the two men.

"I can tell you his fam'ly was real mad six years ago," Bobby said. "They'da done most anything to get back at Jessie for what he told them lawmen and that judge."

By this time another man and two women had openly begun to listen. Beau looked at them.

"Does anyone else have anything to add? Have any of you seen or spoken to Lee Rodarte since he came back?"

Heads shook. No one stepped forward.

Beau straightened his shoulders. "I'll be interviewing the Rodarte family, as well as Lee." He gave Joe and Bobby Starkey firm stares. "Do not take this into your own hands, gentlemen. You don't want to end up in even more trouble than Jessie's killer."

Bobby started to say something but Joe laid a hand on his arm and he backed down. Maybe older brother did have some influence.

Beau started for the cruiser and Joe caught up, asking about his shotguns.

"Later," Beau said. "If they check out clean, I'll get them back to you." Last thing he needed at this moment was to put weapons into the hands of this bunch.

Chapter 5

Beau sat in his cruiser in front of the Starkey home, staying visible while he radioed the department. It took a couple of minutes but he got Lee Rodarte's parents' address and brought up the map of Sembramos on his GPS. It was only one road over and four or five houses down so he drove over there, despite the fact that it was mid-afternoon and he really wanted to be home with Sam right now. They hadn't planned on work taking over their day off together, but then they never did and it seemed to be routinely a part of life.

He rolled to a stop at the edge of the dirt road, in front of another square little flat-roofed house. At least this one showed some signs of TLC, including flower beds out front and tilled rows of a side garden with a haze of green sprigs already sprouting. A thirty-something woman with long dark hair that trailed down her back in a braid was directing a garden hose at a bed of brilliant yellow daffodils. She straightened when she saw him, smiling as he approached. Not typical for someone who has had a lot of unpleasantness with the law.

"Ms. Rodarte?" he said, removing his Stetson.

"Um, sorry, no. I'm Gina Staples." She realized that water from the hose was running across her narrow sidewalk so she stepped to the spigot and turned it off. "The Rodartes used to own this house but they moved away some time ago. My husband and I bought it five years ago."

Beau bit back a remark; the Starkeys might have mentioned that little fact.

"Do you know where they moved? Are they still in town?"

"No. After the thing with Lee they left. Went to Albuquerque, I'm pretty sure. My mother lives three doors down. She and Lee's mother were close. She might have a number for them or something."

"So you've lived here in Sembramos your whole life?"

"Yep, every bit. I was born in the hospital in Taos and grew up here, farming organic produce alongside my dad."

Beau glanced at the large garden. "Looks like it's still going well."

Gina gazed at her neat rows and smiled. "I'm taking a chance, even putting lettuce out this early but it's Butterheads and Romaine, hardy varieties."

"I wonder, have you seen Lee Rodarte back in town in the last day or so?"

"You mean, did he come back here after he got out. I don't know. I heard about Jessie Starkey this morning though. Too bad. But, you know, not all that surprising."

"How so?"

"This town's wound may look like it healed over. After Angela Cayne died and all the ugliness that followed. But it's like a cancer that's still there, under the surface. Doesn't take much at all to get the two camps at odds again. Starkeys and Rodartes. At one time they were all pretty friendly. There weren't really any bitter feuds in this town. But that'll never happen again. It wouldn't be a good idea for either of those guys to come back to town and get the whole mess fired up again."

Beau nodded. His sentiments exactly. Something he would have told either of the men if he'd had the chance to talk to them before they left prison.

"So, Lee's parents. I wonder if they know where he is now. Maybe your mother would give me their number?"

"I'm sure she would," Gina said. "But there's someone else who might be a more direct line. Lee had a girlfriend before he, uh, went away. They have a child together. Sophie didn't want anything to do with Lee after he went on trial, but he really loved that little boy. They say that Lee was calling out to little Nathan when they took him away in handcuffs."

Beau thanked her and accepted her offer to call her mother for the phone number he needed. With that in hand, he got back into his vehicle.

Sophie Garcia lived in unit A of a little six-plex string of apartments near the elementary school. The places were bare-bones, possibly subsidized, definitely minimum-wage-worker dwellings. They all had dingy white stucco and blue front doors, and even from the dirt parking pad out front the place smelled of onions and hopelessness.

From inside the apartment Beau could hear the lively

jangle of a kids' TV show, with an undertone of adult conversation. When he tapped at the peeling blue paint, the voices stopped; the television hummed along. No one answered.

"Ms. Garcia? It's the sheriff. I need to speak with you."

The door opened about three inches and a pretty, young woman with shoulder-length chestnut hair and pouty lips peered around the edge of it. She wore bright pink jeans and a fluffy white pullover.

"Sophie Garcia?"

Her deep brown eyes blinked.

"Could I ask you a couple of quick questions?"

Something shuffled behind the door and Beau's right hand dropped to his holster.

"There's no problem, Sheriff," Sophie said quickly. "My little boy and me, we're just watching some TV."

"Have you seen Lee Rodarte in the last couple days?"

Her eyes shifted and she shook her head.

"Because if you have, I'd like to get a message to him." He watched her face closely. "And if he's here right now, I'd like to deliver that message in person. He's not in any trouble, at least not with my department. But I'm worried about his safety here in Sembramos."

Sophie's eyes flicked to her right.

"Could I just come in and talk to him?" Beau's voice was quiet but firm.

A brown hand touched Sophie's shoulder. "Let him in," said a male voice.

She stepped back and allowed Beau to open the door just enough to get into the apartment. Beau took in the room at a glance, beginning with Lee Rodarte standing with his back to the wall, hands visible. The man had apparently acquired even more tattoos in prison, in addition to the ones Beau remembered from the department photos, which ran all the way down his arms and across his back. Now he had some up the sides of his neck and shaved head. Sophie stepped over to the brown tweed couch and her arm circled a wide-eyed boy of about eight. The kid took in Beau's uniform and gun, but the minute Rodarte spoke the child's eyes were on his father.

"I only came to see my son," Lee said. "Had nothin' to do with Jessie."

"Did you come straight here from Santa Fe? The minute you got out?"

"Pretty much. Sophie and me . . . I want to work things out together." A blanket and pillow on the sofa attested to the fact that he'd spent the night, but apparently not in Sophie's bed.

"Were you here, in this apartment, the whole time?"

Lee nodded. Beau looked at Sophie. She nodded too.

"I brought food, got an Easter basket for Nathan. We sat up a long time, talking."

"You didn't go out early this morning?"

"No, man, I swear I didn't."

"Can you verify that, ma'am?" Beau turned to Sophie.

She glanced back and forth between him and Lee. Whatever answer she gave would be the one her boyfriend wanted her to say. Unsurprisingly, she agreed with him.

Beau sighed. "Okay, then. All I can do is caution you. I'd strongly suggest that you not stick around town. There's an angry group over at the Starkey's house and more than one of them is tossing out the idea that you tracked Jessie out to the woods and shot him."

Rodarte's teeth clenched; a muscle worked in his jaw. "Jessie Starkey cost me almost seven years of my life. My dad sold the house to pay for those lawyers to keep trying to get me out. My little sister gave up her chance at college 'cause they had no money for her. All because Jessie lied!"

"So you—"

"I did nothin'! Nothin', man! Am I sorry he's dead?" Rodarte took a step forward, his teeth clenched.

Sophie Garcia cradled her son's head against herself, her eyes never leaving Lee's face. The cartoon on TV became a ridiculous jangle of noise.

"No, I'm not sorry. But I didn't kill him." Lee's shoulders slumped momentarily. "I don't know how he died and I don't care. I'll leave town, Sheriff, but I don't want to go without them," he said with a nod toward the others.

"Just saying. Be careful." Beau opened the door and walked out. He would, of course, try to check Rodarte's alibi, but it was unlikely that someone had snapped a photo of him asleep on the couch in the early morning hours so if he'd left the apartment it would be up to Sophie to come forward with that information. Sometimes the frustration levels of this job just sucked.

He got into his vehicle and cruised up and down the narrow roads of the small town once more. Didn't see anyone out in front of the Starkey house anymore, so that was good. And the fire station was closed up tight. As long as things stayed quiet there wasn't much he could do about his investigation until he got the autopsy results. He came to the edge of town and radioed that he was 10-7, going off-duty.

* * *

Shadows grew long across the fields of alfalfa as Sam drove toward home. Meeting with Rupert had been fun, although she hadn't exactly gotten the information she'd been after, a list of Bertha Martinez's old friends. But what had she expected anyway? Rupert hung with the art and fashion crowd. Ninety-some-year-old Bertha hadn't fit that mold. She was hoping he might have heard of some local coven or known someone in the mysticism crowd. But at least with the librarian's name she had a starting place.

She also had a new job to do, as of a few minutes ago; however, that would wait until tomorrow. It was too late in the day and Beau had called to say he was on the way home. With luck they might salvage a bit of time together before the weekend was over. Plus, she was eager to hear what was going on with the call that dragged him away during breakfast. She pulled into the long drive and backed her truck up to the tongue of her utility trailer.

Beau's cruiser came to a stop next to her. "Need some help with that, ma'am?" Without waiting for an answer he hopped out and stood behind the truck, guiding her to the right position and hitching the trailer to it before she'd shut off the engine.

"Thank you, kind sir." A kiss showed the rest of her gratitude. "Did you get any lunch, hon?"

"Afraid not. I'm starving."

Sam felt a little stab of guilt for stuffing herself with tea and goodies. She admitted that she couldn't really hold a thing right now, but offered to make anything he wanted. They walked into the house together.

"I'll just wash up and make myself a sandwich," he said, pumping hand soap at the kitchen sink. "How about you get us a drink of some kind?"

She settled on a glass of wine for herself and brought out a beer for Beau when she saw him piling both ham and roast beef slices onto a large slab of bread. He filled her in on the situation up north as he added cheese and lettuce and carried the sandwich to the living room.

"You can't just order Lee Rodarte to leave town?" she asked, taking her usual spot on the deep sofa. Beau was right about starving—he'd wolfed half his sandwich before he spoke again.

"Not really," he said. "He's got as much right to be there as Jessie did, although I did warn him that it wasn't safe." He paused for a swig of his beer. "The guy's not easy to like—I mean, same things that turned the jury against him, I suppose. Covered in tattoos, rough-looking, facial scars that probably came from knife fights, a record of minor drug charges, and an illegitimate child with a pretty girl who probably should have known better than to get involved with him."

Sam waited while he took another big bite of the sandwich.

"But—in this particular case, it looks like he's the innocent man caught up in forces beyond his control. According to the original court testimony, he and Jessie did a few drug deals together—misdemeanor stuff involving recreational quantities of pot. But then Jessie turns on Lee and accuses him of being in on killing Angela Cayne. Lee protests, swears he was somewhere else when it happened but can't prove it, goes to prison. Six years there, the confession is thrown out and suddenly he's free. Life should be good. He wants his girlfriend and little boy back but he gets to town just as Jessie dies and he can see himself getting dragged into court again. He's got a lot of anger—toward both Jessie Starkey and the system."

"So, maybe he did kill Starkey—he sounds angry enough."

Beau shook his head slowly. "I don't know . . . I'm not getting that kind of feeling. But I'll definitely be trying to verify his story."

"If this were me . . . I'd be thinking of ways to get as far from New Mexico as possible."

"You'd think. But as of this moment his heart—or some other body part—is overriding his brain." He set his plate aside. "If his alibi for this morning checks out, I'll see if I can't talk some sense to him. Who knows—another day or so and maybe the girlfriend will be ready to move away with him and there'll be a happy ending to all this."

"So, if Lee Rodarte didn't kill Jessie Starkey and you said it wasn't a hunting accident, who did do it?"

"That's the big question," he said leaning back in his chair. "The fact that it happened within hours after Jessie got home . . . sure sounds like revenge. Which only narrows it down to half the population of Sembramos."

"Couldn't it go back to the original case? When that young woman was killed? Someone thought the real killers had gone to prison, sees them get out and thinks the system has failed, decides they'll take over where the lawyers and courts let them down?"

Beau gave her a serious look. "The mood in that town right now? Yeah, I could easily see one side or the other taking matters into their own hands."

"So, we just have to think through the list of who that might be."

"We?" He grinned at her. "You want your deputy status back?"

"Well, it sounds more appealing than breaking into a house and spending the rest of the week cleaning." She told him about the call from Delbert Crow. "Which reminds me, this one's out in the country somewhere and I need to look it up on the map."

She pulled the note from her pack and stepped to the map on the wall.

"Looks like I have to drive through Sembramos to get there," she said, running her finger along the highway that Crow had named.

Beau sat up straight, then stood up and came to see her notes.

"See, it's about another five miles past town, then Delbert said there would be a driveway with a mailbox. He gave me a number but it's all rural addressing out there."

"I don't like this, Sam." He chewed at his lip.

"You said it was quiet when you left. The people who'd gathered at the Starkey place weren't roaming the streets or anything, right?"

"Well, true." His hesitation made her look up at his face. Worry etched the space between his eyebrows. "Just drive straight through town. Don't stop and don't talk to anyone, and you should be okay."

"What—I've lost my deputy status already?" She kept her tone light, teasing, reaching toward his ticklish ribs.

He tussled with her a moment and tickled right back, but the worry lines were still there.

Chapter 6

Habits—even the ones you don't like—are hard to break, Sam discovered, when she automatically awoke before daylight. She rolled over and snuggled against Beau's back, the warm quilt around her shoulders, and managed to remain in a state of half-drowse until his alarm went off and he turned toward her. A quick kiss; she could tell he was preoccupied already.

Over his breakfast of Cheerios he cautioned her again not to get involved if she saw signs of trouble as she drove northward to the new job she'd been assigned yesterday. She chafed a little at his overprotectiveness but kept a smile on her face as she assured him she would be watchful.

Saturday's weather front had blown through quickly, leaving a clear sky and the promise of warmer temperatures but Sam knew from experience that April could bring nearly anything. She took a spare flannel shirt and tossed her all-weather jacket into the back seat of her truck.

Acres of farmland rolled by, interspersed with wooded patches where trees hugged the streams that flowed out of the mountains. Sam consulted her notes and made the turns Delbert Crow had described. The town of Sembramos appeared, noted by the fact that the speed limit dropped from fifty-five to thirty-five and a rectangular, green highway sign demarcated the town limit. She slowed accordingly and found herself paying attention to little details.

The highway bisected the town lengthwise. On her left stood a one-story school of red brick with a dozen cars in the parking lot. A small bank sat a little farther on. To the right, a variety store and ice cream parlor. A paved cross street led to residential areas of unimposing little houses; the intersection was marked with brilliant yellow signs warning motorists to stop for pedestrians and showing black silhouettes of children.

Beyond the initial cluster of businesses she spotted a small café and two boarded-up retail shops. All had graveled parking lots and no curbs or sidewalks. A block over, in the spaces between buildings, she could tell there were a few more shopping choices and a small park. The entire trip took less than three minutes and she didn't see a living soul the entire time. Eerie for a Monday morning.

It's still early in the day, she reminded herself. The cars parked at the elementary school and the bank gave proof that the town wasn't deserted. But still . . . weird.

She consulted her notes and glanced at her odometer. Crow had said that 5.1 miles beyond the town was a turnoff and that's where her newest break-in project awaited. Sam resumed her highway speed, zipping past fields of alfalfa and apple orchards in full bloom, the trees resembling rows of little old ladies with fluffy white hairdos. Beyond the irrigated areas native sage and piñon dotted the foothills which rose to a climax at Wheeler Peak in the distance. Snow still topped the state's highest mountain; patches of it would probably remain until July.

The orchards gave way to flat fields where in a couple more months tufts of green would begin to show in straight lines along the hundreds of neat rows. Sam began to watch for her turnoff.

Crow hadn't mentioned that the terrain rose fairly steeply to the ten-acre property or that the house was massive, dominating the rocky hill upon which it sat. She steered up a long gravel driveway, topped the rise and pulled into a circular drive overgrown with last winter's dead weeds and the promise of this year's new batch. She killed the engine and stepped out of her truck into the vast silence of open country.

"Wow." Her voice echoed off brilliant white stucco. The mansion reminded Sam of architecture she'd seen in photos of Greece. High walls rose above her, capped by a domed roof and tiled cupola. A pair of matching stairways with concrete balusters curved from the second floor down to the ground, like graceful arms offering a hug to the building. Above an impressive, arched front door, a balcony stretched across the second story, with two sets of double doors opening to it. She pictured the owner—a minor lord or very successful drug kingpin—stepping out to stare down and see who was standing outside his estate.

But that was not going to happen. The whole place resonated with an air of abandoned desolation. The glass doors and windows were blank and dark; not a tire track marred the driveway or parking area. As she studied it more closely she saw that planting beds had been built but never filled and that the central part of the courtyard, where normally there would be a lawn or at least some decorative rock, had never been landscaped. Only weedy earth extended to the footing of the enormous house.

Sam set out to make her customary initial check of the perimeter. An empty swimming pool and round hot tub—marred by a crust of dirt and heaps of dead plant debris—waited behind the house to be filled with water and enjoyed. An elaborate built-in barbeque with tile backsplash and more counter space than Sam had in her kitchen sat coated in dust. The stainless steel grill still had new-item stickers affixed. The house's glass double doors faced the pool and Sam had a momentary vision of what the place would be like in full glory, a party with a few dozen people milling about, the smell of steaks on the grill, the splashes of children playing in clear blue water. A lone cottontail rabbit hopped across the walled courtyard, emphasizing that no such gatherings had ever happened here.

She stepped to the doors and tried the knob. Locked. Cupping her hands around her eyes, she saw that the huge great room, which could have accommodated three or four seating areas or a presidential inaugural ball, was empty. At the far end she saw a kitchen full of appliances; a massive stone fireplace filled the west wall; stairs on the east wall led to a mezzanine that overlooked the ballroom-sized living area, with doors that probably led to bedrooms above.

Whatever the story behind it, her job now was to get inside. It seemed a shame to drill the expensive lock on the front door, but after circling the entire place and trying each door she came to, it seemed the only way. She retrieved her tools from the truck and had broken in within a few minutes.

She stepped into a wide foyer, her sneakers making swishy sounds in the light layer of grit on the tile floor leading to the big room she had viewed from the other side. Her breathing echoed faintly from blank walls to the two-and-a-half story dome overhead. A quick survey of the room showed the fireplace was as sterile and clean as the day it was built; the high-end stainless steel appliances in the kitchen had plastic bags with the operating instructions hanging by their handles; a layer of construction dust powdered the beautifully laid custom tile, and every other surface in the place. Was this a case where the owner had spent every cent to build the structure but ran out of funds before he could furnish it? Perhaps it had been a spec house that a builder had started in more prosperous times and the perfect buyer had never come along. The space suddenly felt extremely chilly.

She walked slowly up the stairs, finding a massive master suite with two bathrooms and dressing rooms bigger than their master bedroom at home. Her earlier chill vanished as she walked into a bathroom where the temperature felt almost sauna-like. Despite a search for a heat source Sam found no reason for the discrepancies between the rooms. Odd. But she'd long ago learned that every house had its quirks.

Back downstairs, she followed a passageway to two more suites, perfect places to entertain guests or spoil your children in spacious accommodation. Beyond the foyer in the other direction were a wine cellar and a series of other, unspecified rooms that could have been intended as study, hobby room, library or maid's quarters; maybe in this league houses simply had places that no one knew what they were for. Sam made her way back to the massive room (she had a hard time thinking of it as merely 'great') and stood there with the sound of her footsteps echoing back at her.

The nice thing about cleaning an empty house was that she had no furniture to work around, no clutter to clean up. The fans near the top of that domed ceiling would be tricky to dust, but since that was a little beyond her obligation to make the place presentable enough for sale she could see maybe two or three days to dust and vacuum, at most. Not such a bad assignment, and she could still probably work in time to visit that librarian Rupert had told her about in her quest to get answers about the two odd wooden boxes.

She placed one of her standard sign-in sheets on the dark granite countertop and went out to her truck for her cleaning gear.

* * *

Beau got off the phone with the Office of the Medical Investigator in Albuquerque and sat at his desk, drumming his pen against the file he'd started on the death of Jessie Starkey. He'd only learned one new thing: the bullet that killed Jessie Starkey was a .357 caliber. One shot to the heart. Yes, they'd retrieved the bullet and it was in good enough shape for matching—*if* he found the weapon to compare to it.

That was the kicker. In a county where half the people hunted and even those who didn't probably owned guns, it wasn't going to be easy to find the right one. The pen tapped and he debated.

As he'd told Sam last night, the most likely motive

was revenge by one of Angela Cayne's friends or relatives, someone who believed the guilty men had been wrongly let go. He tried to remember if she'd had a boyfriend when she died. He didn't recall one being interrogated during the investigation of her death. She'd lived at home with her parents. He turned to the credenza in his office, pulled one of their basic information files and flipped through it. Jotted her address on a scrap of paper. It was a start.

Making his way through the traffic in the center of Taos and heading north on open road, he daydreamed of the possibility that talking with Angela's father would simply get the man to turn over the weapon and tearfully admit that he'd taken it upon himself to rid society of Jessie Starkey. The likelihood was practically nil. He knew that. With a sigh, he drove on.

It was midmorning when he slowed to the speed limit at the edge of Sembramos. Outside the bank, a man getting into a pickup truck paused to stare at the Sheriff's Department cruiser, giving Beau the eye. Beau gave a smile and a nod. The man turned away.

Better take the temperature of the town, he decided, cruising the length of the main drag and turning to travel back along the dirt road parallel to it. A few faces turned at the sight of his vehicle, a couple abruptly changed direction. Sophie Garcia's place looked the same as yesterday, her compact Ford and Jessie's motorcycle out front. A woman coming out of one of the other apartments glanced up, stepped back inside and closed her door.

People were nervous. Had something more happened overnight? If so, no one had reported it.

He decided to make the rounds of the few places he knew. A few cars were parked outside Joe and Helen

Starkey's house, but he didn't see anyone in the dirt yard or peering out the windows. The Rodarte's old house was similarly quiet, no vehicle in sight. Gina Staples and her husband didn't appear to be home but the garden had been watered this morning, he could tell by the damp trenches between the rows. He consulted his note and realized the Cayne family had lived right next door. Had Gina mentioned that? He didn't think so, and wondered if she was hiding something. Somehow he hadn't quite gotten to that part of the old case file in his brief scan of it, and now he was feeling even more out of the loop.

No wonder it was easy for everyone to make the connection between Lee Rodarte and Angela Cayne—they'd been next-door neighbors.

He pulled over to the edge of the road, got out and walked up to the place that looked like a modified double-wide with its white siding and aluminum screen door. It seemed neatly kept, but there were no vehicles or other signs of life at the moment. He was about to tap on the front door anyway when he spotted a little placard, something done by a craft painter. "The Smiths Live Here!" it proclaimed. His knock went unanswered.

He went back to the cruiser and punched up the address finder on his GPS, chiding himself for not doing that in the first place. When he entered the name Cayne only one name in Sembramos came up, a Sally Cayne on Pine Street. It had to be a relative.

Sally Cayne answered the door of her small bungalow, holding a fluffy little brown dog whose high-pitched yipping Beau had heard the moment he stopped the cruiser. The gray-haired woman stood less than five feet tall, with a pronounced hunch to her upper spine, and she had to adjust her hearing aids a couple of times before she got Beau's explanation of why he was there.

"Well, come on in, Sheriff. Bitsy won't bite. She's just real protective, you know." She limped arthritically aside to let him in.

It was usually the protective ones that *did* bite, Beau thought as he edged into an overly-warm living room. Sally reached into her apron pocket, slipped the dog some little nugget of a treat and deposited the fuzzy creature on the couch.

"Now, what can I do for you?" Sally asked after he declined an offer of coffee.

Beau gave the quick version—he was contacting the Cayne family to touch base and make sure there wouldn't be any problem between them and the Starkeys or the Rodartes. It seemed a more benign way to approach the subject than to start with suspicions about Jessie Starkey's death.

"Well, Sheriff, as the young ones might say, I think that boat already sailed." She sank down onto the couch beside the dog, and Beau perched on the seat of an armchair. "The problems between the three families started on June twenty-second, seven years ago. The night our Angela got taken and killed. My son never recovered. Alan blamed himself for not looking after her better, so badly that he lost his job. Used to teach at the school, fourth grade kids. Loved that job. Tracy was an accountant. She had to cut back her hours to take care of Alan. Then Matthew started having trouble in school. A year or so later, right after the trial, they moved away. Went to Houston, thinking a big city would be a place to get lost in, a place with no memories, if you know what I mean."

"Are things better for them now?"

Sally shrugged. "A little, I think. We'd almost lost Angie once, in a car accident, then only three years later she was really gone. At first you can't believe it. Then things are never the same."

Beau nodded. He couldn't really imagine. He let a moment pass. "You heard that Jessie Starkey and Lee Rodarte got out of prison, that the evidence which originally put them away was overturned."

Anger flashed through the old woman's eyes. "I heard it. Couldn't believe it. They confessed! And now they want to take it back? I'll let 'em take it back when I get to have my granddaughter back." She begun stroking Bitsy so hard that the tiny dog yipped. Sally eased off.

"I imagine a lot of folks feel that way, Mrs. Cayne. I can understand. I wonder if you've heard any talk about revenge. If there's somebody in town that would want to get rid of them, would you give me that information?"

"I could hand you the telephone book," she said, lifting her chin higher. "Everybody wants rid of those two."

Except everyone who was related to one of them. He didn't say it.

"Looks like somebody got half the job done right away, didn't they?" A tiny smile touched her lips.

Beau didn't want to get into details about Jessie's shooting, not the way news flew around this town. Better to keep the fact of the high-power bullet to himself. He couldn't see Sally Cayne limping into the forest on a cold spring morning to stalk and kill Starkey, but he still had to ask questions.

"Do you own a gun, Sally?"

She gave him a hard stare.

"I have to ask everyone. Rule out the innocent." He met

her gaze and didn't back down.

"I've got one. An old .22 rifle my husband used to use when coyotes would come around our livestock. Back in the day, we had chickens, a few goats, sometimes a few lambs. It's a person's right to protect their property."

"Yes, ma'am, it is." No point in asking to see the gun. Wrong caliber. "Be sure you keep that gun safely stored now," he said, rising. "Wouldn't want some bad person getting his hands on it."

Sally looked as if she would love the chance to face off with someone who tried to disarm her. Truthfully, Beau didn't blame her for that attitude; he just didn't want to see this situation escalate further. He warned her again about being careful.

He felt her watching him as he got into the cruiser and drove away, wishing he had a simple fix for the little town that had been hurt so deeply.

That wish turned into anxiety when he passed Sophie Garcia's apartment on his way to the Starkey's house. He'd decided to ask Joe Starkey the same question about what else they owned besides the shotguns he and Jessie had taken hunting. Sophie's car was gone, but now he saw that something was burning on the front sidewalk. He whipped to the side of the street and got out.

A hunk of plastic and cloth had melted into a puddle about ten feet from Sophie's front door. The flames were gone but the rest was smoldering vigorously. When Beau stomped out the fire it appeared to be the remains of a baby doll. It might have been an attempt at sick humor, but Beau got a real feeling that it was a personal warning. Someone threatening to harm her child because of the harm done to theirs?

He scanned the area. No activity on the street, maybe a curtain falling into place at that house across the street . . . At least no one stood nearby, taunting him. He circled the strip of apartments, making sure no one lurked outside Sophie's back windows. All seemed quiet.

He returned to his cruiser and grabbed an evidence bag from the cargo space, bagged the crispy remains and tossed the bag into the vehicle. It wasn't really evidence of any crime that he knew of, but before all this was over who knew what part it might play in the whole picture?

He decided to cruise by the Starkey place, get a feel for things there, see if someone holding a can of lighter fluid opened the door. He'd just put his SUV in gear when his cell phone rang.

Sam's name showed on the readout.

Chapter 7

Sam's first hitch in her cleaning project came when she plugged in her vacuum cleaner and discovered the huge house had no electricity. She uttered a little curse, mostly at herself for not thinking of that. Obviously, if no one had ever lived in the place and if the taxes were in arrears . . . well, she should have planned better.

She owned a generator that she'd used on more than one occasion in these situations, but it was in the barn at home right now, not on her utility trailer where it might have done her some good. She stood at the open front door, staring toward her vehicle and estimating the distance across the long front courtyard to the driveway. With her longest extension cord she might—*might*—be able to reach the outlet nearest the door. There was no way she could piece together enough of them to cover all areas of the ten-thousand-plus square feet inside. It would have to be manual labor.

She groaned at the thought and strode out to the truck to retrieve her brooms and dustpan. Giving the house a critical eye as she returned, her idea of finishing this off in a few hours disappeared. Every doorjamb and window frame was filled with an accumulation of years' worth of dirt and she now noticed that the windows themselves were a grimy mess. She sighed and attacked the first of the window sills with her whisk broom. An hour into it she'd finished the master suite's numerous windows and doors, deciding on a change of scene downstairs before tackling the acres of tile floors.

Humming helped fill the silence and when she discovered that the great room had the acoustics of a concert hall, well, she couldn't resist breaking into a medley of Patsy Cline tunes. She'd finished 'walking after midnight' and 'falling to pieces' and was about to think she was going 'crazy' when she caught a flicker of movement outside. Down on the highway, far below the house, a white vehicle cruised slowly past. For an instant she thought it might be Beau's department SUV. But it didn't have the brown logo and lettering as far as she could tell at this distance, and it definitely didn't have the light bar on top. She turned back to her work but found herself really wishing that Beau had come by. Her back was aching and his company would have provided a welcome break.

Once the idea of taking a break entered her mind she couldn't let go of it. Lunch would be a good idea. There was a café in Sembramos. It would probably be open now and she could order a sandwich to go. She leaned her broom against the wall and locked the house, dropping the shiny new key into her pocket. There would be paperwork to do later, signage to install, and a lockbox for the key—but for now she just wanted food.

She guided her truck carefully around the looping circular drive; despite the ample space, a crew cab truck with a utility trailer was too large a rig for some places. Since she wouldn't need the lawn mower or garden tools for this job maybe she would just take the trailer home and leave it before she came back this afternoon.

At the highway she paused to look back up at the large white house, a mansion by any standard and unique in design compared to everything else in this county. Hard to believe she'd never known the place was here. She looked both directions but there wasn't a single car in sight as she made the left turn and headed toward town.

The acres of cultivated fields ran from the edge of the roadway all the way to the forested foothills of the Sangre de Cristo range. Somewhere in those woods was the spot where Beau said the suspicious hunting accident had happened. Ahead, she came to the north end of the little community, marked by another set of speed limit warnings and a few little businesses.

Two men stood outside a taxidermy shop, their conversation punctuated by gestures; one of them pointed toward something, which drew Sam's attention. The front window of the shop was broken out, with violent-looking shards of glass hanging menacingly from the frame. Looked as if a brick had gone right through the middle of it. Below the broken glass, something had been painted in vivid red.

She couldn't read it, if indeed the red lines were words, and she realized she'd nearly steered off the roadway. She corrected and drove on. In the next block a white-coated man stood outside his barber shop, arms crossed, eyes darting nervously. Across the road, Sam caught sight of three figures ducking between two buildings. What was going on here?

She spotted the café ahead and edged off the road, looking for a large enough place for her truck and trailer. Picking up her phone she hit Beau's cell number. He'd mentioned coming up here today to ask more questions. If he was in town maybe he would meet her for lunch. If not, she would definitely order something to go and take it back to her job. Things in town felt a little too edgy for her taste.

"Hey, darlin'," he said. Was there a tightness to his voice? "How's your job going?"

"I decided to take a break for lunch. Forgot to bring anything from home this morning and my aching back was screaming for a break. This one is all manual labor. I'm near that little café in Sembramos—I thought I'd grab a bite. So, where are you right now?"

"I'm in Sembramos too, interviewing witnesses. Ran across something real strange awhile ago."

He said something else but suddenly her driver's side door flew open and a hand grabbed her sleeve, jerking her sideways.

"What!" she shrieked and her phone went flying.

A tall man in a dirty flannel shirt and jeans held a fistful of her jacket. "Tracy, what the hell are you doing in town?" he demanded.

"I'm not Tracy! Let go." Sam yanked her arm out of his grasp, grabbing the steering wheel to keep from falling out. "What do you want?"

He seemed momentarily at a loss—clearly he'd thought she was someone else—but his bravado returned. "I asked what you're doing here." He leaned toward her.

She sat up straight. Whoever this was, he wasn't going to intimidate her. "You've mistaken me for someone else. I simply want some lunch. This is a restaurant, isn't it?" She nodded toward the wood-sided building.

A flash of red, then Beau's cruiser bounced off the edge of the pavement and skidded to a stop on the dirt. He was out of the SUV, hand at his holster, in one smooth move.

"Bobby Starkey—you just simmer down. What's going on here?" Beau demanded.

The grizzled man dropped his hands to his sides, not quite meeting Beau's stare.

"I asked you a question," Beau said.

"Uh, nothin' really. Thought I recognized this—"

"He grabbed me and called me by someone else's name." Sam tugged her jacket straight. "Someone named Tracy."

"Are you all right?" He looked her up and down for verification.

"I think so. Just surprised."

Beau gave her another long look. "Okay, then. Move along, Starkey. I better not hear about any more trouble from you."

He stood firm until Bobby Starkey shuffled away, sending malicious glances back at Beau. When the man turned the corner at the end of the block, Beau turned to Sam.

"You're sure you're okay?"

She nodded. "Yeah. It was just so weird. I'm talking to you and all at once my door flies open. I never saw him approach."

"I warned you about being in town—remember? I don't

know how this will go down but things are really tense."

Confirming that, Sam caught someone staring out a window at the small motel across the road.

"What *is* going on, Beau? Who was that man who grabbed me?"

"I don't have time to go into the whole thing now, and I don't want you out on the street. That was Jessie Starkey's uncle. Some in that family are blazing mad and more than a few pints of whiskey have now begun to figure into the equation." He glanced around inside her truck. "Get your phone—I want you to have it on you at all times. I'll escort you to the edge of town so no one else starts something, then I want you to go home and stay there. Don't come back up here."

"But—my work—"

"It'll keep. And if that USDA guy of yours gives you any trouble, I'll speak to him personally."

"Beau—?"

"Not a good time. This town's a powder keg right now and I can't have you in the middle of it."

Sam clenched her teeth. "I only wanted to say that I don't like you being in the middle of it either. Do you have backup?"

His expression told her that up to this moment he hadn't believed he would need it. Now that Sam had been accosted, he wasn't so sure. "I'm a radio call away from my deputies. If it gets out of control, State Police will assist."

He stepped in close enough for a quick hug.

"Beau, you smell like something burnt. Has there—"

"Nothing major. I was just on my way to have a little chat with the Starkeys. Now, I think I'd better find Lee Rodarte instead. I'll fill you in when I get home this evening." He opened the door of her truck and waited until she got behind the wheel.

"Do you think we're in danger in Taos, too?" she asked as she clipped her seatbelt in place.

"I doubt it, but please don't take chances. If Bobby Starkey mistook you, then so could someone else. Can you just sit this one out at home? Jessie's funeral is tomorrow—after that things should calm down."

Another quick kiss and Sam started the truck and steered onto the highway, glancing back in the direction of the big white house she was supposed to be tending. But Beau was in his cruiser now, only a few feet from her bumper. No way was she going anyplace other than home. For the time being. She chafed but drove, slowly and carefully, with him behind her. In her rearview she saw that he pulled over at the edge of town, then made a U-turn after she was a mile or so down the highway.

* * *

Beau let Sam's truck get nearly out of sight before he turned around to face the rest of his day. He would have loved to go home with her, settle in with a game on TV and let this whole mess in Sembramos work itself out. But he couldn't do that. It's what his predecessor would have done. Padilla's lack of attention to detail might have been what led to the sloppy police work that created today's situation in the first place. Beau drove back toward Sophie Garcia's apartment, hoping she would tell him that Lee had followed advice and left town.

Even if that were the case, Beau knew he needed to

verify Lee's alibi. Until it could be corroborated that he'd spent the night at Sophie's, he was still number one on the suspect list for Jessie's death. Arresting Lee would probably calm the Starkeys, but it would surely inflame the half of the population who believed in his innocence. This was getting stickier all the time. Maybe he should put the State Police on alert, just in case.

He zigzagged a couple of streets and stopped across the street from Sophie's apartment. Her car was in the drive now and a bicycle rested against the wall near it. No sign of Lee's motorcycle. This could be the news he wanted.

As Beau was getting out of the cruiser a white Volkswagen passed him slowly and turned in at the drive of the single-family home where he was parked. The driver—a woman with blonde hair up in a bun, wearing dark blue scrubs—walked toward him, looking concerned.

"Is there a problem, Sheriff?" she asked. "My son—"

He asked her name—Claudia MacNeill. "No, it's nothing to do with your son. I'm looking into the death of Jessie Starkey."

She nodded, weary lines settling over her features. "Sorry," she said, yawning widely. "I just finished a double shift. It's been a crazy week."

"You work at Holy Cross?" he asked.

"Yeah. Night nurse in the ER. *Usually* nights—twice I've had to pull the seven-to-three as well. And then a couple days ago the whole schedule got messed up when Kathy went home sick and now I'm doing a half shift on what was supposed to be my day off." She smiled and shifted the purse strap that hung on her shoulder. "But you don't care about all that, do you?"

"I'm checking with neighbors of Sophie Garcia's," he said. "I know her boyfriend has been around recently. I'm wondering if you saw his bike coming or going over the weekend—Easter Sunday morning?"

She stared skyward for a moment. "I did. That was the day I got called in for an extra shift. They woke me up. I went in around two in the morning. Once we took care of a rollover carload, things weren't so busy so I was able to get out of there around five. Thought maybe if I rushed home I could get my husband and son up in time to go to the sunrise service in Taos. But they were so sound asleep that I didn't have the heart to wake them, *and* to drive back where I'd just come from." She realized she was rattling on. "Anyway, yeah. The bike was parked in the driveway, in front of Sophie's car, both when I left and when I came back. The apartment was dark except for the outdoor lighting that's on all night, all the time. They might have left for awhile, but in the middle of the night? Why would they?"

Beau could think of one reason but to have shot Jessie Starkey, Lee would have had to leave and tail the hunters out to the woods. And he'd have needed to make record time getting back here before Claudia MacNeill came home. Besides, neither Sophie's little car nor Lee's Harley was exactly suited to quiet travel over mountain terrain. It wasn't proof positive that Lee was innocent, but it went a long way toward backing up the story the ex-con had told him. Beau thanked Claudia for her time and she gratefully headed toward her front door.

Voices across the street caught Beau's attention and he saw Nathan Garcia come out of the apartment and mount his bicycle.

"Stay right here on our block," Sophie called out to him. She looked up and saw Beau.

He made eye contact and walked over.

"Can we talk for a minute?" he asked.

"I guess." She backed into the apartment, standing aside so he could enter. "I don't know what I could tell you that's any different from yesterday."

Beau looked around. "I notice Lee's bike is gone. Did he leave?"

"I don't know. I mean, he didn't bring much stuff with him. A few clothes that he carried in his saddlebags. He loves that bike." She moved a stack of folded towels from the armchair and motioned for Beau to sit.

"He's had it a long time?"

"Long time. Even back when we first started dating. He left it with me when they sent him away. Nathan was a baby then and Lee told me if things ever got really hard for us that I could sell the bike. That was my first clue how much he loves Nathan. He wouldn't give up that bike for anything or anyone else."

"Things must have been difficult for you, more than once I would imagine."

"Yeah, well. I've got my job at the bank. It's steady even if it doesn't pay a whole lot. My folks helped me out some too. Mom watched the baby for me until he started school, so that was really good."

"And now that Lee's back?"

"I don't know." She'd perched on the arm of the couch and now she ran her fingers through her hair, scraping it back from her face. "I still have feelings for him. We might be able to make it work. But I told him he can't put Nathan in danger—no matter what. I don't want to move away from my family . . . but I don't know if we could stay here. I just don't know anything right now."

"If it's any help, I was able to verify Lee's alibi for Sunday morning."

Relief washed over her. She truly hadn't been sure that he had stayed on that couch all night long, Beau realized.

"Sophie, I think the way out of this whole mess is if we can go back to the old case, when Angela was killed. If we can find out who really did it, I'd hope that the whole town could get on with life and put this situation behind them."

She nodded. "Otherwise, I'm afraid it's going to be one payback after the other."

Smart girl.

"So," he said, "what do you remember from back then? Did you know Angela Cayne?"

"Oh sure, slightly. Everybody knows everybody in this town—I'm sure you've heard that before. Angie was a few years younger, you know, so we were never in the same classes. But when I started going out with Lee—we were seniors in high school then—I'd see Angie around. Her folks lived right next door to Lee's. Cute girl, pretty popular as I remember. I recall her getting into some kind of trouble over a drunk driving incident . . . she was probably about sixteen."

"Her grandmother said she was in an accident once and they thought they might lose her."

"Oh, gosh, that's right. That's what it was. Angie was driving and there was a bad wreck. Her best friend died. I was away when that happened, taking training courses for my job. Lee went to UNM for a year and I think he was gone then too. College didn't work out for him. He finally went to work for his buddy who owns that bike shop in Taos."

"So, moving up to the time when Angela was abducted and killed . . . what do you remember about that?"

"My world and Angie's were pretty different. I'd gotten pregnant with Nathan, but Lee and I were having problems. I couldn't decide if getting married was a good idea or not. I guess my hormones were going all crazy, but I just didn't want to make that commitment until after I had the baby. Then one thing and another. I went back to work, my mom was keeping Nathan during the day . . . you know, I rarely got over to Lee's parents' house in those days so I hardly ever saw Angie. The first I knew about the tragedy was when a customer came in the bank, all scared and shaky and said she'd just heard that Angie Cayne was kidnapped. I mean, no one believed it at first. The gossip went wild—she'd run off with a boyfriend, she'd run off with an older man, she'd run off to get away from her parents—that kind of stuff. No one truly believed that anything bad had happened to her until her body was found a few days later. Then it was shock—total shock."

Chapter 8

Sam hit the accelerator a little too hard as she watched Beau's cruiser turn around. Being ordered back home didn't sit well with her, but a niggling feeling told her that it wasn't Beau she was angry with, it was the situation. And she couldn't very well be angry at a situation that didn't realistically involve her. And yet, just a few minutes ago, she had become involved.

At the bottom of it all was fear. What if the man who'd pulled her out of her truck was the killer? And what if he'd grabbed her with evil intent, and what if Beau hadn't come along at that moment?

That's what spurred her emotions now.

The road curved and her truck swayed across the yellow line. *Get hold of yourself, Sam.* She eased off the gas and concentrated on the road, dashed lines on pavement, flowing past, calming her mind.

At the ranch, Nellie and Ranger sat up on the porch as Sam pulled up the driveway. The minute she got out of the truck, both of them bounded toward her, tails in motion, smiles on their faces.

"Hey you guys," she said, bending to give them some attention. "You know how to brighten a mood, don't you?"

They circled, slowing her progress to the front door. She let them come inside and she dropped her pack on the couch. Frustration welled up again. No lunch, little progress on the job at the big white house, and now Beau was put out with her for being in Sembramos at all.

She stood in front of the open refrigerator door, contemplating the contents—didn't she used to get after Kelly for doing the same thing?

Make up your mind, Sam, and just get on with the day!

She picked up a plastic container of leftover potato salad, not exactly the lunch she'd anticipated. Wandering through the house with fork in hand, she polished off the contents as she debated what to do next. Despite the best of intentions, she wasn't in the mood for spring cleaning. She took the empty Tupperware to the kitchen and put it in the dishwasher, looked around, felt her impatience rise again.

A slip of paper on the counter caught her attention.

It was the name Rupert had given her, the reference librarian. Well, doing a little research sounded like way more fun than cleaning. She picked up the phone, dialed the number at the Harwood Library and was put in touch with Cora Abernathy.

"Oh, yes, Rupert Penrick," the woman with the elderly-sounding voice said. "He comes around now and then. I have to say, he does have some of the strangest requests for information."

Sam could see this line of conversation going a thousand directions—interesting ones, yes, but since she already knew the plots of most of Rupert's books, she figured she better lead Cora toward her own needs.

"Well, my request might turn out to be an odd one, too," she said with a chuckle. "I met a woman here in Taos—Bertha Martinez. She died almost two years ago and I understand that she was possibly involved in the occult. People said she was reputed to be a *bruja*."

"Hmm . . . I've never heard of her. I suppose I could check the New Mexico history texts, see if her name comes up."

"I don't know that it would," Sam said. How to approach this without actually telling Cora about the wooden box? "I doubt Bertha was anyone very important, although I could be wrong. What I'm mainly interested in knowing is how I might find other people who knew her. There's not some kind of local witches club around here or anything, is there?"

"That would be called a coven. I'm not aware of any. Still, you never know." Cora sounded slightly distracted. "I'm making some notes. Let me do some checking and I'll get back to you."

The librarian took Sam's phone number and promised to call back, whether she found out anything or not. At least it was a start, Sam figured, as she hung up.

The idea of there being a local coven really hadn't occurred to Sam before now, so on a whim she set her laptop computer on the dining table and decided to give that a try. A search for "witch covens Taos" led to two websites, one of which seemed to be wiccans who seriously studied the practice of modern day witchcraft; the other looked like a bunch of schoolgirls who fancied themselves to be Harry Potter's girlfriends. Neither seemed a likely match for a woman in her nineties who had probably practiced the oldest of the old New Mexico traditions. To have been a contemporary of Bertha Martinez, Sam guessed she would be talking to someone over seventy.

She closed her browser, unsure whether she was on the right track at all. A rumor about Bertha being a *bruja* was a far cry from knowing it for a fact, and an even farther leap to the notion that the wooden box had anything at all to do with such practices. Sam decided to put the whole thing out of her mind unless she heard back from Cora Abernathy and got any truly useful leads. There were more important things requiring her attention—her business, for one.

Aside from the two weeks she was away on her honeymoon, this was the first time she'd gone a full day without being at the bakery. She dialed Sweet's Sweets. Jen didn't answer until the fourth ring and Sam could hear a clamor of voices in the background.

"Things are busy, I gather?" She could picture the sales room full of people and Jen dashing around to fill orders. It was, after all, mid-afternoon and there was often a rush of coffee-and-dessert folks about now. "Just call me back when it settles a little."

"No, Sam, wait!" Her voice went lower. "We have a little situation. Can you talk to Becky a minute?"

Situation? Uh-oh.

Becky came on the line, sounding frazzled. "Oh, Sam, I'm afraid I lost an order. There's a lady here who's giving Jen what-for out front."

"Take a deep breath and tell me what happened."

"This woman comes in—this was about fifteen minutes ago. She's got, like, five or six friends with her. She says she's here to pick up her divorce-party cake. Jen comes back with a blank look on her face. I don't remember the order either . . . And now this woman is throwing a fit and all of her friends are making comments like 'why did you order from *this* place?' and stuff like that. I'm afraid they'll all leave here and tell people that Sweet's Sweets is a terrible bakery. She keeps saying that the party is tonight and if there's no cake she's going to—I don't know what, but she's pretty angry."

Sam's mind whirled. She didn't remember any divorce-party order either, but with the Easter rush and everything else that had happened in the past week, she just couldn't be sure.

"Becky, calm down. Has the woman described what she ordered? Can we pull something together quickly?"

"She says it was like a wedding cake, three tiers. Only the bride and groom aren't standing together on the top, she's pushing him off, like he's falling down the stairs and breaking his neck."

This customer sounded like a lovely woman to be married to. The guy was probably thrilled to be taking the stairs out of there.

"Okay, Becky, walk over to the fridge and tell me what we have on hand."

"Two dozen vanilla cupcakes iced in chocolate, a red velvet half-sheet that isn't decorated yet, four eight-inch layers . . . those aren't decorated yet either. Oh, and two fruit tarts. All of that was going to be part of our stock for tomorrow."

It was an adequate amount for the usual walk-ins who wanted birthday cakes and family desserts. Sam's mind tried to put it all together into something coherent.

"Good. Now we're going to fudge a little with the customer." An out-and-out lie, really, but you had to do that sometimes to save the day. "Go in there and tell the woman that you hadn't realized the owner had taken her order home to personally finish it. Tell her to come back at five and it will be ready."

Becky let out a whimper.

"I'm on my way. I'll be there in fifteen minutes. Meanwhile, pull out all the cake toppers we have and see if anything can be adapted to the bride-and-groom scenario she wants. If not, get out the modeling chocolate and you and Julio do your best to sculpt figurines. I'll handle the cakes, if you can do the other. And Becky? Don't panic. We can do this."

Sam glanced at the clock as she hung up. Three o'clock already. But at least she finally felt like the afternoon had purpose. She wondered how soon Beau would be home. He'd ordered her to stay at the ranch so there wouldn't be trouble with the Sembramos crowd, but surely this didn't count. She picked up her pack and the keys to her bakery van. *See? I won't even be driving the same vehicle—no one will know me. Yeah, how far is that argument going to go?*

She walked through the back door at the bakery to find Becky and Julio bent over the work table shaping bits of colored claylike material.

"I take it the customer accepted the plan?"

"Barely. I think she still gave Jen an earful."

Sam peered through the curtain, where Jen was furiously polishing away at the bistro tables.

"You okay?"

Jen looked up and nodded. "Thank goodness you came

up with this idea. The woman actually seemed a little bit pleased that her order was being personally handled by you."

"Thanks, Jen. I'm sure you handled it as well as anyone on earth could have."

"We never did find an order form for this, and I swear I never saw this person in the shop before."

Whether the lady was mistaken about which bakery she'd visited, or whether she was the type who operated by throwing tantrums all around town to get what she wanted, Sam would probably never know. For now, she would have to come up with something to save her reputation from being trashed.

She'd been forming an idea as she raced out of the house and drove to the shop. Now it was time to implement it.

"Julio, do we have plenty of white buttercream?" she asked.

He pointed to a tub that Becky had wisely taken from the fridge. Sam pulled out the sheet cake and the four layers. Smoothing buttercream on the sheet first, she then stacked three of the layers on top of it, butting their edges together into a cloverleaf formation. They all received a buttercream coating, then the final eight-inch layer went on top. Sam filled her biggest piping bag and went to work with flowers and large, full-blown roses. The design began to take shape nicely, and it really did scream 'wedding.'

Julio, meanwhile, had created a groom in tuxedo. The little man-figure's legs were splayed and his arms seemed to be grabbing air. Julio held him beside the cake and, for all the world, he looked as if he'd just been knocked down a flight of steps. Becky's bride-figure had her hands on the hips of her white gown and a furious expression on her face.

"I got her hair color and features from the real one," Becky said with a satisfied little grin.

Sam set the figurines in place, piped on a couple more little details, and stood back to evaluate. "It seems pretty vindictive to me."

"So did this customer. Maybe we should add some blood," Becky said.

Julio eyed the cake. "I think the guy's lucky. The real one, I mean."

The bells at the front door tinkled and female voices filled the shop. The clock said five.

"Shh," Sam warned. "I'll take it out there. Either she'll love it or I'll be back in a minute with half my ass missing."

That drew a chuckle and the others turned to clean up the mess the flurry had created on the worktable.

The customer seemed in an entirely different frame of mind this time. She greeted Jen as if her parting words had not been rude and threatening, and she gushed over Sam's cake design to the point that Sam decided the group must have started the party a little early at a bar somewhere. At any rate, the lady paid for the cake and left and Sam's entire staff had survived. Smiles and relief showed unanimously. Sam was in the middle of handing out congratulations all around when her cell phone rang. Beau.

Oh boy. Was this going to be their first real clash of wills?

Chapter 9

A deep rumble vibrated the apartment's windows. Beau looked out and saw the familiar Harley roll to a stop. Lee swung his leg over. Sophie's son, Nathan, sat on his bicycle at the edge of the roadway, watching the man and machine with fascination.

"Like father, like son." Resignation in Sophie's voice.

Beau waited inside. Lee took a long look at the sheriff's SUV, glanced toward the apartment, came up to the door anyway. Sophie let him in, standing at the open door a few extra seconds and sending some kind of non-verbal mom signal to her son.

"Sheriff," Lee said, slapping dust from his jeans.

Beau asked what his plans were.

"I told you, I want to be near my son. I have as much right to be here as anybody."

"You do. And legally I can't make you leave. But, think about it. Is it smart to be here? Jessie's dead already. I don't think you or Sophie want you to be next on someone's hit list. The mood around town is getting uglier all the time."

Sophie spoke up. "I won't have you putting Nathan in danger. You can't stay here in the apartment."

Rodarte looked as if he wanted to say something, but he glanced at Beau and closed his mouth.

"Look, how about if you got yourself a place in Taos? Close enough to get together with Nathan, but maybe it would be far enough to keep you safe."

"I'm not—"

Beau raised a hand. "We don't know that you're in danger. But we don't know that you aren't. And if somebody comes after you, here in this apartment, you *will* be putting Sophie and your boy in danger."

"How can I clear my name if I can't even be here in town?" Lee's arms crossed over his chest.

"That's what I'm here for, to try to get to the bottom of all this and find out the truth once and for all."

Rodarte made a derisive sound.

"Look, I didn't want to mention this," Beau said. "But someone's already been here." He told them about the burned doll on the front sidewalk.

Sophie's face went two shades whiter. "That does it. Go! I don't care where, at this moment, but you can't be here." She stepped toward the front door but Lee didn't budge.

Beau really didn't want to see this degenerate further. "Lee, take my advice. Please. Leave this town for awhile. Jessie's funeral is tomorrow and things will surely settle down after that. And my department will keep working on this. We'll do our best to get it settled. Meanwhile, I'm afraid

I have to insist that you leave the apartment. The lady wants you out and it is within my authority to make that happen."

Rodarte's belligerent stance wilted. "Sophie . . . come with me? I don't want to lose you."

Her dark eyes became liquid pools. "Not now. For Nathan—"

Beau moved to the door and opened it. "Get your stuff. I'll keep an eye on Sophie and Nathan for awhile. You two can make your plans, but let's not aggravate the whole situation right now."

Lee picked up a ratty backpack from behind the armchair, hugged it to his chest and walked outside. Beau followed, cautioning Sophie to keep her son near and to lock all her doors and windows.

"Take a minute with your boy if you want," Beau offered.

But when Lee approached, the child backed away slightly. Lee gave him a rueful smile and a little knuckle-tap to the handlebar of the bicycle before walking away to stash his pack on the Harley. Beau followed the biker to the edge of town and watched him roar down the highway. Three broken hearts and not a thing he could do to reassure them it would soon get any better.

He cruised back by Sophie's apartment. The bicycle was chained to a porch railing and the place seemed buttoned up tight. At least one of them was taking his warnings seriously.

Now for the Starkeys.

At the small food market, a raised pickup truck with huge tires sat near the door with two rough-looking men in it. One of the men looked a lot like Joe Starkey. A woman with a cartful of bags rushed to her car and began to toss her purchases inside. Beau slowed, making sure they noticed him, waiting until he saw the woman get safely into her vehicle. Another Starkey male came out of the store with a twelve-pack of Bud and waved at Beau as he joined the others in the truck.

Little signs of trouble continued as Beau drove through town—spray paint on a wall where none had been before, with the words 'get Jessie's killer'; two motorcycles lying on their sides, not yet discovered by their owners. He circled the block to the Starkey house where the high pickup truck sat among a cluster of vehicles that had all seen better days. Beer cans littered the space around a large barrel. Clearly, no basketball players in this crowd. Beau parked, radioed his location and stepped out.

"Not too happy to see you takin' care of that Rodarte scum," Joe Starkey said, swaggering his way over to Beau.

"It's my job to take care of everyone in this county," Beau said. "I just stopped by to see how you all are doing."

Helen Starkey appeared from beside the house, her face contorted in anger. "Take care of us?" she shouted. "You did a helluva job taking care of us so far."

Beau took a deep breath. "Helen. I know this hurts. Eventually it'll get better."

"Better? My boy is dead and you think this will ever get *better*?"

Beau started to apologize for his poor choice of words but Helen interrupted.

"My life hit its best point seven years ago. It's been nothin' but downhill since then. And *your* department's done diddly-shit to make it *better*. Get out of my sight, Sheriff!"

A younger woman wearing skin-tight jeans and a baggy man's shirt stepped forward and touched Helen's shoulder. "Come on inside, Helen. Let's get you somethin' to eat."

Beau surveyed the faces in the crowd of a dozen or more, spotting Bobby's wife JoNell, who placed restraining hands on the arms of two long-haired teenage boys. This could get real dicey, real fast. He raised a hand in a conciliatory gesture.

"Listen, all of you," he said, working to stay in command. "We're doing what we can. I got Lee Rodarte out of town. I'm putting my whole department to work on solving Jessie's murder. Nobody in town wants trouble and I'm asking all of you to remember Jessie with dignity, not to let this thing get out of hand where somebody else ends up hurt and a lot of folks end up with regrets." He met the patriarch's stare, straight on. "Joe? You keep 'em in line?"

Joe Starkey nodded slowly but the sneer on his face didn't reassure Beau in the least.

"Okay, then. I'll put some of my men around town, make sure Rodarte doesn't come cruising for trouble. After the funeral tomorrow I'll expect everyone to get back to business as usual and do your best to put this behind you and just let us do our jobs."

A couple of the men shuffled slightly, scuffing toes in the dirt like young bulls, testing. Beau wanted to give a warning about the amount of alcohol at the gathering, but this didn't look like the time to press his luck. Hopefully the message about extra law enforcement would get through. He touched the brim of his hat and turned toward his vehicle, making a show of getting on the radio before he drove away.

With the order in for teams of deputies to take turns patrolling Sembramos overnight, he made another run past Rodarte's parents' old house, Sally Cayne's, and the few others he knew to be connected. All quiet. So far.

Pulling over in the parking lot of the now-empty elementary school, he used his cell phone to call home. No answer.

He dialed Sam's cell. "I called the house and you weren't there. I thought we'd agreed on that." He realized that, technically, he'd issued orders which she hadn't exactly said she would follow.

"Sweet shop emergency. I'm on my way home now," she said.

"We'll talk about this when I get there." He hung up without waiting for a response and pulled out onto the two-lane road.

Twenty minutes later he arrived at the ranch. Sam's red pickup truck sat in its usual place but her bakery van was gone. He fumed, getting out of his cruiser. He'd said he didn't want anyone on the highway to recognize her truck and give her trouble. Did she have to take his words so literally?

He greeted the border collie and Lab with pats on their heads and went inside. This whole day was really beginning to wear on him. Pouring a short Scotch into his favorite crystal glass, he carried it upstairs and started the shower. When he emerged, in a mellower frame of mind, he heard sounds downstairs. He also smelled pizza.

"I brought it from Giuseppe's," Sam said, pointing to the box with the fantastic smell.

It was, of course, his favorite combo and when Sam launched into the whole story of the crazy lady at the bakery who was about to drive all her employees off the cliff, he held back on the list of warnings he'd been planning. And when, after pizza and a couple glasses of wine, they found themselves in the bedroom, he forgot the lecture altogether.

"I'm sorry I worried you," Sam said afterward, running a finger down the middle of his sweaty chest. "I didn't intend that."

He started to say something about wanting to keep her safe, but the sex had been great and he was in a much more expansive mood now. There was no point in prolonging the discussion and letting it degenerate.

"I could make us a special coffee," she offered. "Or hot chocolate?"

Sam put on a robe and Beau slipped into his jeans and an old, soft shirt before following her downstairs. He scooped food for the dogs, filling her in on the latest in Sembramos.

"So, do you think Lee Rodarte will stay away?" She located some cookies she'd brought home a few days ago, to go along with the coffee.

Beau shook his head. "No idea. I doubt it. I've got deputies assigned to the funeral tomorrow and I'll try to be there too but, realistically, I think the only way this thing is going to calm down is if I can find out who really did kill Angela Cayne seven years ago. Basically, everyone in that town has taken a side—some on Lee's, more on the Starkeys, a lot who feel for Sally Cayne and that family's loss. Everyone wants justice. If I can catch whoever set the whole mess in motion, maybe we can give them that."

Sam poured coffee and carried mugs to the living room.

"I just wish I had the manpower to devote to a cold case. I don't know where we're going to find the evidence we'll need. And we've got new cases all the time. With budget cutbacks, it's all I can do to serve warrants and handle traffic."

"So, what if you and I started going through the file, reviewing it? We might come up with something that was missed the first time around. You said Sheriff Padilla didn't seem to work this one very hard."

"Yeah, well that was my perception at the time, as a new deputy in the department. It did seem like he raced through it. And I was always uneasy about that confession."

Sam reached for a notepad and pen. "The file's here. Let's do it."

Beau brought the thick folder to the coffee table and unfastened the metal brads holding it together. "This thing's impossible to hold on your lap and even more impossible for two people to read at once. Let's divide it up. The pages are numbered—we'll just put it back together when we're done. Besides, maybe looking at it in some other order than the way it is now will give us a few new ideas."

He handed Sam a half-inch thick chunk of pages and took one for himself.

Sam read two pages and immediately decided she would have to take notes. A half hour later they paused to compare.

"I'm reading Lee Rodarte's statement after he was picked up," Sam said. "After Jessie implicated him during the confession. Lee says he had ridden his motorcycle out toward the gorge bridge that night, wanting a little time alone. He said no one was with him, no alibi, but we should find out if anyone was even asked whether they could give him one."

"Make a note about that—a list of unanswered questions. We may come across the answers as we read, and we could check them off, but I want to be sure everything fits together before this is all over with."

Beau thumbed through his set of pages. "This section basically describes the crime scene. Angela Cayne was found in a ravine near the creek. She'd been badly beaten and strangled. She'd been there nearly three days before she was found.

"From my interviews in town, she was reported missing within two hours after she was taken, and that seems to fit with the timeline in the initial report. The parents had gone to Taos and she had stayed home. Her grandmother was staying with them at the time but she'd not been feeling well and went to bed early. I met Sally Cayne and can attest to the fact that without her hearing aids she wouldn't have necessarily heard a scuffle in another room."

"Lee swears he's innocent, every time they talk to him, in all the pages I've read," Sam said. "Yet no one seemed to be listening to him. Every question from Padilla comes back at Lee with the fact that Jessie Starkey told them Lee was guilty."

"Are Jessie's statements there? With your pages?"

She shook her head. "Haven't come across them."

An hour later, Sam's eyelids felt like they had lead weights attached. "I'm not making sense of this anymore," she said. "Nothing seems to be filed here in sequential order and my brain isn't working. It's been a long day."

Beau smiled up from his set of pages. "I know, darlin'. Go ahead upstairs—I'm right behind you."

He didn't have to suggest it twice. Sam set her pages down and trudged to the kitchen with their coffee cups. She'd brushed her teeth and smoothed the sheets from their earlier visit, and was about to settle herself into sleepy bliss when she heard his footsteps on the stairs.

"Well, this adds an interesting wrinkle," Beau said, coming into the room. "At the time Jessie Starkey confessed, he tested positive for cocaine."

Sam gave a puzzled look.

"That little fact never came up at the trial," Beau said. "And the lab report was shoved between two other pages, in a spot completely unrelated to the confession."

"So you think someone tried to cover it up?"

"That would be my guess."

Chapter 10

The revelations in the Angela Cayne case file might have kept Sam awake but that didn't turn out to be. Her head hit the pillow and she didn't even roll over until gray dawn began to filter into the bedroom. When she reached out for Beau she discovered that he was not in bed. No light from the bathroom; he must be downstairs. She found him at the dining table with pages from the file spread out in stacks.

"Morning, baby," she said. "Did you actually settle into bed last night at all?"

"Oh, yeah. A few hours. Kept waking up though. Finally, it made more sense to let you sleep without all my tossing and turning."

She kissed the top of his head. "Coffee?"

Not waiting for his answer, she went into the kitchen and found that he'd already brewed some, just hadn't remembered to pour it. She doctored two mugs and carried them to the table.

"I'm trying to organize all this into a timeline," he said. "It's almost as if somebody took a dozen little folders and a hundred loose pages and just gathered them up any old which way and stuck them together with a cover over it all. There's no sequence to it whatsoever."

"Glad you said that. Last night I was beginning to feel like it was my fuzzy head that wasn't making sense of it."

"Wasn't you." He paused for a sip of his coffee. "You know, taking over this job, half the time I wonder how much of this stuff was Padilla's incompetence and how often he might have been purposely covering up something. I find this kind of sloppy work all the time. If the defense lawyers were never given Jessie's drug test results, that alone could have changed the outcome."

"If money were no object you could hire a staff just to go through files and organize them all."

He snorted. Money was always an object and he was lucky his current staff hadn't been cut further. Two of his older deputies had retired within the last year and he'd been informed that he couldn't replace them. Let the rest of the department pick up their duties. So, no. Finding someone to go through old case files wasn't going to happen.

"How can I help?" Sam offered. "Looks like you have a system going there."

"Yeah, kind of. Once I get each interview, report, evidence list, etcetera, put into one of these piles, we can both read through them." He looked up and sent her one of his winning smiles. "Maybe something to eat?"

"You got it." Food wouldn't be such a bad idea, Sam decided, thinking to clear her own cobwebby brain.

She found that they were out of eggs, bacon and bread—when was the last time she'd stopped for groceries? But there was pancake mix and enough butter and syrup to make one of Beau's favorite breakfasts. She heated the griddle and soon had two nicely browned stacks ready; it didn't take a second call for Beau to show up and take his spot at the kitchen table.

"I just wish I didn't feel like I was starting so late in the game with this one," he said halfway through his fourth pancake. "It's like everyone in Sembramos was there from day one—they know all the history, and I'm the unsuspecting guy who's just walked into the trap. They'll tell me only what they want me to know."

"At least you can't say that it's one little town united against the lawman. Nobody in that place seems to agree on anything." Sam swiped a wedge of pancake through her puddle of syrup. "You know, I remember reading about this in the papers, back when it happened. I wonder, if we had copies of those articles maybe we would get another angle on it?"

"We couldn't use news reports to build a legal case," he said.

"I know. But maybe the press talked to someone back then, somebody the sheriff didn't formally interview. I could go down to the newspaper office and get copies of whatever is in their archives."

Beau looked a little skeptical but gave a knock-yourself-out approval to the plan. "Meanwhile, it's late and I better get to the office and find out what new catastrophe is facing me today."

He carried the dishes to the sink, leaving Sam with her thoughts and her coffee. She ran through her own checklist for the day. Get out to the monster house and try to finish cleaning the windows and floors there—she'd sworn to Beau that she would drive straight through Sembramos without stopping. Go by the newspaper office; check in at Sweet's Sweets and hope no new disasters had shown up.

Upstairs, she put on the same jeans and work shirt she'd worn yesterday. Rummaging in her drawer for a pair of clean socks she touched the deputy's badge Beau had given her once when she helped him with a case. At the time she'd suspected that the old piece of metal was hers more as a spoof, something to semi-officially give her access to evidence that she shouldn't otherwise see. She didn't actually work for his department.

On the other hand . . . maybe it wouldn't be such a bad idea to have it with her now, as long as she had to drive through Sembramos a couple of times a day. She pinned it to the waistband of her jeans and let the shirttail cover it. Just in case.

The April weather had taken another of its sudden turns, Sam discovered when she walked outside. Clouds scudded in from the west, driven by a brisk wind that whipped the tender buds on the apple tree by the barn. So typical of the Rocky Mountain climate—March winds, April showers, and May flowers, all at once, all competing. She buttoned her jacket and checked her truck and trailer for supplies.

Since the big house had no landscaping or electricity, there really was no need for lawn mower, rakes or vacuum cleaner. She pulled brooms and her biggest mop and bucket from the trailer's storage box, stashing them in the back of the truck. It would be far easier to maneuver the circular drive up there on the hill without the trailer. Taking a minute to consider the job, it occurred to her that without electricity up at that house, there would be no way to pump water from the well and that would mean taking water with her for mopping. She filled a couple of five-gallon buckets that had lids, checked the dogs' water bowl while she had the hose uncoiled, then took a deep breath, climbed in the truck and headed out.

Sembramos seemed quiet this morning. Sam gave a little wave to Deputy Rico when she passed his vehicle, parked in front of the patched-up taxidermy shop. He raised two fingers in acknowledgement. Otherwise, she saw what appeared to be a normal scattering of cars at the grocery store, the bank and in the school's parking lot. She hoped Beau was right—things might settle down once the Starkey family had buried Jessie. She wondered if this little town had its own cemetery or if the service would take place in Taos.

Beyond the town limits the highway was clear, not a single car passing Sam as she drove north. She spotted the white dome of the house from more than a mile away. Easier, now that she knew what she was looking for. She wondered about it—as she often did with these properties. Who had gone to the effort and expense to build such a place and then never move into it?

She steered off the highway and her truck climbed the hill to the circle that led to the open courtyard and the massive front door. Her new key worked smoothly and she carried her brooms inside. The place seemed even larger today, with the prospect of having to manually sweep and mop all that tile. She'd decided to start with the kitchen when her phone rang. Delbert Crow.

"What's the progress on the LG property?" he asked, not bothering with a hello first.

"The what?" Her push broom fell over, the wooden handle hitting tile with a loud clatter.

"LG Properties. That's how the ownership is listed. I hear it's quite a place."

"You could say that." She gave a quick description of what she'd found, including her estimate that she had nearly ten thousand square feet of dusty tile to clean. "What's the story with it anyway? It's new construction. No one's ever lived here."

"Weird." Papers rustled in the background. "It's not a loan default. The land and property were paid for. It's going to auction for back taxes."

"I wonder how long it's been here, empty like this?"

"No idea," Delbert said. "My file just shows taxes in arrears for four years. So, that's what I'm calling about—we need to push this thing. The auction is set for a week from tomorrow." No appreciation for the extra effort, just a click as he hung up.

Sam stared at the expanse of dirty floor in front of her, wondering as she started to work why she hadn't been assigned the job earlier. A little more lead time would have been helpful. An image of her wooden jewelry box popped into her head. She hadn't called upon its powers since their trip to Ireland, when she'd discovered that another box existed. Something about that—and the fact that she'd almost obtained the second one as well—had spooked her a little. Until she knew more about the powers of those things she wanted to be careful.

She'd hardly finished that thought when her phone rang again. As if the woman had read her mind, it was Cora Abernathy. The hairs on her arms rose.

"Ms. Sweet?" The elderly librarian's voice sounded

excited. "I think I've found some information for you, if you want to stop by later on."

Not the best time to drop everything and rush off in search of Bertha Martinez's acquaintances, but Sam had set this ball in motion and the woman had gone to some work on her behalf. She explained about being tied up with the job and being away from Taos at the moment, but promised to get by the library within a day or so.

Cora seemed a little disappointed that Sam wasn't a block away and ready to rush over at that moment. She probably found herself becoming interested in the subjects she researched for her patrons and shared in their excitement when she was able to find what they needed. Sam made a mental note to take the lady a bakery treat when she went by to pick up the information.

Thinking of the bakery reminded her that she hadn't checked in with her crew since yesterday's crazy-divorcée incident. A quick call assured her that things were running smoothly so far. The day was young, though, she reminded herself as she told Jen to call her if they hit a snag.

She'd finished the kitchen floor and thought she might tackle the master suite upstairs—putting off the inevitable task of that massive great room—when her phone rang yet again. What did people do before cell phones? Came home to dozens of messages, as she recalled.

Beau asked how things were going, said he was checking to be sure no one had bothered her in town or up at the property. He asked if she would want to meet him in town for lunch in thirty minutes. She begged off, describing the amount of labor ahead of her. She'd tossed two granola bars into her pack this morning. That would have to suffice for a few more hours.

She did take a moment to ask how things were going in Sembramos.

"At the moment, all is quiet. The Starkey clan seems pretty subdued. I saw a bunch of them milling around the house this morning, some actually wearing suits. The funeral service is in Taos at two o'clock. Then burial in the Sembramos cemetery. After that, I imagine the drinking will start and that's when I expect we'll see what the real mood is."

"I don't envy you."

"Well, if you can, finish up and get through town before it gets too late—"

"I'll do my best."

Among the choices—going through the old case file on Angela Cayne, stopping at the newspaper office to follow up on that story, visiting Cora Abernathy to find out what the librarian had to offer, or sweeping and mopping floors— Sam would have chosen nearly anything except the one she was stuck with at the moment. Tomorrow, she would call upon the box for help.

She stepped up her pace and had finished the master suite by noon. Taking a break for granola bars and water, she convinced herself that was enough lunch and then tackled the main room. She'd mopped about half of it when she ran out of clean water. Checking the time, she decided Beau was right. It was four o'clock and she should get going. She collected her empty buckets and left the other tools behind. Her lower back and shoulders were screaming and tomorrow loomed as another very long day.

This time, driving through Sembramos she followed Beau's directive and went straight through without a pause. Once again, she saw Rico's patrol car at the side of the road, and this time there were almost no other people in sight. Maybe the whole town was on alert for trouble from the Starkeys. Maybe the Rodarte sympathizers were somewhere else, brewing up trouble of their own. Sam only knew she didn't have the energy for any of it.

She arrived at home, accepted kisses from both dogs, and went straight for the shower and the ibuprofen. She now felt clean and achy. She picked up her jewelry box from the bathroom vanity and held it for a long moment. When the wooden surface began to glow and Sam felt the warmth travel up her arms she set it down, aches and pains only a dull twinge now. She almost had the energy to drive into Taos and check with the librarian, but it was late and the woman would have gone home. There would be another day for that.

She wandered downstairs, slightly at loose ends until Beau came home. *If* he was able to break away anytime soon. She picked up her phone and speed-dialed his.

"So far, so good," he said when she asked about the situation. "Starkeys just got back to their house from the cemetery. Joe got a little loud when he saw my cruiser on their street. I'm waiting on Withers and Rayburn to come out and give me a break. I should be home by seven."

She said she would have dinner ready. A peek into the fridge and pantry narrowed the choices to leftover pizza or canned soup. She really needed to get to the store. The pizza didn't look appealing so she opened the soup and added a little extra seasoning to it; biscuit mix could be dressed up a little to go with it and she could make it seem like a real meal. Fortunately, Beau was pretty easy to please in the food department.

Unfortunately, he called at six-thirty to say that there

was no way he would get home for awhile. Someone had set the Starkey house on fire.

Chapter 11

Beau came dragging in around eleven. Soot clung to his uniform and outlined the wrinkles near his eyes.

"Lee Rodarte and four of his cousins rode through town on their motorcycles, very noisy and visible, and naturally they had words with several Starkey supporters," he said as he hung his jacket on the rack near the door. "The fire broke out shortly after, although no one saw who threw the beer bottle full of gas through a back window."

"Oh my gosh, Beau. Was it bad?"

"Everyone got out okay but half the house is in ruins. Helen and Joe had to move in with Bobby, Joe's brother. I give that about two days before everyone starts bickering."

"Two whole days?" She wiped at the black smudges on his face.

"The squabbling among the Starkeys is the least of

my worries. I couldn't believe Lee came back and started trouble. I thought Sophie had him convinced to stay away until things cooled off." Beau started up the stairs and Sam followed.

"Did you get anything to eat?" She offered the remains of the chicken noodle soup and biscuits.

"The guy who owns the café sent his wife over with burritos for us. I had the whole department out by this time. For the night I've got State Police from Taos. This gets much worse I'll have to call them up from Espanola and Vegas too. At least for the moment I think all the Starkeys are sleeping it off over at Bobby's place." He peeled off his smoky clothes and tossed them into the laundry basket, then stepped into the shower.

One whiff and Sam knew she couldn't sleep in the room with the dirty uniform. She carried the basket down to the laundry room.

On the end table by the couch, Beau's cell phone rang. The readout said it was Rico so Sam answered it.

"When he gets out of the shower, tell him we didn't have any luck apprehending Lee Rodarte or any of his group. The bikes cleared out. If the sheriff wants to release me to go back to Taos, I can search for them there."

Sam passed the message along as Beau toweled himself off.

"Nah. Not tonight. I wouldn't send Rico after them alone anyway—too dangerous. We'll let things cool off overnight, get whatever evidence we can collect from the fire, and I'll pursue this in the morning."

"Beau?" She made him meet her gaze. "I don't like it, you being in the middle of this."

"Darlin', it's going to be fine. I can take care of myself.

We can't just sit back and let anarchy take over."

For every lawman killed in the line of duty, she would bet most of them had uttered those words. She crawled into bed and held him very close.

* * *

Beau followed Sam's red truck the next morning, from their driveway all the way through to the northern end of Sembramos. He didn't like the look of the town. Windows were broken in more than one shop, and signs of a small fire showed at the gas station. His body tensed as he surveyed the damage. He needed to get Sam away from here and then call a meeting of his men. He dialed Sam's phone and cautioned her again to lock herself into the house where she would be cleaning most of the day.

"Call me when you get ready to leave. Depending on the situation, I can have an escort bring you back through and get you home safely."

She started to say she would be fine, but he wished he'd taken some time to familiarize her with one of his pistols and insist that she carry it. It was something they should address soon. He watched the red truck until she went around a bend in the road, then he U-turned and found Rico's cruiser parked by the bank.

"Some things going on here that I didn't hear about?" he asked, approaching his deputy but keeping an eye on everything around him.

"Sheriff, sorry. Every time I stopped to call you something else happened. We were getting calls from dispatch all night. Broken window over here, next thing it's a B&E over there. It felt like we were stomping out fires all night."

"Literally. I saw the one by the gas station."

"Luckily, the volunteer fire department had just come from the Starkey place early this morning. We don't know if the gas station fire was accidental or on purpose. A lady was filling her tank and then started screaming. Station attendant got right on it and kept it small. FD came along and checked it out. The woman could have been so nervous that she messed up. We don't really know."

"We have anyone under arrest for this?" He nodded toward broken shop windows across the street.

"No one. Every time something happened we'd rush over, but whoever did it would be gone. It's almost like they were purposely running us around."

"Any major incidents?"

"Mostly little stuff. And I'm not sure we know all of it yet, boss. Calls were still coming in an hour ago, someone waking up to find a car vandalized or lawn furniture all broken up."

Seemed like everyone in town had taken a side in this mess and was now causing grief for the others.

"I'm calling in some help," Beau said. "You guys need to go home and get some rest."

Rico looked relieved at the suggestion.

"Hang around another few minutes," Beau said. He keyed his radio and put in a call to the state police in Taos. The chief agreed to send enough men for a day shift to relieve Beau's deputies. Once that was arranged, Beau told Rico he could leave.

He watched the deputy drive away, then Beau made a

slow cruise through town. Two other deputies reported the same kind of news Rico had given. After speaking with each man he released him to go home, told him to get some sleep and plan to be back by dark. If the violence escalated he would call in the National Guard.

Belatedly, Beau decided he should coordinate all this with the town bigwigs. He couldn't recall ever having met the mayor or town councilors. He checked the county telephone directory and found the number for the town hall. A cautious female voice answered. As soon as Beau explained who he was, the call went right to the mayor. Within a minute, Beau had directions and an appointment.

"I just can't believe this is happening in our town," said the short woman with the pageboy haircut and lipstick that was a tad too bright. She'd introduced herself as Consuelo Brown and ushered Beau into a room off the lobby of the so-called town hall.

The entire facility occupied one section of a small strip shopping center, next to the ice cream parlor. Beau couldn't believe he hadn't seen it on his other passes through town, but that's how small it was. The governing offices consisted of a lobby with a desk, where people probably came to pay their water bill or get a permit for something, and the office where he now sat with the mayor. Across the room, a table with four chairs crowded around it probably served as the town council's meeting space.

When he mentioned the state of lawlessness that had prevailed overnight, Ms. Brown became flustered. "I got elected here, Sheriff, because nobody else ran for the office. Really, the most complicated thing I've done in months is to give a speech at a boy's Eagle Scout induction. I have no idea how to handle this, and two of my three councilors are out of town right now."

He recapped what Rico and the other deputies had told him, ending by telling her about calling in the state police. Her hands fluttered above the surface of her desk and he swore her lip trembled a little more with each thing he revealed.

"I suggest that we call a town meeting," he said. "See if we can't calm things down. If that doesn't work, I'll have to call in the National Guard to keep order."

Her lip was definitely trembling now.

"I'll do the talking if you'd like," he said. "Now, how shall we get the word out about the meeting? Where and when would you suggest we hold it?"

With something definite to think about, Ms. Brown settled down a little. "Well, there's the automated telephone system we use to advise when we have weather closures for school. Every family with a child in school gets called. When the trouble started last night we used it to cancel school for today. We could telephone about the meeting and word our message to suggest that they tell their neighbors. We would pretty well reach everyone that way."

"Good. That's an excellent plan."

A little encouragement and she went on. "I'd suggest the park, on Third Street. The gazebo there makes a good podium, gets you up above the crowd a little. I'll get the school janitor to set up the PA equipment and test it."

"I think we should do this before dark tonight," Beau said.

"Yes. How about five o'clock? We'll catch most people on their way home from work and we won't interrupt their dinner hour."

Heaven forbid that dinner be late because of a

crime spree. He withheld his smile, merely nodding. "I'd appreciate it if you will handle those details," he said, standing. "I'm going to meet with the state police and coordinate a schedule. Even if the meeting goes well and we have everyone's cooperation, I plan to keep heavy patrols throughout town tonight."

Mayor Brown swallowed hard, nodding but clearly still rattled.

* * *

Sam approached her task with a better attitude and a shot of energy from handling the magic box this morning. Finishing the floors in the massive great room took half the morning, then she started on the smaller rooms in the other wing, the two guest suites, plus ones she'd named the nursery, the sewing room and the library. By three o'clock she was able to stand back and survey her work. Not bad. The place had a fresh feeling to it and was nearly done. She would come back one more day and wash all the windows. If her energy held and the wind let up she could come back one final time and chop weeds, plus do some touch-up work on the exterior. That should please Delbert Crow and the taxation department.

She filled out a line on the sign-in sheet, packed away her brooms and mops and locked the door, remembering as she was pulling out onto the highway that she had agreed to check in with Beau. He sounded busy, saying something about being in Taos at the moment, coordinating a schedule with some officers, and that he had to be back in Sembramos at five o'clock. A meeting of some kind. He would fill her in when he got home. She assured him that she would drive right on through.

With a few hours of free time, she mentally reviewed the things she'd thought of last night. Buying some food would be tops on the list. She couldn't really keep offering canned soup for dinner every night. She bypassed the turn to their driveway and continued straight into Taos.

The newspaper office was another stop, and she would need to get there before they closed. She turned off near the county offices and pulled into the parking lot of the place, familiar from the times she'd come to place ads for her shop. Britney, the young woman at the desk, recognized her and seemed happy to take her to a room where back issues were tightly archived.

"How far back does this story go?" she asked Sam.

"Six to seven years."

"Ah. You're in luck. Everything older than eight years goes to our storage building. Everything newer than three years is on the computer. You can find the middle stuff here in the microfiche."

Yeah, lucky, Sam thought as she followed instructions to thread the rolls of film into the machine. A computer search would have been so much easier.

Left alone, she soon figured out the system; it helped that she and Beau had just been through the murder file and she knew the exact dates to look for. She scanned pages and enlarged every article that featured the names Cayne, Starkey, Rodarte or Sembramos. Pages printed out and she gathered them and went back to the desk to pay for the printouts. Britney made change for her, glancing at the sheet at the top of her stack.

"Huh. That's interesting," she said, closing the drawer of her register.

"What's that?"

"This article about a real estate deal near Sembramos. I had no idea big real estate deals ever happened up there. My dad used to know that guy, Linden Gisner," Britney said, pointing to a name in one article. "He was well known in real estate here for awhile. Dad called him the wheeler-dealer of Taos county."

The name seemed vaguely familiar but Sam's mind was already dashing ahead to the rest of her errands as she went back out to her truck. She glanced at her dashboard clock. It was almost five, traffic was picking up, and she didn't really feel like driving to the bakery or checking back with Cora at the library. Her earlier burst of energy was gone. The supermarket posed challenge enough for the moment.

Chapter 12

The PA speakers squawked when Mayor Consuelo Brown handed the microphone to Beau. He held it a little way from his mouth and surveyed the crowd. A small group of Starkeys—minus Helen, he noticed—stood at the left-hand edge of the crowd. The men looked a bit the worse for wear after what had probably been an afternoon of heavy drinking. Sophie Garcia stood at the opposite side of the park, edging as far away from them as she could get, and two unfamiliar men in biker leathers stood near her. They looked enough like Lee Rodarte to be related, but Beau didn't see Lee in the crowd. Between the two factions stood fifty or so of the townsfolk, by Beau's estimate. Ringing the perimeter of the crowd, all of Beau's deputies and six state officers—all uniformed and armed—kept watch.

"Thank you for the introduction, Mayor Brown," Beau

said, "and thank you all for coming this afternoon."

He watched faces in the crowd. No one looked happy, no matter where their loyalties were.

"There was trouble here in Sembramos last night. We were fortunate that no one got hurt. But it's the kind of trouble none of us wants to see."

Low muttering came from the Starkey side. Losing two rooms from their house hadn't exactly been painless.

"You all can work out your differences however you see fit—it's not really my business—as long as people don't get hurt and property doesn't get destroyed. When someone breaks the law, it becomes my business. I've been elected to keep the people of this county safe. So tonight, we're asking for a voluntary curfew of nine p.m. Do your shopping, go out to dinner . . . but be home by nine o'clock. Please. I'm asking nicely. But just in case 'nice' doesn't work, my department will be patrolling your streets, along with officers from the state police. And if things continue to get ugly around here, we can bring in more help to restore order. That's really all I have to say. Obey the curfew for a night or two, calm down, and we won't have to be in your backyard any more."

"By 'more help' you mean the National Guard?" someone shouted from the middle of the crowd.

"Yes, sir, I do." Beau stepped back and handed the microphone to the mayor.

She cleared her throat a little nervously, but Beau was the only one who heard that part. When she brought the mike up, her voice came out clear and strong. "We all need to calm down, try to put old events and old feelings aside and let ourselves heal. Let the town get back to the way it used to be. Sheriff Cardwell is being very helpful. Let's show that we can put our own house in order and get along like grownups."

She thanked the crowd again and turned off the microphone. Beau remained on the raised platform while the mayor stepped down to shake hands and speak softly with her constituents. At the back of the crowd, Beau spotted a white van from one of the Albuquerque TV stations. Great. How did they know about this and how long had they been here?

Movement among the Starkey contingent caught his eye. Helen Starkey had joined her husband. Joe and Bobby glared toward Sophie Garcia's little group. The two bikers glared right back. Sophie, he noticed, was speaking quietly to them. As if that would stop them if a brawl began. Beau took a stance and gave them a no-nonsense look. One of the bikers noticed, said something under his breath, and they both strolled toward their motorcycles.

Bobby Starkey started to mouth off, but Helen aimed an elbow at his ribs and the verbal exchange turned into a battle of nasty staring. Eventually, Joe gave his brother a little punch to the shoulder and their group moved away. Within ten minutes the entire crowd had dispersed. Beau gathered his men and gave instructions. Any trouble, he was to be called on his cell. He hoped for an evening at home, strategically placed between the trouble in Sembramos and anything else that might happen in Taos. He didn't actually believe he would end up relaxing much.

* * *

As long as she was caught up in the bustle of the supermarket, Sam decided to really stock up. Who knew what the next week would bring? She picked up Beau's favorites—steak, potatoes for baking, ice cream—along with a resupply of nearly everything for the pantry. As soon as he called to say he was on the way, she lit the gas grill, seasoned the steaks and opened a new bottle of wine.

As it turned out, he declined the wine. He was still technically on duty, but he managed to put away all of his meal and a double serving of ice cream with caramel sauce. When the phone rang, both of them groaned in dismay. They had hoped the trouble wouldn't flare up quite so soon. But the call was from Texas.

"Samantha Jane, *what* on heaven's earth is going on out there?"

"Mother? What's wrong?"

"It's on the news—*CNN!*. Beau standing up there telling the whole county he's going to bring in the National Guard. The TV said somebody was killed and there's nearly been a riot. I thought you lived in a quiet little town. Your daddy's just fit to be tied."

"Mother, there hasn't been a riot. And the National Guard—"

Beau's eyes widened and Sam shook her head, resigned to letting her mother finish saying whatever was on her mind.

"I think you should just get yourself home, right now. It's too dangerous there, with these two killers on the loose."

"Mother, they—"

"I mean it. Things are safe here in Texas, not like that *wild* place where you are now."

Sam let her go on. Texas hadn't been home for Sam in more than thirty-five years, and Taos so seldom had anything 'wild' happen that Nina Rae's statement was ludicrous. But there was no way to get a word into the one-sided conversation. After ten minutes or so, her mother ran out of steam and began repeating.

"Mother, we're fine. Beau's department has everything under control. There were some protests last night, that's all."

Protests? Beau mouthed the word. That Albuquerque station must have sent their footage out to the major networks.

Sam shrugged and signaled that she couldn't get her mother to quit. Beau reached over and took the phone.

"Nina Rae, hi." He used his soothing voice, the one that he'd developed in training to stop prison riots, and eventually he began to talk more as Sam's mother relinquished phone time. It took five minutes of re-explaining but finally he hung up.

"Whew-ee," he said, setting the phone down. "That woman is strong willed."

"Told you," Sam said with a grin. The call seemed funny, now that her mother wasn't actually harping in *her* ear. "I was smart to leave home at eighteen."

He picked up the empty ice cream bowls. "No comment. In the remote possibility that you ever repeat my words to your mother."

She laughed out loud as he went into the kitchen. When she heard him loading the dishwasher she turned to the dining table, where they'd left Angela Cayne's case file spread out. At a glance, she knew she would need to write down a listing of the events—there was just too much material to keep it straight in her head. She found a yellow notepad.

Beau came out of the kitchen with two cups of coffee. "I don't know if you had much chance to look through this stuff yet. Basically, I've been grouping the pages by subject: Crime scene evidence; the Cayne family's story; Jessie's version of it; Lee's version of it; anything other witnesses told us."

Sam retrieved the printouts she'd gotten at the newspaper office and told him about her idea for organizing the material. She picked up the Cayne family's stack. "I assume the first event would have been the Caynes reporting that Angela was missing."

Beau nodded, looking up from the main file where he was still sorting. "There's an initial report. The deputy who responded would have filled that out."

Sam paged through until she came to it. A hot summer night. Mr. and Mrs. Cayne had gone to a choral program at church. Angela stayed home with her grandmother who wasn't feeling well. Sally Cayne said she had gone to bed very early and never heard another thing until Alan and Tracy came home and woke her to ask where Angela had gone. With the front door standing open and the living room in disarray the family's conclusion was that the twenty-year-old had been kidnapped. They immediately called 9-1-1.

Sheriff Padilla's thoughts weren't included, naturally, but Beau remembered that his boss hadn't made a big deal of the girl's disappearance at the time. He'd openly stated at the squad-room meetings that most likely Angela had run off with a boyfriend and would call her parents from Las Vegas in a few days to announce that they were married. Parents were often the last to have a clue that their kid was unhappy at home. Although Angela was hardly a child at that point, Padilla had assigned a deputy to canvass the neighbors and to question Angela's friends; that was about the extent of it for the first forty-eight hours.

But the Caynes had remained insistent. Fed up with the sheriff's lack of answers, they called the state police and initiated a search and rescue operation. SAR members had been the ones who found Angela's body lying out on open ground in a wooded area near a stream, a little over six miles from town.

An embarrassed Sheriff Padilla had quickly backtracked on his earlier halfhearted measures, calling in everyone who could possibly be a suspect.

"He grilled them relentlessly," Beau said. "I remember poor old Roy Watson being dragged in there, having to question the same witnesses over and over again, even when he would tell Padilla that someone was clearly not their guy. This case was what pushed Watson to an early retirement."

Sam picked up the transcripts from Jessie Starkey's interrogation. The gist of it was that Jessie 'didn't look right' in the sheriff's estimation. Someone had spotted him near the Cayne house that night—a long-haired, skinny guy with a lot of tattoos who was acting jumpy. The witness thought he'd seen Jessie approach the Cayne house—for sure the front door was open, with only the screen between Jessie and that poor, innocent girl. That statement was enough for Padilla to haul Jessie in. From the transcript, his tone and manner were third-degree.

Jessie's answers were all over the place—he'd gone to see Lee Rodarte; he'd gone for a long drive alone in his truck; he'd been in Taos at a bar, not in Sembramos at all; sure, he'd always thought Angela was pretty hot; he'd asked her out a few times but she was always busy; yes, he'd bought some cocaine that night; he didn't remember how much of it he'd used—so before the end of the hours-long interrogation the man couldn't seem to keep anything straight. By dawn he'd signed a confession to taking Angela Cayne from her home, with the help of Lee Rodarte. Jessie's court-appointed lawyer didn't meet him until two weeks before the start of the trial.

Lee Rodarte's interrogation was even more disturbing. He swore he'd been with his girlfriend, Sophie Garcia, in the early part of the evening. Sophie wouldn't give him an answer about getting married and that had upset Lee. He'd left her house and gone for a ride on his motorcycle. He stayed consistent with this throughout, despite the so-called 'facts' that the sheriff kept throwing at him from Jessie Starkey's confession. Lee had to admit that he dealt a few drugs now and then, that he'd sold Jessie both cocaine and pot at times, but not that night. Unfortunately, from the time Lee left Sophie's company at around eight p.m., no one could vouch for his whereabouts the rest of the night. Except for Jessie Starkey. Lee was toast.

Sam jotted all this on her timeline. From Deputy Watson's canvass of the neighborhood, through the interviews at the department and interrogation of the suspects, more than two dozen people had offered information, but nothing she'd come across so far would have conclusively exonerated either man.

"Maybe I should keep a separate list of everyone who was interviewed throughout this whole investigation," she told Beau. "I'm getting them confused and I haven't even been through a fraction of this yet."

"Good idea." He yawned and looked at his watch. "It's after eleven. No calls from either front, so I'd say that's good news. I better try for some sleep." He set the file pages down.

Sam was scribbling names as she came across them. "The minute I finish with this stack of neighbor interviews, I'll be joining you."

But she soon gave up. Her brain felt dull after the hours of reading so she set her lists aside and turned off lights as she walked through the living room and made her way upstairs.

"I'll get back to the witness list in the morning," she told Beau as they brushed their teeth at the double sinks. But at some point she needed to finish her caretaking project and submit a final report to Delbert Crow, and then there was the matter of keeping her bakery business alive too. She'd better put in some time there. She fell into a sound sleep until the tone of Beau's phone woke them both.

A hint of dawn showed at the windows and the clock said it was 5:47. Beau groaned and picked up the phone. Two seconds later he sat up, alert. "Shit!" He gave quick orders.

Sam came fully awake. "What is it?"

He set his phone on the night stand and stood up. "Lee Rodarte's body was found in an alley a little while ago."

"Oh, no."

"I know. It feels like this just won't end." He grabbed the uniform he'd left on a chair last night and started pulling on pants and shirt. "I've ordered deputies back to town and we'll have to wake up Lisa early, gather whatever evidence we can secure before the scene gets disturbed."

"Back to town? So it happened in Taos?"

He nodded and was out the door. A minute later red and

blue lights flashed across the ceiling and she heard gravel spin as he drove away. Sam ran her fingers through her hair, realizing that sleep would never come back now. She got up and tried to decide which of her many obligations to handle first.

Chapter 13

Knowing that Beau was probably right now standing over the body of Lee Rodarte, and wondering how this would spark the tinderbox situation in Sembramos, Sam knew her mind would never settle down enough to concentrate on decorating cakes this morning. Nor did she think her husband would be pleased if she headed toward the big white house, having to drive right into the powder-keg up north. She stared into the bathroom mirror, feeling that there was so much work she needed to do, yet stymied as to what to prioritize.

Coffee. That would help.

The temptation to stay in pajamas and robe, nursing endless cups of warm comfort, tugged at her; simply letting her mind and body take a break would feel so nice. Good in theory, impossible in real life. She dressed in jeans and a work shirt. If she could get the go-ahead to finish her caretaking project, that would be a big relief and would keep her from having to make that drive ever again. All of this went through her head while the coffee dripped into the carafe.

She poured a mug of the black brew and dumped in plenty of sugar. Pacing the living room, hoping a plan would present itself, her gaze fell to the notes she'd been writing the night before. She debated continuing, but decided her thoughts wouldn't settle down enough. Some important detail would get away from her.

Her cell phone sat on top of one stack of paper, reminding her of her mother's call last night. Sam picked up the remote control and switched on the television, scrolling to a news channel. Tornadoes across the plains dominated the first story—and Nina Rae thought Sam lived in danger. She turned her back on the images and picked up the witness list she'd written. Beau would probably recognize the names; he'd been interviewing the citizens of Sembramos for a couple of days now.

Sam thought a few sounded familiar, probably because he'd mentioned them. For some reason, the thought of the big white house came into her mind, and the unanswered question of why its owner had abandoned it. Another thing added to her to-do list was to find someone associated with LG Properties. It was always possible they hadn't received the notices and weren't aware of the impending auction.

The television interrupted her thoughts. "The violence continues to escalate in Taos County, New Mexico, with yet another murder. Lee Rodarte was released from the state prison less than a week ago, one of two men convicted in the murder of a young woman in that small northern town.

We go live to the scene in Taos, New Mexico."

A reporter holding a microphone stood shivering on a street corner, one Sam recognized. It was only about four blocks from her old house. A chill went through her, realizing that Kelly might have passed the very spot where Lee died if she'd been out last night. Sam missed some of the reporter's words, and when the phone rang she missed the rest of it.

"Sammy?" Her father's voice came through. "Your mama wanted me to check on you this morning. Everything okay?"

"Fine, Daddy. I suppose you guys are watching the news again." It had to be the reason for the call. She could hear her mother's voice in the background and a moment of shuffling as the phone was handed over.

"Samantha Jane, I'm worried."

Sam glanced at the TV screen but the coverage had moved on to something in Washington.

"I know, Mother. But, believe me, the trouble isn't nearly as widespread as the news people are making it sound. It's a very small town about a half hour away from us. The people are upset, yes, and Beau's men are there to keep the peace."

"But this news lady this morning, she said a murder happened in Taos. I don't like it that you're living there so close to all this."

Sam sighed. "We don't know what happened with that one yet, Mother. Beau's checking it out."

She wanted to point out that murders happened everywhere but that seemed callous. A death was always personal to someone. But it didn't have to mean that everyone nearby was in danger. There had to be connections between Lee and Jessie and Angela, although it certainly didn't seem as straightforward as Sheriff Padilla's original theories made it out to be. She realized that her mother was still talking. Sam's head began to hurt.

"I need to go now, Mother. I'll talk to you again soon. Don't worry." Sam clicked off the call before Nina Rae could repeat her worries for the umpteenth time.

She rubbed her temples, forcing herself to relax. Her parents were getting older; of course they would worry. The coffee in her mug had gone cold and the smell of it suddenly turned her stomach. She switched off the TV and went looking for something more nutritious.

An apple and a bowl of yogurt later, she decided she had to get out of the house. If she couldn't go to Sembramos she could at least check in at the bakery.

She drove through the outskirts of Taos, slowing as she approached the plaza, watching the side streets to her left. A block away, down San Fernando, she could see Beau's cruiser and a few other vehicles, along with a strand of yellow tape cordoning off the alley behind The Rooster, a small bar that Sam had never been to. The team seemed to be working quietly, and most motorists on the main drag went on by without even noticing. She itched to go over there and find out what happened, but this wasn't the time. Beau would call her when he finished at the scene.

Sam made a right-hand turn and circled a block to enter the alley behind Sweet's Sweets. The familiar scents of sugar and cinnamon filled the kitchen and she breathed it in, realizing she'd really missed her business the past couple of days.

"Hey, you're back," Becky said, looking up from a tray of brownies onto which she was piping small milk chocolate roses. Becky noticed Sam looking at them. "It's for the Chocoholics book group. Do you think this will be okay? Ivan didn't say what he wanted."

"He never does. We just make up whatever we want to, as long as it's chocolate. He'll love these—they all will." Sam wiped up a smudge of the frosting from the table and tasted it. "Ooh, nice. What did you do? Let me guess . . . a touch of coffee?"

"It's okay?"

"Yummy." Sam looked toward the basket of order sheets on the corner of her desk. A satisfying stack of pages sat there, enough to say that business was good, not so many that it would overwhelm her crew if she didn't put in a lot of hours this week. Julio was in front of the big bake oven, waiting for the timer to ring so he could take out a large pan of muffins. He nodded toward Sam and smiled.

"Hey, Sam, I thought I heard your voice." Jen stood in the doorway to the sales area. With a glance to be sure no customers awaited, she asked, "So what's all this on the news about some trouble up in Sembramos?"

"Yeah, well, there's been some conflict among the residents. I'm really surprised that the national media picked up on it."

"My uncle used to live up there," Becky said. "When I was a kid he would bring us the best peaches from his orchard. I guess it's a hard life though, farming. He got too old to handle it and none of his kids wanted to do it. I wonder what ever happened to that orchard."

The front door bells tinkled and Jen left to serve the customer. Sam looked through the order sheets; they seemed like standard items the others could handle. She walked into the sales room to check it just about the time Jen had bagged three scones and rung up the sale for the lady who had come in. When the woman left, Jen asked about Sam's newest caretaking project.

"Strangest thing I've seen," Sam said. "It's a brand-new house—huge—and no one has ever moved into it."

"Seriously?"

Sam described the site, the layout and the rooms. "It would have been an amazing place, furnished, with some art and decoration. I could imagine it as a place where you could host fabulous parties. Well, if you were into that sort of thing." Personally, she'd never hosted anything larger than the grand opening for the shop.

"Wait a minute," Jen said. "Is it a big white place, like you might see around the Mediterranean?"

"Yeah—you've seen it?"

"Only in pictures. When I worked at the gallery, there was this man who would come in to look at art. Sometimes his wife was with him. I can't think of his name . . .

"Whenever he came in, the gallery owner would rush out of her little office and insist on waiting on him herself. He only looked at the most expensive stuff, so of course she didn't want to share a commission with me. Didn't matter. I never really liked talking with those snotty rich types anyway." She wiped a crumb from the top of the glass display. "But, wait . . . you were assigned that house because—?"

"Back taxes. I guess things went downhill for Mr. Important."

"Wow. I *guess*. I mean, that's one guy I would have never expected for that."

"Yeah? Well, I have no idea what happened." Sam looked at the beverage bar and saw that everything was in order.

"You know, I did overhear some gossip. Now that I'm thinking about the guy. He'd asked Lily to hold several expensive pieces for him and said he would come pick them up in a few weeks, once the house was done. He never came back and my boss was telling another client that if he didn't take it soon the painting she wanted would be available. So anyway, the other lady was saying 'don't hold your breath.' She went on and on about how his real estate deals had fallen through. Something about the guy's family falling apart, his wife died or left, or something like that."

"It must have been a long time ago. The taxes haven't been paid in four years."

"Oh yeah, longer than that. I don't remember exactly. I worked for Lily seven years—can't believe I did that—and I've forgotten the details."

Sam nodded. It was a puzzle indeed. She complimented Jen on the display cases, offered to carry the brownies next door to Ivan at the bookshop, and left her crew to handle the rest of the day. She got into her truck and let it idle while she decided what to do next.

Two other things hovered at the edge of her awareness. One, she'd told Cora the librarian that she would stop by for the information the woman had taken the trouble to gather. Since the old Harwood Library wasn't far from the shop, it would be easy to do that now. The other thing was to track down the owner of LG Properties, just to be sure he knew about the tax situation. Maybe Jen's bit of gossip was true, but it didn't feel right that the man would lose the house he'd worked so hard for and cared so much about. At least Sam would feel better if she knew that he was aware of the problem and was letting go of the place willingly.

During the drive of two blocks, Sam tried to focus her thoughts on what she'd wanted from Cora Abernathy. Her goal was to learn something about her wooden box and where it had come from. As far as she knew, Bertha Martinez was the only connection to it here in Taos but maybe Bertha had friends who might know something. It was a tenuous connection. From what Beau had told Sam when they first met, the old woman had been a loner. But it was worth a little of her time to find out.

Cora Abernathy looked much the way Sam had pictured from her voice. The gray-haired woman was of medium height and reed-thin, with arthritic hands and the sort of peachy complexion that meant she'd always been careful to wear hats outdoors. She greeted Sam enthusiastically and thanked her for the pink-frosted cupcake Sam had brought in one of her bakery bags.

"Here is the information I found for you," Cora said, turning to a bookcase behind her desk. Neat stacks of books and papers filled two shelves and the woman knew just which one to reach for.

"These two books are on witchcraft, with emphasis on beliefs in New Mexico. In modern-day practice, there are many types of witches. Wicca, for instance, is actually recognized as a religion. Some practitioners study very seriously and even acquire degrees in wiccan studies. There are some covens in our area." She picked up a sheet of typing paper upon which she'd written notes. Pointing at the page she said, "This first one is pretty easy to find. They don't seem to be secretive and they even hold a festival each year, sometime around the feast of Beltane."

Sam assumed that reading the material would give her a clue as to what that meant. The coven names looked familiar, probably the same ones she'd found online.

"I've also included a list of books that could give more in-depth information. I'm sorry we didn't have all of them in our collection."

Sam couldn't see herself becoming interested in a study of the craft; she really only wanted to know whether Bertha Martinez had ever mentioned the origin of the wooden box to anyone. She tamped down her impatience and smiled at Cora.

"Here's another thing I found interesting," said Cora, "The covens usually use a place in the woods for ceremonies. I'd had that impression, you know. But one of the women I spoke to, she told me that for the winter solstice ceremonies, if it's too cold outside they are allowed to find a place indoors. But it has to be a place with the right ambiance."

"I wonder what she meant by that?"

"She didn't really say. But the way she said it— *am*biance—I guess the mood and setting have to be just right. You know, for the magic to work." A cute little sparkle showed in her eyes.

Sam picked up the books, thanked Cora for the information, and walked out to her truck. She remembered a certain room at Bertha Martinez's home, a room with white symbols painted on red walls. Maybe that was the sort of setting the witches wanted.

Chapter 14

Discouragement settled over Beau like a heavy garment as he watched the bag containing Lee Rodarte's lifeless body slide into the medical investigator's vehicle. There would be an autopsy but it seemed pretty clear that the man had been beaten to death. Dammit—just when he thought things might cool down.

Lee had followed instruction, come here away from Sembramos. Seemingly, the curfew had held; his men had reported no trouble. So why this? Why now?

He hoped to have the answers to those questions soon. He'd sent his deputies to round up all of the Starkeys and anyone else in Sembramos with attitude. The department would be pandemonium; Beau wasn't looking forward to wading into it. He watched Lisa, his crime scene tech, as she packed up her kit full of samples and snapped a couple of final pictures.

"Anything else, Sheriff?" she asked, opening her SUV's door.

"Just process it quickly. I'll be in after I question some folks here." He would also need to find out where Lee's parents had moved and contact the authorities there to notify them, then get up to Sembramos and inform Sophie Garcia. Her son was Lee's closest kin around here. Poor little kid—meeting and losing his father too many times.

The bartender sat inside at the bar, nursing a cup of coffee and not looking happy about it. Beau didn't blame him. The guy probably hadn't gone home until the wee hours and had been called back at six. Daylight coming in the front windows and overhead lights glaring down revealed every beer stain, every dingy patch on the thin carpet, the fact that the walls hadn't seen fresh paint in years, everything easily concealed by neon and soft lighting at night. At least the wood surface of the bar itself was gleaming and the glassware on the shelves behind was spotless.

Toby Quintana introduced himself and offered Beau some of the coffee. It was actually quite good.

"I can't believe this," Toby said, wiping a droplet off the bar. "We've never had trouble here. My place is a family hangout. We don't get the rough crowd or the druggies. Mostly it's, you know, guys who'll stop by for a beer after work. They go home for dinner, maybe bring the wife by later for some dancing. Saturday nights we got a local Western band that plays and everybody lets loose a little. Most nights we're empty by eleven, I clean up, get home at a reasonable hour.

"Last night. Do you remember this guy?" Beau pulled out Lee's official mug shot. The crime scene photos were too gruesome to show around.

"Sure," said Quintana. "First time here, as far as I know. He sat at that end of the bar, alone, looking sad. Had a beer. Added a shot of tequila, then another."

"Was he drunk when he left?"

"Didn't seem like it. I mean, he was walking okay. Exchanged a few quiet words with me when he paid his tab."

"Did he talk to anyone else? Start up a conversation?"

"Nah. Just sat there. Well, wait a second. At one point, two guys came in. They wore leathers, 'do-rags. Walked right over to your guy and talked a minute. Seemed like they were all friends. By the time I got around to them, asked if they wanted anything, the conversation seemed to be over. They said no, thanks, to the offer of a drink and walked back out." He seemed more surprised by the 'thanks' than any other part of it.

"What time was this?"

"Oh, gosh. I lose track, you know, get busy. I'm guessing maybe around ten? Could have been earlier."

Beau glanced toward the small front windows. "Did you see what they were driving?"

"Nah, man. After dark, I hardly get a chance to look up. Way they were dressed, I would guess bikes."

"And the victim—what time did he leave?"

Toby blew out a puff of air. "Maybe half-hour after the others were here?"

Beau thanked him, handed over a business card, and asked Toby to call him if he remembered anyone else who might have talked to Lee Rodarte or followed him out of the bar. He walked out into the bright sunshine and surveyed the area for a minute. There was a residential neighborhood one street over, but it seemed pretty far away for anyone inside their home to hear a beating taking place. Especially what had happened to Lee.

The MI had surmised that Lee had gone down with one blow to the back of the head. After that, they'd kicked him repeatedly, all over his body. The whole thing could have happened fairly quietly, especially with traffic noises less than a block away. And Beau didn't yet know whether this was one assailant or many. He would try to get the word out, ask citizens to come forward if they'd seen anything. You never knew—sometimes a guy was out late, walking the dog or something.

He climbed into his cruiser and drove toward his office, parking in the department lot at the back of the building. Two deputies who'd been on patrol in Sembramos last night were sitting at desks in the squad room. Beau signaled them to come into his office and close the door.

"What've we got?" He settled into his chair and shuffled the little stack of phone messages that awaited him.

"We pulled Joe Starkey and Bobby Starkey out of bed this morning. They're in the interrogation rooms. They both swear they were at home all night. A couple more cousins are in a cell, held for questioning at this point but we haven't gotten around to them."

Since the fire at Joe and Helen's home, the couple had been staying at Bobby's house a few blocks away. It would make sense that the family members would alibi each other. Beau didn't remember the bartender saying whether the men who'd talked to Lee where Anglo or Hispanic, but he didn't see biker leathers as being the style of anyone in the Starkey clan. They went more for the mountain-man look.

More telling was the fact that the two men had been polite and had spoken to Lee as friends. That definitely didn't sound Starkey.

On the other hand, nothing really pointed to the two men in the bar being the same who'd beaten Lee. Which left all of the Starkeys right up there on the suspect list.

* * *

The idea of tracking down the owner of the big house wouldn't leave Sam alone, and the county courthouse wasn't out of her way. She pulled into the parking area of the big, new complex and spent a few minutes finding her way to the records division. A clerk helped her find the information she wanted, based on the legal description and a plot map of the county.

"LG Properties, Inc., is all it shows?" Sam asked when they came up with the name on the deed. "There's not a person's name listed?"

The clerk gave a shrug. Sure, businesses could own property. Did it matter? The physical address of record was the rural address of the house. Billing and communication went to a post office box in Taos. Sam could have gotten that much from Delbert Crow. She wrote it all down anyway. The post office was also on the way home so she stopped and posed her question to the clerk at the window.

"We can't give out box-holder information," he said in his best postal-worker voice.

"Let me talk to the postmaster." Sam raised her shirt-tail to reveal her deputy badge.

She was shown into a side office where she shook hands

with a man in Taos's version of a business suit—dark slacks, white shirt, string tie.

"All I really need to know is whether LG Properties, Inc., still holds this post office box and if the mail is being picked up regularly."

Between the badge and the fact that she knew the company's name, Sam got him to turn to his computer and do a search.

"Sorry. LG Properties relinquished the box a few years ago. It's registered to someone else now. And no, LG didn't rent a different box. If they gave a forwarding address it expired after six months."

"So it's been too long ago to get anything current on them?"

"That's right." He seemed almost happy to deliver that news.

She drove toward home, feeling that she hadn't come very far in either of her searches—the ownership of the mansion or further information on her wooden box. She wondered if Beau was doing any better with his investigation. She needed to get out to the big house and finish the windows, but didn't relish the idea of any type of confrontation in Sembramos—with the residents or with her husband.

There was one way to find out if the coast was clear, she decided as she set the library materials on the coffee table in the living room. She dialed Beau's phone. Not surprisingly, it went to voice mail. Was this entire day going to consist of frustrations and non-answers? *Screw it*, she decided, *I'll go anyway.*

Gathering her supplies she loaded window cleaner,

squeegee and clean rags into the truck and set off with a somewhat fatalistic attitude. Washing windows this time of year was a useless task anyway; sporadic rains and whiffs of dust from the roads usually turned any sparkling glass or a clean vehicle into a spotted mess within a few days. But this way she could tell Delbert Crow that she had completed the job and submit her invoice to be paid.

The two-lane highway into Sembramos had little traffic and Sam noticed two state police vehicles parked strategically where they could see who came and went. In town, it looked as if normal life had resumed. Two women stood chatting in front of the variety store and a number of cars were moving about, coming and going from the bank and gas station. Sam drove through slowly, remembering Beau's warnings about stopping. No one seemed to notice her red truck, and she had cleared the town's northern limit within five minutes.

A woman walking an Australian shepherd paused and called the dog to sit as Sam approached the turn for the driveway to the LG property. With her side window down, she heard the lady say hello as she turned. Might not hurt to ask . . .

"Hi there," Sam said. "Pretty dog."

"Thanks." The woman beamed and sneaked the dog a little treat for sitting so quietly. "Um, if you're going up to see someone, well, nobody lives there."

"Yeah, I discovered that." Sam gave the one-sentence version of why she was there. "I've been trying to locate the owner but I can't seem to find out his name or how to reach him. The property is listed in a business name."

"Oh, odd. There used to be a man who came around all the time, back when they started construction. I'd see him talking with the builder and his crew. But, you know, it's been years since then and I haven't seen him recently."

"Do you know his name?"

"No, never met him. I heard it once, something kind of funny. I thought he lived in Sembramos, but I haven't seen him around there in ages either."

Sam chewed at her lip.

"You know, there are rumors the place is haunted," the lady said with a crooked little smile.

"Seriously?" Sam thought of the unusual hot and cold spots in the house.

"My daughter and her friends claim they've seen lights in there at night, like candles or firelight." She chuckled. "Of course, don't all twelve-year-old girls like to believe in haunted-house stories?"

Sam laughed along with her but Cora Abernathy's words came back, the parts about witches finding places with the right ambiance for their indoor festivities. An elegant, abandoned house might be just the ticket. She rubbed at the goose bumps that rose on her arms, said goodbye and continued up the long drive.

Staring at the huge windows that overlooked the valley and the highway, Sam could almost imagine a coven of young witches, dancing by candlelight on a winter solstice night. Almost. Any number of people could have keys, from construction workers to the owners. But she'd noticed no sign of anyone being in the house, certainly not a burned candle or evidence that the fireplace had been used. The local kids were just having a good time with ghost stories, that was all.

Chapter 15

A string of swear words erupted from Interrogation Room 1, just before Beau put his hand on the doorknob and walked in.

"Joe. The colorful language isn't going to get you out of here any quicker," he said, motioning to his suspect who was pacing the small room. "Take a seat. Let's talk."

"I already talked all I'm wantin' to." Joe Starkey seemed more unkempt than ever, his beard stained with tobacco and his hair sticking out at odd angles. He must have dressed quickly when the deputies came for him in the wee hours; his shirt was mis-buttoned and the jeans looked like they'd been in a wad on some floor. "I want to quit talkin' and get my brother and go home."

"A man is dead, Joe, and your family had threatened him. I have to ask the questions."

"My Jessie's dead, too, Sheriff. And nobody's found out who did that. My family wants answers too. Did you ever stop to think that maybe the same person killed that Lee Rodarte is who killed my boy?"

Beau actually had considered that very possibility.

"Any ideas who that would be?" he asked.

Starkey's bluster dimmed a little. "Well, somebody who didn't want to see 'em leave the pen. Somebody who was happy about their trial going the way it did. That prosecutor who sent 'em away, for instance."

Beau gave him a steady stare.

"Okay, so maybe that prosecutor got better things to do, wouldn't want to risk his fancy-pants career. What about somebody else in town?"

"Again, who?"

"Well, I don't know. But why aren't you up there asking questions?"

This was about to start going in circles, Beau realized. He was almost relieved when the desk officer tapped at the door and told him there was a phone call he would probably want to take.

Beau stopped Rico on the way to his desk. "Go ahead and release Joe and Bobby Starkey, but warn them—strongly— that there better not be any more trouble and that they can't leave the area. Radio the guys patrolling Sembramos, tell them to make frequent passes by the Starkey house."

Rico nodded. Beau stepped into his office and picked up the phone.

"We've received the body you just sent down," said the medical investigator in Albuquerque. "and there's one thing I thought you might like to know right away. We found a note stuffed into the victim's waistband. Don't know how our man at the scene missed it, but it was probably left by the killer. I'll fax you a copy of it and send the original by courier."

"Thanks, appreciate it." Beau hung up and stepped out to the fax machine in the squad room. Within a minute, a page rolled out.

They deserved to Die. You support these two scumbags, you Die too!!!!

It was handwritten in shaky lettering. A nervous hand, or someone trying to disguise handwriting? Beau couldn't tell. Once he received the original he might be able to get a handwriting expert's opinion. Or, he could leave that to the lawyers who would have to build a case around the evidence his department managed to gather. He walked into the hallway, where Rico was herding Joe and Bobby Starkey toward the front desk.

"Just a second," Beau said, catching up. He held out the facsimile of the note, watching the two faces as they saw it.

Joe Starkey's face went a little pale; he looked at his brother.

"This look familiar?" Beau asked.

They both shook their heads. He wasn't sure whether to believe them. He raised two fingers to his eyes, then pointed to the men. *I'm watching you.* He nodded to Rico to see them out.

His intercom line was ringing when he got back to his office.

"Sorry, Sheriff, there's an Alan Cayne on line one."

Beau punched the red button and picked up the handset. "Sheriff Cardwell."

"Sheriff, my wife and I are *very* upset." The male voice was shaky with emotion. "We just heard that Angela's killers were freed from prison. How could they do that? How can those two be running free now?"

Clearly, the family had not been monitoring television news. Beau gave him the condensed version of the reasons for the release, ending with the fact that both men were, in fact, not running free anymore.

The air seemed to go out of Alan Cayne. Beau could hear small background sounds, as if Cayne were rubbing a calloused hand over a days' growth of beard. "I'm glad to hear it," he finally said. "I'm happy, actually. Happy those two scumbags are—dead. They deserved to die!"

Beau's gaze fell to the fax on his desk. Almost identical to Cayne's words. A chill went up the back of his neck. Could a vengeful father have come back here and done both murders, covering his deeds with this phone call and pretending he knew nothing of it?

Alan Cayne thanked Beau enthusiastically and hung up before Beau could formulate a question. He sat there with the receiver dangling from his fingers until the line began to beep at him. He set it down and looked up the number for the Houston PD, placed a call. With a short explanation that Alan Cayne might be implicated in something in New Mexico, he asked that the man be questioned for alibis on Easter Sunday morning and again for last night.

Beau sat back in his chair, thinking. This rapid turn might provide a huge break in the case. After all, who would be more upset about the two convicts being released than the family of their victim? And who more likely to come looking for revenge than the young lady's father?

He thought of the only Cayne member still living in Sembramos, the grandmother, Sally. It was ludicrous to think of an old woman of Sally's size and build beating a man like

Lee Rodarte to death, but it didn't mean that Sally couldn't have been reporting all along to her son in Houston. And certainly either of them could have recruited someone for both the beating and the shooting in the forest.

* * *

Sam never wanted to see another big plate-glass window in her life. As she moved through the rooms, she thought about the dog-lady's story of strange lights in the house at night. Witches? Or maybe just the home's owner, coming back now and then to check things over? The latter seemed far more likely, except that there were still so many unanswered questions. Why, if he'd paid in full for the home, had he not moved in? Or, if he never planned to use it, why not sell it? Why let the taxes lapse after paying them for a number of years? Why, why, why . . . it was driving her crazy.

She rubbed at her aching shoulders, wishing she'd broken her resolve about not using the powers of the magic box. C'mon, surely all rules were off when one was faced with washing a million windows.

Finished with the ground floor, she decided to take a break before starting on the equally big second story. She ate two cookies and called Beau again. Once more, his cell phone went to voice mail. She gazed around the now-spotless kitchen, her thoughts drifting back to the deed she'd seen at the county records department. How could she find out who the person was behind LG Properties? She fiddled with the phone in her hand and decided that, if she couldn't reach Beau, maybe Rupert could point her in the right direction. He answered on the first ring.

"It's a corporation?" he asked after she posed the question. "Well, have you tried the corporations department in Santa Fe?"

How did a guy who wrote steamy romantic books know about this stuff?

"The information might be on their website . . . wait a second . . . What's the full name of the business again?"

Sam could hear computer keys clicking in the background, punctuated by a couple of mild oaths.

"Okay, Sam, got it. Now, what did you need to know about this corporation?"

"Who owns it, how to contact them."

"The registered agent's name is Linden Gisner." He spelled it for her and she fished in her pocket for a pen. "No phone number but the legal mailing address is 12489 County Road 12, Sembramos, New Mexico."

The address matched the property where she was standing at the moment. No help.

"Is there any alternate address?"

"Sorry, no."

At least she had a name, which was further than she'd gotten yet. She thanked Rupert and told him his next cupcake fix was on the house. When she'd clicked off the call, she stared at the inked note on her left hand. Gisner. That sounded vaguely familiar—but in what context?

She stared at the stairway leading to the second floor, feeling no enthusiasm for more windows today. Let Delbert Crow scream, she decided. She would finish the job tomorrow. She locked up and got into her truck, sending a silent plea to the cloudy sky that no rain come along and mess up all those newly cleaned glass panes.

Miles of familiar-feeling highway rolled past, bordered

by the same old orchards and tilled fields. Sam slowed her speed at the northern edge of Sembramos, staying watchful. Nothing seemed much different until she spotted Beau's vehicle at the side of the road. He was stopped beside another department cruiser, chatting with the deputy inside. Sam pulled in behind, and Rico waved at her as he drove away.

"Hey, darlin'," Beau said, getting out of the SUV and walking over to her window. "I saw your calls, just didn't have a minute until right now."

"I know. I didn't really expect you to call me right back. So . . . bad morning?"

"Yeah. I feel like I've been asking questions all day and getting no answers. We had the Starkey men in for questioning about Lee's beating but they go all wide-eyed and claim their innocence. Then an angry call from Angela Cayne's father, furious about Lee and Jessie being released. If he weren't in Houston, I'd pin him for both deaths. As it is, I'm having it verified that he really is *in* Houston. Can't discount the possibility that he heard the news and came out here."

"I saw the two state police cars on my way through this morning."

"It's going to stay that way for awhile. If there was trouble from the Starkeys yesterday, I have a feeling tonight every buddy of Lee's could show up asking for more of the same. His cousin, Bono Rodarte, is one rough dude. I don't dare leave the town unguarded, so it's all of my men plus the state patrols. I'll need to be here with them."

"Really?" Her anxiety ramped up a notch.

"Afraid so." He stared up the road for a few seconds. "Look, you go home, lock yourself in. Relax."

She had to chuckle. "Lock myself in, but relax?"

A battered white pickup cruised by slowly, the grizzled man at the wheel staring hard at Beau.

"President of my fan club," he said with a wry smile. "Joe Starkey."

"Beau—be careful."

"I am. They won't try anything against a lawman, darlin'. I'm just worried about what they'll do to each other."

"Don't these people have jobs? Something to do all day besides cruise around and give you the evil eye?"

"I suppose I could suggest that they get out and pull weeds in their fields or something."

He was trying to keep it light, Sam knew, to keep her from worrying. But it really wasn't working. He patted the side of her truck, sending her on her way. She kept a watchful eye all the way through town but didn't see Joe Starkey's truck again.

At the ranch, Ranger and Nellie came off the porch to greet her and she invited them inside. Maybe Beau was right. Her truck had been seen in town several times now—big and red, it wasn't exactly inconspicuous. She'd parked at the side of the house, out of view from the road, but still—having two large dogs at her side felt comforting.

The upside of Beau's working tonight was that Sam had the whole evening to pursue her own interests. She booted up her computer and prepared a small salad. An Internet search for Linden Gisner didn't net much. Who on the face of the earth wasn't on Facebook these days? She found one piece, a reprint of a five-year-old article where he'd bought a big commercial property outside Santa Fe and signed a deal with a developer who wanted to create yet another shopping mall. In it, Gisner was referred to as "a prominent northern

New Mexico land developer" which didn't exactly tell her anything she didn't already know. And it didn't include any possible leads on where to find him now.

She was about to turn her attention to the books on witchcraft when her phone rang.

"Hey, Mom. Everything okay? Haven't seen you in a few days."

With Sam's bakery right next door to Kelly's job at Puppy Chic, it was rare that they didn't touch base almost daily.

"I guess you've heard on the news about Beau's current case, the killings related to those two Sembramos men? That's eating up most of his time. Me, I'm just trying to locate the owner of one of my properties." She briefly described the huge house.

"You gotta get a smarter phone, Mom. There's an app for that."

"You're kidding, right?"

"I don't know. What's the name?"

Sam told her.

"And he's in New Mexico?"

"That, I'm not sure about."

"Hang on, let's see." Kelly's voice went into musing mode, with a couple of da-dum, da-dums while she did something. "There's a Linden Gisner right in Taos."

"Seriously? It was that easy? I checked online and the phone book."

"He probably doesn't have a land line, but maybe this info comes from his cell phone contract or something. I don't know."

Or some sneaky government agency out to track the

moves of everyone on the planet. Sheesh, Sam wondered. How much do they know about *me*?

"Mom? You want the address or not?"

"Yes! Definitely." She grabbed a pen and wrote down what Kelly told her.

"You want directions? The map's right here."

Oh god, that *was* invasive. But she wrote it all down. Then she walked around the house and closed all the shades.

Chapter 16

Sam carried her salad plate to the dishwasher, wanting to erase the disturbing feeling that had settled over her. What if that creepy Starkey guy had one of those gadgets and looked up Beau's home address? What if any of the many lowlifes and villains he came across did the same thing? She double-checked the locks all around. Took a deep breath. This voice in her head was sounding too much like her mother's.

Settling on the sofa with a cup of tea and the books Cora Abernathy had given her, Sam flipped one of them open. Maybe plain old-fashioned witchcraft wasn't as scary as other things these days. But the words didn't hold her attention and she decided maybe it was better use of her time to make some phone calls.

Cora's notes had given information on two covens. The

one that held an annual festival seemed a little too New-Age and public for Bertha Martinez's style, so Sam called the other contact person, listed only as Mary.

She had a little difficulty explaining exactly what she wanted. Mary kept letting Sam talk without actually answering anything.

Finally, she said, "We take oaths of silence, you must understand. Few of us would give out our names, much less discuss what goes on in our rituals."

"I'm sorry—" Sam stammered. "I don't want personal information. What I have is more of an artifact, I guess you might say. All I know about it is the name of the woman who gave it to me."

"Perhaps this woman—you said her name was Bertha Martinez? It could be that she was a solitary practitioner. Many witches do not care to work with others."

"I don't even know that Bertha considered herself a witch, but I have a feeling you might be right about a solitary practice. Do you have any ideas how I might learn more about this item?"

The woman at the other end of the line paused for a long time, considering. "I can take a look at it. It might have something to say for itself."

Sam was beginning to wonder if this was the right track for her at all, but she agreed to meet Mary at a local coffee shop the following afternoon. She tried to formulate questions to ask of the witch when they met, but by this time her attention refused to focus. She let the dogs out the back door, stepping outside, herself, to stare into the black sky. The long, brilliant tail of a meteor turned her thoughts from the troubling forces of man to the more soothing forces of nature.

When Ranger and Nellie returned, with a chill on their fur and happy smiles on their faces, Sam settled them into their crates for the night, rechecked the locks and went upstairs. Snuggled into the lonely king-sized bed, she called Beau to make sure all was going well on his nighttime patrol and to tell him goodnight. He sent her a kiss—clearly, he was alone in his car—and told her to sleep well. She did, for awhile.

In the dream she was back in Ireland, in the very masculine study at her uncle's home. Terrance O'Shaughnessy came into the room, wearing the nightshirt from the last time she'd seen him, with a striped robe of rich fabric and leather slippers. He greeted her familiarly, joy lighting his lined face.

"Uncle Terry, you promised to tell me the story behind this," Sam said, holding up the carved wooden box she'd found in his bookcase. The twin box to her own.

"Ah, yes child, I did. And I shall." He moved to the fireplace in the corner and bent to strike a long match to the stack of kindling and logs. "Come, sit," he said, pointing to the pair of armchairs near the comforting glow.

Sam carried the box with her and walked toward him.

"You know, Samantha, that I traveled the world while I was alive," he said, settling into his chair. "I had the opportunity to visit many interesting places. I collected many fine pieces of art, many fascinating items. This one— it does things. Things that I cannot explain, things no one else would believe."

Sam felt her pulse quicken. Yes! She wanted to tell him how well she understood what he was saying. But she woke up.

No—no, no.

She stared around the bedroom, seeing only faint

outlines in the near-perfect darkness. For the second time, she felt robbed of the truth. Terry had been ready to share this story with her last fall. And then he died. She sat up and raised the comforter to her face, burying the urge to cry out.

With a sigh, she got up and made her way to the bathroom, finding her carved box on the vanity by the glow of the tiny nightlight in the corner. She pressed her palms against the top of it and closed her eyes, hoping for a vision of her uncle, for some words from him. But nothing came. After a time, she gently patted the box and went back to bed.

The dream never returned and Sam was surprised to wake at daylight, refreshed by an uninterrupted sleep. By the time she had brushed her teeth and dressed she began to wonder if she had imagined the episode. Was it possible to dream that you'd had a dream?

She dumped out her jewelry and carried the box downstairs, reviewing her plans for the day as she tended the dogs and gathered the witchcraft books and papers. Finish the windows at the big house—and yes, she would call upon the energy from the box; her muscles still felt the effects of yesterday's labor—then back to town for her meeting with Mary. She debated whether to tell the woman about the Irish connection or last night's dream.

That decision could be made later; right now she wondered how the night had gone for Beau. She dialed his cell.

"It stayed pretty quiet here," he said, his voice sounding weary enough that Sam almost felt guilty for her night of solid sleep.

"Can I buy you breakfast?" she asked. "If the café there is open?"

"It is and you may. If I don't get a lot of coffee in me soon, I'll be asleep in this car."

"I'll be there in twenty minutes." She made space in her pack for the wooden box, then headed out the door.

She could smell the coffee almost the minute she got out of her truck, which she parked beside Beau's cruiser in front of the building with its Old West wooden façade. Toward the back of the single room she spotted Beau at a table.

"Long night, huh," she said, rubbing his shoulder as she stepped over to take the chair across from his.

"Too long. I don't know which is worse—trouble flaring up or sitting around with nothing to do but make myself stay awake." He nodded at the offer of a refill from the teen waitress who approached.

"So, no new leads about Lee or about Jessie?" Sam asked as she studied the menu.

He glanced around the near-empty room and lowered his voice. "Can't remember if I told you, I had an angry call from Angela Cayne's father yesterday. Guy sounded mad enough to have come after both men. At first I assumed he was calling from his home, in Houston, but then I got to wondering. I'm waiting for word from Houston PD on whether they can confirm that. Story of my job—waiting."

"Beau, do you think there could be some sort of *avenger* up here, somebody local who truly believes he's doing everyone a favor by getting rid of both Starkey and Rodarte?"

He turned thoughtful, considering the idea, but then the waitress came back, looking fresh and perky. Beau ordered bacon and eggs.

"You need some rest," Sam told him after ordering

French toast and watching the girl head for the kitchen. "Can someone relieve you for a few hours?"

"That's the plan. We'll keep one man in town today while the night crew gets a little time off. I'll probably go home and crash. For later, we'll see how the day goes before we decide whether to keep patrols here another night."

"Well, I'd offer to trade you a day of washing windows for a night of sitting in the car, but I have a feeling that, really truly, neither of us would take that deal."

He smiled, the dimpled grin and those ocean blue eyes sending a pang right to her heart. Their meals arrived, along with a table full of diners—locals who were dressed like construction workers—so their conversation waned. Twenty minutes later, they parted outside by their vehicles, Beau promising to keep her posted as the day went on, Sam saying she wouldn't wake him up to ask.

Her squeegee and Windex waited on the kitchen counter at the big house, right where she'd left them. If the place were haunted, it sure would be nice if the spirits would come in at night and do some of this work. But they hadn't.

Sam unzipped her pack and took out the box, closing her eyes for a moment and then holding it close to her body. Immediately, the wood began to glow and warmth traveled up her arms. She felt the suffusion of energy more quickly than usual—was it because she hadn't used these powers in a long time? As the small red, green and blue stones on the box began to glow Sam set it down. She rubbed her hands together to diffuse the tingle, then put the box back into her pack. When she looked up, the kitchen was filled with sunny yellow light.

It was almost tangible and Sam reached out a hand, testing to see if it was real, like smoke. No, it was more as if someone had turned on theatrical lights with a yellow filter. She walked toward the large windows that overlooked the valley and when she turned, the great room also had an aura, this one a disturbing, murky orange. Sam's heart began to race.

She opened the door to the terrace and stepped outside. She backed away from the house; she'd seen auras around people before, and they often conveyed feelings, such as love or fear, sometimes motivations, like dishonesty. But a house? How could a building have emotions? She stared out over the open meadows below and breathed deeply twice. Three times.

When she turned toward the house again, the windows revealed only clear air and the normal appearance of the place.

Okay, that was weird.

She went back inside, a little tentatively, feeling hyper-aware. The room felt cold, much colder than when she'd arrived. She stared at the doorways to the other rooms. The place was hollow and deadly quiet. Up the stairs, the same. She walked through every room and looked inside every closet. No one was here with her.

All right, Sam, you gotta shake this off and get to work.

After fast-walking out to her truck and back she shook her arms, rotated her shoulders, and went back inside. No colors, no chills.

She cursed her too-vivid imagination, picked up her cleaning supplies and marched up the stairs. Two hours later, every window on the second floor sparkled to within an inch of its life. Sam rechecked that entire level and decided it would pass muster.

Downstairs, the kitchen and great room still looked

normal and Sam began to question whether she'd really seen any colors at all. Maybe with all this talk of witches and magic her imagination had simply been working overtime. That had to be it.

She started to take her cleaning supplies to the truck but remembered that she hadn't yet done windows in the smaller rooms in the other ground-level wing. She picked up clean towels and headed that direction. She would start with the rooms nearest the back, the guest suites, and work her way toward the front door.

The first guestroom door was closed and when she opened it, the entire room filled with a hot, red haze.

"Whoa!" She backed away, slamming the door, feeling her eyes go wide. Her breath came in short huffs.

Down the corridor, near the home's front door, she glanced into the wine cellar. The air in here was clear but the moment Sam stepped into the chamber, it began to take on a purplish tint and before she could back out, the air had become murky with the stuff.

"Okay, this is ridiculous. I do not need to be here this badly." She deposited her cleaning gear back in the kitchen, picked up her pack and left.

Out in her truck, logic prevailed. What had just happened in that house? Evidently, there was some type of reaction to each room as soon as Sam entered it. The colored fog and variations in temperature vanished once she left the space. But it didn't happen everywhere; she'd spent time upstairs with no bad effects. Not to mention that she'd been here multiple times in recent days and perceived nothing out of the ordinary aside from warm and cold. Unless one counted an abandoned multi-million dollar house as typical. So, what was different?

She glanced at the seat beside her. The box. Even deep in her pack, in the kitchen, that house could sense the box's presence. Sam did a quick little snap-out-of-it head shake. The whole notion was crazy, impossible, preposterous. Utterly ridiculous. She unzipped the pack and took a look. The box sat there, ugly but benign. Minding its own business.

Oh, Sam, Sam . . . what are you doing trying to imagine the box's thoughts? Instead of meeting up with a witch this afternoon you need to get yourself to a psychiatrist.

No, you need to get yourself away from this house. The place was flat-out weird. She stuck her key in the ignition and started the truck. Normalcy—that's all she wanted right now.

She headed toward home but partway there remembered that Beau was trying to catch up on a missed night of sleep. She had far too much pent-up energy to sit quietly around the house for several hours. So—the bakery was the one place where excess energy could always be put to good use.

Sweet's Sweets looked like a happy little oasis of normal as Sam drove past the front, with its purple awnings and cheerful displays of cakes and pastries in the windows that faced the sidewalk. She parked at the back and entered her world of sugar and spice, happy to be away from things that couldn't be fixed with an extra teaspoon of vanilla extract.

"Hey, Sam," greeted Julio.

"Can't stay away, huh?" Becky teased.

Sam rolled her eyes, getting off with the explanation that after washing windows all morning she was ready for something that tasted good. "I've got a couple hours before I have to get to an appointment. Who needs my help?"

Becky held up a wedding cake sketch on an order form. "I've got the flowers made for this one, but it calls for a whole lot of traditional piping and you know how nervous I get doing the string work."

Piping parallel swags of thin icing strings was a technique that took a lot of practice and an extremely steady hand. Sam ran a few practice rows of them on a cardboard form, amazed that her hands were a whole lot steadier than her gut felt. Then she tackled the actual cake.

"Oh my gosh," said Becky, an hour later. "I am so glad you came in when you did."

Sam stepped back. The four tiers were gracefully draped with triple rows of perfect swags. She breathed a sigh of satisfaction. This was her real calling, not going into strange houses and encountering oddball, unexplainable things. Maybe she should drop the idea of investigating anything magical.

Becky brought the flowers for the cake from the fridge and Sam set them in place, forming cascades of peach and ivory, adding a spritz of pearlescent powder with the airbrush. She compared it with Jen's sketch to be sure she hadn't left out anything the bride wanted.

"Good to go?" she asked Becky.

"It is gorgeous. I'm supposed to deliver it at three."

Sam thanked Becky for taking the initiative, then walked out to the sales area to check on the displays. Jen reported a decent morning's sales, which reminded Sam to review her supplies and place an order with her wholesaler. That done, she realized it was time to go meet Mary the witch.

Chapter 17

Whatever Sam expected of a witch—somewhere along the spectrum between the curvy young creatures on *Charmed* and a black-clothed crone with pointy hat and warts—Mary was none of those. The woman who approached Sam on the sidewalk outside Java Joe's Joint was nearing sixty and wore a soft cotton pastel yellow skirt, blue top and earthy sandals. She carried a cloth drawstring bag. Her all-gray hair hung in waves to her shoulders, with a strand on either side pinned back from her face with glittery tiny clips. She looked more earth-child than conjurer. Mary seemed a little more wary of Sam than Sam was of her. They decided on a booth at the back of the room.

Java Joe didn't seem the least bit put out that both women ordered tea. He went behind the bar and came back with a small pot for each of them.

"You're the lady who owns that adorable pastry shop near the plaza, aren't you?" Mary said after they'd established a little common ground. "I love that place, especially those chocolates you sell around Christmas."

Who knew a witch could also be a chocolate fanatic? Sam wasn't about to tell the woman that the chocolates, first introduced to the shop by an odd Romanian chocolatier who had shown up to offer his services, seemed to have an addictive effect on most everyone.

Once their tea arrived and Java Joe had retreated to his own duties, Sam introduced the subject of the wooden box.

"Ah, yes, the curious artifact you wanted me to look at," Mary said.

Sam unzipped her pack and took out the box, careful to handle it minimally, lest it start to change color in the presence of a stranger. She wanted to know if the box reacted the same way with someone else.

"Well, it's an interesting piece." Mary turned it over and looked at all sides of it. "Not exactly a piece of fine craftsmanship."

An understatement. At best, the quilted pattern in the carved wood was fairly symmetrical. But the stain used on it was an ugly yellowish-brown, which had settled into the grooves unevenly, and the colored cabochon stones must have been mounted by an amateur as none of the prongs were finely crafted. Sam made no comment on the dramatic changes that came over the box when she handled it.

"The woman who gave it to me was reputed to be a *bruja*. I may have mentioned that on the phone. Someone else once asked me if she might have actually been a *curandera*."

"I didn't recognize the name you gave me—Bertha Martinez, wasn't it?" Mary raised the hinged lid of the box and examined all sides of it.

"That's right. I'm trying to find out something of the history of the box and wondered if there were friends or . . . would you call them colleagues? . . . of Bertha's in town."

"I'm afraid most of this is out of my league," Mary said. "My beliefs are religious. We study the pagan gods and goddesses that pre-date Christianity, a very nature-based belief system. While that goes along somewhat with the Native American ideologies, they really are two different areas of study and practice."

"So, Bertha wasn't affiliated with any group that you know of?"

Mary set the box down and shook her head. Sam watched carefully over the rim of her tea mug. The witch showed no sign that the box had energized her or warmed to her touch.

"There's something else I've been wondering about. Just recently I've been assigned as caretaker for a house that seems to have a sort of . . . I don't know how to describe it . . . Well, I've observed hot and cold places in the house." How much to reveal? "And colors . . . something I can best describe as an aura, except I thought only people had auras surrounding them."

Mary regarded Sam, mouth pursed slightly, head tilted.

"Where could I find out more? I mean, I'm wondering if the place is haunted or . . ." Sam couldn't think of a better way to describe it.

"You wonder if a house can be spiritually active, maybe inhabited by forces from another world?"

Sam shrugged. "I guess."

"Many things are possible, and it's unwise to discount any of them entirely," Mary said with a soothing voice.

"A neighbor near this particular place says there have been odd lights at night, like perhaps someone has been holding candlelight ceremonies or something there."

Mary smiled indulgently. "Maybe the neighbor just watches too much television. I'm afraid TV and movies have really distorted what our practices are truly about."

She started to pick up her bag. "Nothing in my own practice relates to what you are asking me, Sam. I'm sorry. But I will keep my senses tuned to your request. If I come across anyone who might have known your Bertha Martinez, may I have them contact you?"

"Certainly." Sam waved off Mary's cash. "The tea is my treat. I appreciate your time." *You have no idea how much your handling the box has told me.*

"Blessings on your day," Mary said as she stood up.

Sam stowed the box back inside her pack. Should she have mentioned to Mary that there were two boxes? The information probably wouldn't matter. Something told her that the witch's answers were true; she really didn't know anything of use to Sam's search.

* * *

Sophie Garcia had called the sheriff's office when Lee's parents got to town. Now she paced the floor of her apartment, meeting Beau's eyes now and then.

"I feel so . . . conflicted," she said. "I'd given up on Lee and started my own life. It was part of the reason the Rodartes moved away, because I was never a hundred percent sure that Lee wasn't guilty, because I didn't fall apart when he went to prison. Things became very tense between us—me and his parents. And now they're here."

"What caused your doubts?"

She walked to the window, turned. "I wasn't sure of his story—that he rode out to the gorge just to think. I mean . . . it wasn't impossible, but it didn't fit his nature, really. I don't know. I've thought about this for years."

"And when he was released—did your feelings toward Lee change?"

"When he came back, last week, and they said he was innocent after all. I—" her voice cracked.

Beau gave her a moment.

She wiped at her nose with a tissue grabbed from a box on the end table.

"For a little while, when I saw him with Nathan. The joy Lee felt at seeing me again . . . Yeah, I really did consider giving it a second chance. Sheriff, I was so crazy in love with him before, when we'd just gotten out of school and had our whole lives ahead of us. But there was all the history— the way his parents feel about me. I couldn't decide. And now he's—"

Beau waited while she got past a bout of sobbing. Surely she hadn't specifically called him for a session of grief counseling, but it seemed rude to interrupt and ask what she'd wanted of him. She looked up at him with reddened eyes.

"Sophie, has there been trouble with the parents? Or someone else?"

She nodded. "It's Nathan. Kids at school started pushing him around, saying his dad was a killer, really being cruel. Yesterday was bad. I kept him home today, but then the Rodartes showed up and wanted to spend some time with him. They're completely broken up over Lee so I said they could take Nathan out for ice cream. Then I thought maybe if I talked to you . . . I don't know . . . school problems aren't probably your worry, but then you hear of such awful things happening to kids at school these days. Sorry I'm bothering you with all this."

"No, it's okay. You were right to let me know. Did you talk to his teacher or the principal?"

She nodded. "They said they would hold a session and talk to the kids about being sympathetic when someone loses a parent. I'm sure the kids are just repeating things they hear at home."

Sad. Down to the youngest ones, this town was still ripped into different camps.

A vehicle slowed out front and Beau automatically stepped to the edge of the window. It was a late-model Chevy sedan. It stopped and Nathan Garcia got out, followed by the grandparents. Would this be yet another confrontation, people waiting to take out years of anger on the nearest symbol of the system that had put their son away? Beau braced himself.

"We have funeral plans to make," Sophie said, watching them come toward the apartment. "I told them I would help, even though they plan to take Lee to Albuquerque for burial."

Sophie introduced Kathy and Leroy Rodarte, and Beau's concerns of hostility eased. These were people whose grieving had begun years ago according to the deeply etched lines on faces that looked at least a decade older than their true ages. Both wore simple clothing of the Wal-Mart variety. Kathy's makeup was minimal and her short hair had probably been done in the same pixie style for thirty years and colored only when the gray began to show up. Leroy's salt-and-pepper had many more strands of salt these days.

Nathan grinned at his mother with a chocolate-rimmed mouth and Sophie hustled him off to the bathroom to wash up.

"Sheriff, thank you for speaking with our son when he came back," Kathy said. "He had called us. He said you were very kind to Sophie and Nathan." She lowered her voice. "Lee had his rough spots. You know, young men. He got in with that group and the big motorcycles. I was afraid he might try drugs."

Leroy made a move to shush her but Kathy merely smiled sweetly at her husband.

"I'm just saying," Kathy continued. "it seemed like he was turning all of that around. When he met Sophie we were so happy, and then little Nathan—"

Leroy nodded at that.

"Well, we just thought it was going so much better until all the trouble started."

"It was hard, leaving our hometown," said Leroy. "We both grew up here. But then the girls went to college in Albuquerque. It seemed better for us to be near our daughters after Lee was sent away."

The sadness in Kathy's eyes came back, full force. "I never dreamed it would end like this."

Beau nodded sympathetically. A lot of what they said was probably true, much of it was obviously parental blindness.

"We did our best to make a new life." Leroy forced optimism into his voice, for his wife's sake.

Sophie and Nathan came back into the room. "Are we ready? Our appointment's in thirty minutes so we better move along." She glanced at Beau. "Funeral home."

He said goodbye and repeated that they could call him

if they needed to. They followed him out the door and the family got into the Chevy. Beau crossed the street to his cruiser and checked in with his dispatcher before putting it in gear. No new calls. He decided to make the rounds—it wouldn't take long to cruise the streets of Sembramos and make sure things had stayed quiet all day.

He turned from Cottonwood Lane back to the paved highway. The businesses along the main drag looked normal for this time of day, quiet. At Third Street he made a right and went by the Starkey place. The battered white pickup sat out front. Helen should be back at work at the grocery store now, but maybe she walked the three blocks to get there. Scary, Beau thought, how quickly this little burg had begun to feel familiar to him, how he was already recognizing patterns.

He stayed on Pine parallel to the highway, cut over on Fifth Street, the last named one in town, and made his way over to Cottonwood again where he saw Gina Staples watering her garden at the Rodarte's old house. He briefly wondered whether the Rodartes had come by here on their earlier trip for ice cream. Gina waved at him but otherwise didn't divert her attention from her work.

Next to the old Rodarte place was the former Cayne house. Seeing it reminded him that he hadn't heard back about Alan Cayne's alibis for the times of either of the recent killings. He would have to call Houston PD back if he didn't get something soon. He stared at the house. Alan Cayne wasn't the only one who'd been furious with Jessie and Lee. What was it someone had said about Lee Rodarte and Angela's brother getting into it? Another mental note: check the testimony from the witnesses back in the murder file at home.

Three killings, all related. Tied together, unfortunately, by nearly everyone in this town. So difficult to pin all the events back to any one person. He shook away the cobwebs. Even though it felt as if one person could have been responsible, it was far more likely that Angela's death was one thing; Lee and Jessie's killings were most likely the result of the current flare of hot tempers, accusations and years of pent-up anger. What a tangled mess.

Beau completed his circle of town, again passing in front of Sophie's apartment. He pulled over beside the adjacent park and took a few minutes to check in with dispatch. No word from Houston PD yet, and no new calls for Beau. Two deputies were on duty, handling routine things in Taos, the others were home catching up on sleep in case Beau wanted them back in Sembramos again tonight. He told his desk clerk to have everyone meet at the station at five o'clock and he would give out assignments. So far, things in Sembramos were quiet.

Even as he said it, though, he looked up and scanned the area. Perhaps things were too quiet.

Chapter 18

Sam sat in her truck after watching Mary the witch drive away. Interesting meeting, although she was a little disappointed that it hadn't given her a solid lead to anyone who'd known Bertha Martinez. Curious, though, that Mary had detected nothing unusual about the wooden box, and clearly she'd gotten no reaction like the electric-jolt feeling that had shot through Sam the first time she ever touched it.

All these questions about the box were beginning to make Sam wonder why she was bothering with this. She'd gotten no reaction when she handled the other box, the one at her uncle's house, even though it looked almost identical to hers. The thought had crossed her mind more than once that Bertha's words, saying that Sam was intended to own the box, meant more than that the old woman was giving Sam a simple gift. There was a relationship—although that sounded weird to her—between herself and this particular item. Maybe there were dozens of these things out in the world, each supposed to bond with a different person. But then, that was too much like believing she'd been chosen for some higher purpose. Her head started to ache whenever she got into the whole convoluted mess of thoughts.

She reached into her pack for her keys and came across the scrap of paper where she'd written the name and address of that man who owned the big white house. Now *there* was something she could do that had absolutely no woo-woo factor at all.

Maybe she *would* have to get one of those phones with maps integrated into it, Sam decided as she tried to follow the written directions in an area where half the roads were named but didn't happen to have signage. After a couple of missed turns, she spotted someone's hand-written sign that corresponded to a name Kelly had given her. Apparently the residents were tired of having visitors and deliveries lost along the way.

A curve in the road, another turn where the sign was obscured by shrubbery and she finally came to a spread with a long white fence surrounding at least forty acres of horse pasture, with a rambling adobe house as the centerpiece. She rechecked the address. This was where a man lived who was letting his other house go for back taxes?

You never know, she reminded herself, pulling into the long driveway that led to a circular roundabout with a bubbling granite fountain at its center. The house was laid out in two symmetrical wings, one of which contained a five-car garage with rustic wooden doors that faced perpendicular to the road. Outside one of the garages sat a gleaming antique car—maybe a Rolls Royce or Duesenberg—Sam wasn't sure. The residence's front door was eight feet wide, consisting of two elaborately carved Mexican-style panels with curved wrought iron hardware. Now *that* was a lock that would not be easy to pick.

She pressed a button beside the door and cringed as the notes of "La Cucaracha" echoed through the interior. Uck. Just when she believed the estate to have been done in exquisite taste. Her second clue to her mistake came when the door was answered by a man in surfer shorts and sandals, holding a margarita. He wore his faded blonde hair longish and combed straight back from an extremely receded hairline.

"Oh, hey," he said. "I thought you'd be Val. Guess he's running late."

"I'm looking for Linden Gisner," Sam said.

"You got him. C'mon in. It's happy hour—or at least it's five o'clock somewhere. Like, right *here*—in my salon." He chuckled at his own hilarity as he turned his back, assuming she would follow. She closed the door behind her and trailed along through a wide foyer tiled in Saltillo so shiny it might have been underwater. At the back of the house a room lined with windows faced south—what was with this guy and windows anyway? Furnishings consisted of wicker pieces with lots of turquoise, yellow and red cushions, and a long Mexican bar filled one side of the room. Gisner had stepped over to it and was about to pour Sam a margarita before asking whether she wanted one. She declined with a smile.

"Your loss. I make an amazing margarita."

She would have to take his word for it.

"Rest of the gang should be along soon. Julia said she'd try to make it today. Val's definitely coming."

It dawned on Sam that he was talking about some of the Hollywood elite who loved to hang around Taos. If she didn't get her questions answered soon, she wouldn't get the chance. She gave the quick rundown on who she was and why she'd stopped by.

"Ah, Sembramos," he said. "I named the house Heathermoor, after my wife. Well, then the bitch ran off—I'm sure it was with that jackass electrician who came around all the time—and I was left to raise a child *and* try to finish the house *and* handle my business, which was keeping me going twenty-four-seven." He stared out the windows where four thoroughbred horses grazed on grass so brilliantly green that it had to be sucking water out of the aquifer like crazy. "It all came to a stop when my daughter died. I could not think, much less keep juggling all the balls at once."

"I'm sorry to hear it." Two awkward minutes passed while Sam tried to think of something comforting to say.

Gisner raised his margarita glass. "Well, here's to times past. Luckily, times present are far happier."

He looked toward the foyer, where a young blonde woman with lots of tan skin crossed to another room, giving him a flirty smile on the way. He smiled right back and the solemn moment vanished.

Sam cleared her throat. "Well, I just wanted to let you know about the tax auction. If you want to get things caught up, you could save the place." She handed him one of the cards that the USDA had issued her when she began her contract with the agency.

"Yeah, yeah, I suppose I should do that." But his eyes were on the doorway where the blonde had disappeared.

The whole time she was telling him about tax payments

she had to wonder—if he had this kind of money and connections maybe the other house truly didn't mean that much to him. He certainly didn't act like it. She thought of the rumors of big real estate deals, Jen's story of the man who'd breezed into the gallery to shop for expensive art, the empty white mansion. A completely different world.

The "Cucaracha" door chimes went off again, and Gisner happily floated off to answer. Shouts and enthusiastic greetings attested to the likelihood that the guests had started happy hour somewhere else. Sam didn't want to get caught up in this odd, artificial place. Being at home and seeing Beau had great appeal right now. She edged to the doorway and when ten lively partiers drifted into the salon she slipped out, pleased to see that their Jaguars and BMWs hadn't blocked her truck.

The sun sat low in the sky when Sam reached the other end of town and turned toward home. The sight of their comfortable log house and the two dogs on the porch warmed her heart; she'd had a full afternoon of oddball people and situations. Beau rose from the long dining table and held her close.

"Rough day?" he asked.

"Strange day. But then, we've had a lot of those recently, haven't we?" Sam glanced at the pages from the Angela Cayne file where he had been working. "Want some help with that?"

"Later. I'm starving."

While they prepared a salad for dinner Beau told her he'd met Lee Rodarte's parents. "They've lived with grief for so long; there's just a permanent air of sadness around them. But not hostility. I don't ever like to discount the idea that anyone can commit murder, but I just don't see these as the people who would have taken a high-power rifle out to the woods to get rid of Jessie Starkey."

"Sure doesn't sound like it." Sam set their plates on the kitchen table. "So. Do you feel any closer to figuring this out?"

"Not really. Jessie Starkey was only back in town a couple of days before his killer caught up with him. Someone who harbored the old resentment might have heard the news of his release and started to stalk him, but they would have had to be well organized. I mean, it's not easy to take a gun on an airplane, so for it to be Angela Cayne's father he would have had to drive from Houston, which is a day and a half at least, or fly in and risk a paper trail or have someone ready to give him a weapon. You can't buy one that fast, with background checks and three-day waits and all. So he would have almost needed advance word that Jesse was getting out. I've got the Houston police checking his alibi for Easter Sunday morning, but I'm thinking he's less and less viable as a suspect. Not ruling him out entirely though."

"And Lee's killer?"

"Well, we know Cayne couldn't have done that. We'd already started looking at him, and the Houston cops assure me he hasn't left the city in recent days."

"And, from Mr. Cayne's standpoint, would there be any point to coming out here to get rid of one of his daughter's killers unless he stayed to get them both?"

"My thoughts exactly," Beau said, absentmindedly swabbing a lettuce leaf into salad dressing.

"So, if the Cayne family is clear—"

"Wait a second . . . I'm thinking all along about Alan and Tracy Cayne, the parents. But Angela had a brother too. He was in his teens—" Beau dropped his fork and rushed into the living room.

By the time Sam caught up with him he was riffling through one of the paper stacks.

"Someone had mentioned . . . hang on . . . Here it is." He ran his finger down one of the newspaper article copies Sam had brought home. He quickly read the piece and looked up at Sam. "Matthew Cayne approached Lee Rodarte in the hallway at the courthouse, as the trial was getting started. The brother was only fifteen at the time but he got right in Rodarte's face and threatened him. Words to the effect that he better not think he could get away with this."

"So, he may have harbored that anger over the years and when he heard the two men got out of prison . . ."

"Exactly." Beau tapped his fingers against his thumb, counting. "He's twenty-two now. I better see what he's doing these days."

He dropped the page, picked up his phone and within a minute was in conversation with the detective he'd been working with in Houston. Sam went back to the kitchen, realized that the remaining salad on their plates would never be touched, so she dumped the scraps and put the dishes into the dishwasher. She was measuring coffee into the filter basket when Beau walked in.

"Bits and pieces," he said, picking up a cookie from the bakery box she'd set out. "Alan Cayne's alibi for the weekend checks out. He never left Houston. I asked if the son, Matthew, still lived at home. Detective Barnes didn't recall, but he will check on that. He says he'll get back—"

His phone rang and he made a dash back to the living room. By the time Sam was pouring from their little two-cup carafe, he'd come back, a gleam in his eye.

"Well, this could get interesting," he said. "Matthew

Cayne no longer lives in Houston. He joined the Air Force. And he's stationed at Kirtland Base, in Albuquerque. Less than three hours away. He has firearms training and access to the local news. I'd say it's worth a bit of my time to drive down there in the morning."

Chapter 19

The miles peeled away, dry desert becoming drier as Beau went south. Without some rain soon, the whole state might be in for a bad fire season again. And typically, if that rain didn't fall this month, it probably wouldn't come until after the searing heat of June and July had baked the landscape even crisper. At the outskirts of Albuquerque he adjusted his thinking and his driving to cope with the packed traffic on the corridor of Interstate 25 that ran through the center of the state's largest city.

Kirtland Air Force Base, which actually housed soldiers from several branches of service, was simple to get to. Stay on the freeway all the way through Albuquerque. Exit at Gibson, near the airport, which shared its runways with the base. He'd called ahead and gotten the name of Matthew Cayne's commanding officer who, by the time Beau got there, should have arranged a meeting. Two soldiers who looked as if they shouldn't even be shaving yet stopped him at the gate, asked for ID, checked his name against a list, and made a phone call before issuing him a guest pass.

His own military stint was twenty-five years in the past but the layout and procedures still felt familiar to Beau. Some things were indelibly imprinted on your mind, he supposed. Either that, or some things never changed. There were more women walking around and the base housing looked nicer; those were about the only differences Beau noticed. He followed the set of turns described by the guard and pulled up in front of a two-story generic tan, concrete block building. A young man with a shaved head, wearing fatigues and staff sergeant stripes, met him and eyed Beau's uniform. After no-nonsense introductions, SSgt Lopez showed Beau into a depressing square room with shiny beige paint, a rectangular table and four metal chairs. Beau stared at posters touting equal opportunity and warning what-all constituted sexual harassment these days. Five minutes later the staff sergeant was back, leading a young man with two stripes and a spine made of rebar.

Matthew Cayne addressed him as Sir and stood at attention until Beau suggested they sit at the table that ran the length of the small room.

"I'm looking into a couple of recent incidents in your home town," Beau began.

Cayne's eyes scanned the insignia on Beau's uniform, apparently thinking he meant Houston.

"Taos County. I need to know if you've left the base here in the last week."

"Yes, sir. We were on maneuvers."

"Where was that?"

"In the desert near Holloman, sir." The other military base was near the southern end of the state, at least a six-hour drive from Taos, each way.

"Were you ever away from your unit?"

"No, sir."

Beau made eye contact with Lopez. "Can we verify that?"

The man gave a curt nod and left the room. In the silence behind him, Cayne waited without a word, hands clasped on the table top. Beau leaned back in his chair, hoping Matthew would relax a little.

"Have you been back to Sembramos at all since your family moved away?"

"No, sir."

"You're certain?"

"Yes, sir."

Had the young man been briefed to only provide yes and no answers? Beau felt as if he were up against a brick wall.

"I don't know if you've heard about the problems up north, but we think these incidents go back to your sister's death, seven years ago."

"I've heard the news reports, sir. I don't know anything beyond that."

The staff sergeant returned. "Sheriff Cardwell, it looks like Corporal Cayne's statement is true. His unit was on a training mission—ten days under desert conditions, reporting to and from Holloman."

"Thanks." Beau tamped down his frustration. It felt like every lead was coming to a dead end in this case. "Matthew—could we chat informally for a minute? I have to admit that we're looking for ideas now. Do you remember, back when

Angela died, anyone who had reason to kidnap her? Just tell me anything you remember from that time."

Now that his own alibi had checked out, Cayne's shoulders relaxed. "My parents worried that question constantly, sir. They talked about it, over and over. Myself, being fifteen and more concerned with what my buddies and I were doing, I started to tune them out after awhile." His spine finally touched the back of his chair and the tight jaw became less rigid. "It was scary when it happened, sir. I was in my room, headphones on, music mix blasting away. Grandma Sally was staying with us. I don't remember if she was recovering from some kind of surgery or just hadn't been feeling well. Mom was taking care of her, but Grandma went to bed early so Mom and Dad went to something at church. They wanted me and Angie to go along, but then they decided it would be smart for someone to be home in case Grandma needed something. We both talked our way out of doing the church thing, so we were both there with Grandma."

He picked at a shredded cuticle now. "So, I'm in my room with the door closed—what can I say? You know teenagers, I wanted my privacy. Next thing I know Mom's coming in, all freaked out, asking where Angie went. And I have no clue. I've been in my own zone the whole time. But then I go out to the living room and it's a mess. There's a glass of Coke tipped over on the table by the couch and Angie's fashion magazines are all scattered on the floor. The couch is kind of crooked and the coffee table is tipped over."

"And you never heard this happening?"

He looked a little embarrassed. "I used to turn the music up to where my brain would vibrate. Stupid, I know.

Between that and working here, around turbine engines and loud machines, the doc says I already have pretty bad hearing loss. I'll probably be one of those deaf old men you laugh at, except that I'll be thirty when it happens."

"What about Angie's friends? I suppose your parents checked with all of them?"

"Yeah, well, she didn't have a lot. Her very best friend was always Molly Gisner, but she got killed in that accident. Her dad went all weird over it, so our two families really weren't friends afterward. Angie, she was, you know, popular in school but she was also kind of distant. She wanted to wear cool clothes and all, but she mostly read books and kept to herself. And she'd graduated a couple years before all this happened. Most of her classmates had scattered."

Beau gave an understanding nod. "Were you or Angie friends with either Jessie Starkey or Lee Rodarte?"

"The Rodartes lived next door—you probably already know that. I looked up to Lee because he was older, a cool guy with a motorcycle. You know. At fourteen, fifteen, all that seemed important to me. My dad wouldn't let me hang out with him though. Later, when I heard that Lee was doing some drugs, I guess I could see my dad's viewpoint." He gave a little shrug. "The whole Starkey family was sort of intimidating. We were this conservative, church-going family and they always seemed on the wild side. I think Jessie had a crush on my sister when she was in high school. He'd be over at Lee's and I'd see him really giving her the eye."

"Did she show an interest in him?"

"Angie? No way. She used to wrinkle her nose when she'd see him down the street, like she could smell him from far away. She dated a few guys in high school, but nobody like Jessie Starkey."

Beau's antennae rose. "Did Jessie ever push it? Come on strong to her?"

Matt shook his head. "Not that I ever saw. Seriously, I doubt he ever even asked her out. He was enough older that he'd have probably gone for girls his own age anyway. I really don't know."

Beau could see that Matthew Cayne had run out of information; how much could he expect a younger brother to remember anyway? He pulled out a business card. "If you can think of any names, friends of Angie's who might remember something from that time, could you give me a call?"

He walked out to his cruiser, feeling the buzz of electricity from the new revelation. Jessie Starkey, interested in Angela Cayne? Not one of his other witnesses had mentioned that. He needed to get back into that case file at home; maybe someone had been named and questioned at the time, someone who might have made the same connection that Matt had noticed. He left the base and found a McDonald's a block away where he indulged in the rare treat of fast food.

A half-hour later he was on the road northbound, mulling over everything since he'd received the call about Rodarte and Starkey being released from prison. Less than a week, and yet so much had happened. He barely remembered driving through Santa Fe or Espanola and, shortly, he was arriving at the outskirts of Taos.

Clouds had begun to build, heavy and dark over Taos Mountain. Maybe that rain would come after all.

* * *

Sam had awakened, feeling half tempted to ride along with Beau to Albuquerque and the interview with Matthew Cayne, but her own duties nagged at her. She'd been stalling—she knew this—about going back to the big white house, leery of a repeat of the weird auras she'd encountered last time. The place was beginning to give her the creeps, especially since she'd met its owner face to face and didn't exactly get warm vibes from him either. However, until she finished, the responsibility would continue to hang over her. Eventually, she had to face up to it and just go there. She sighed and began cutting carrots and potatoes into stew-sized chunks.

Looking at the situation with an analytical eye, she reminded herself that she'd never encountered the strange colors except the one time she went there with the wooden box in her possession—had, in fact, used its power to get through her work more quickly. Today, she would leave it home and simply wash windows under her own steam. Tired arms, yes. Unexplainable happenings, no. Tired seemed like the better answer. She dumped the vegetables into the slow-cooker. At least dinner would be ready when she got home.

She cruised through Sembramos, the way becoming more familiar with each trip. Patterns had begun to emerge. The blue Explorer at the bank meant that its owner worked there. Same with the white sedan at the variety store and the Moped at the ice cream shop. Depending on the time of day, kids might be at the crosswalk aiming their attention toward those afternoon treats. School buses from Taos would be delivering the high-schoolers home later in the day.

The police presence, too, was beginning to feel normal. Sam waved at Rico when she passed his cruiser.

Linden Gisner's house—it felt odd to attach a name

and image of the man to it—stood majestic as ever on its hill. Now that she'd witnessed the man's lifestyle, his casual party-mode attitude, she puzzled more than ever why he'd never moved in. The kitchen and great room and the large suites were perfect for that sort of entertaining. Maybe this location was a little too remote, too far north for the Taos crowd. And maybe Sembramos held too many painful memories; reminders of losing both his wife and his daughter would be right in his face every time he drove down the hill for a gallon of milk. She gave up trying to guess, parked her truck and went inside.

A little tentatively, she peered from the foyer into the great room. The air was clear and bright through her freshly washed windows. The earthy tans of the flooring and the deep browns of the fireplace and granite counters—all looked absolutely normal. No weird colors. She let out her pent-up breath and carried her window-washing supplies down the hall toward the guest suite and library where she'd left off.

The hours passed—guest suites done, library done, sewing room and nursery (although since learning his story and meeting Mr. Gisner in person she would have to rename those last two). She emptied her water bucket a few times and refilled from the supply she'd brought. When she came to the wine cellar she was happy to skip it—no windows in there. Finally, she declared the job finished. She was rechecking the rooms, making sure she'd left no dirty rags behind, when her phone rang. What did Delbert Crow want now? She took the call.

"I've emailed you a document," he said without preamble. "Did you get it?"

"I'm on the job right now." She felt a testy attitude creep

into her tone and she tamped it down. "I'll be sure to check for it when I get home."

"You said you'd located the owner of that property out by Sembramos, right? Well this is something he needs to sign. Since he doesn't answer mail, I need you to take it in person. Get him to sign it and then put it in the mail to me."

Sam gritted her teeth. Once in awhile a 'please' would be nice. She'd hoped that doing the windows was the last of this commitment for awhile, but she agreed to get the document and the signature. *Then* she could be done.

It was midafternoon when she pulled into the driveway at home. Beau's vehicle wasn't there—not surprising— although she'd hoped he might get back early from Albuquerque. She gave each of the dogs an absentminded pat on the head as she went inside and hooked her laptop to the printer on Beau's small desk.

While everything booted up she wandered to the kitchen and stirred the beef stew, turning the pot down to keep-warm mode. Back in the living room, she hit a few keys to open the email from Delbert and five minutes later she was out the door again, the two-page form in hand. Going by Gisner's "it's five o'clock somewhere" mantra, she figured she could catch him at home this time of day.

The wind was picking up as she reached the south end of Taos and began the series of twisty roads to her destination. The blonde with the long, tan legs answered the doorbell.

"Amber, where the *hell* are the *limes*?" Linden Gisner's voice echoed from somewhere deep in the interior of the house just as the door opened.

The young woman flinched, glanced over her shoulder. "Um, can you wait a second?" she said to Sam. She disappeared, leaving the door open and Sam standing on the tiled veranda.

Voices drifted toward her, the female sounding conciliatory and pleading, the male coarse and demanding. After an exchange or two Amber must have reminded him that someone was waiting at the door. Gisner approached Sam with his smile in place, except that this time it seemed forced.

"Ms . . . sorry, I don't remember your name. Anyway, what can I do for you?" He didn't exactly look as if he wanted to do *anything* for her.

She held out the pages. "My supervisor said these need to be signed."

Linden snatched up the papers. "I'll see about it." He started to close the door.

"I'm supposed to get them signed now and put them in the mail myself. Apparently it's something that's needed right away. It looks like a simple release form of some kind." She stepped forward. "I'll be happy to wait while you read through it."

His mouth opened, but apparently he thought better of what he was about to say. He grumbled a little and opened the door wider.

She trailed him into the salon where she'd been before. A blender full of pale green liquid waited beside a pair of salt-rimmed glasses. Linden held the pages in his left hand and poured himself a drink with the right, this time not offering one to Sam. She perched on the edge of one of the wicker chairs while he leaned against the bar, reading.

Amber came in with a small plate heaped high with lime quarters, gingerly setting it near the blender. Gisner gave her a glare that seemed to say that their earlier discussion wasn't finished. He flipped to the second page of Sam's form.

"Get me a damn pen," he growled at Amber.

The girl scampered away and came back a few seconds later. He scrawled a signature and thrust the pages back at Sam. She almost followed Amber's lead, wanting to slink out of the room, but why did she think she had to fear this guy? He was the one behind on his taxes, in trouble with money or for whatever reason.

"I suppose you might be happy to see the last of Sembramos," she said as she reached the foyer. "There's been some trouble up there recently. Too bad, because it's a cute little town."

He gave Sam a strange look, then turned on Amber. "Get those drinks finished!" he shouted.

"She didn't deserve that," Sam said quietly, facing him squarely.

"It's none of your damn business what I say to her." His face was suddenly fused with red, his voice reaching a manic pitch.

"Okay, you're right. It isn't. She must be willing to stick around for some reason."

He strode ahead and yanked open the front door.

Sam was happy to comply. She scooted past him and got into her truck, keeping an eye on Gisner as he stepped to the edge of the veranda. She reached the property boundary and pulled out to the county road before she let out her breath. So weird. What *was* this guy's story anyway?

Chapter 20

Dark clouds roiled over the top of Taos Mountain and the first drops of rain splatted against her windshield as Sam turned east, off the highway. Beau's cruiser sat in the drive, and her mood lifted. Dealing with angry people wasn't her strong suit and although she'd steamed over Gisner's treatment of his girlfriend, he was right—it wasn't her business. If Amber put up with him, it was her choice. Meanwhile, Sam looked forward to a quiet evening at home. Done with her caretaking job, she didn't intend to go back to Sembramos for a good long time.

Besides, her shoulders ached and she was ready for a hot shower.

"Rough day, darlin'?" Beau took her jacket and pack and hung them on the coat rack, then pulled her close.

"Tiring. I had hoped to be home an hour ago." She

tilted her head up for his kiss. "But I am now. And as soon as I get out of the shower, dinner's ready."

"I was going to say, something in that kitchen smells really good."

Over dinner, Sam told him about her encounters with Linden Gisner. "I'm not surprised his wife ran off with another man. The guy runs hot and cold, and today he was all over the case of the girlfriend." She pointed her fork at him. "You ever start that, I'd be out of here so fast."

"What about the part that included 'for better or worse'?" At least he said it with a smile on his face.

"That applies to external forces, not to one partner abusing the other. Plus, I never said that—we wrote our own vows." She broke off a piece of the cornbread she'd made to go with the stew. "Your turn—was the trip to Albuquerque productive?"

"Well, Matthew Cayne had a solid alibi. He was out on a training mission more than three-hundred miles from here, with fifty other guys."

"Sorry to hear that all the leads are turning out to be dead ends."

"At least Matt did tell me a bit more about the night of his sister's death. Unfortunately, even though he was in the house he didn't hear or see anything. He delivered a bit of a shocker—told me that Jessie Starkey had a romantic interest in Angela."

Sam felt her mouth open.

"She didn't reciprocate, according to her brother, but I plan to re-read those interviews carefully. I still think that *somewhere* among Angela's circle is where we'll find her killer. Murders by strangers are far more rare than you would think. Statistically, you have a ninety-five percent chance of being murdered by someone you know and love rather than a stranger."

Her spoon clattered against the side of her bowl.

"I'm not saying there aren't weirdos, predators and psycho stalkers out there. Just that most of us never encounter them or don't become their targets. Most killings are done for the basic reasons—love, money, jealousy . . ."

What a cheery thought. Sam cleared the empty bowls and put on a kettle for tea. When she walked back into the great room, Beau was sifting through the pages of Angela Cayne's file again.

"The answer has to be here somewhere, doesn't it?" she said softly.

"Matt said that his sister didn't have a lot of friends, mainly one girl named Molly Gisner. Said the two of them—"

"Gisner?" Sam stood still.

He held out his small notepad where he'd written the name.

"That's the name of the man who owns the house I've been tending. Just outside Sembramos. It's an odd enough name that there has to be a connec—" She paced the length of the room. "Okay, somebody mentioned that this guy's daughter had *died*."

"Has to be the same one. Matt said Angela's friend died. His sister was very withdrawn after that."

"So, Linden Gisner's daughter died, his wife ran off. Now I see why he wouldn't want to move into that house and spend time in Sembramos after that. It's a little easier to feel sympathy and understand the prickly attitude."

"I wonder where the wife went." Beau studied the witness list. "I'm sure she was never interviewed during all this. If we could locate her, she might have some idea of who might have come after Angela Cayne."

"I'm curious about the whole time frame," Sam said, musing aloud. "Did Mrs. Gisner leave before or after Angela died? Maybe it was before her own daughter died . . . in fact, I think Linden said . . . how did he phrase it? I think he said that his wife abandoned both of them."

"I think I need to talk to Sally Cayne again."

"Good idea. A grandmother is going to know more about a granddaughter's set of friends than probably anyone else around here."

The tea kettle whistled and Sam ran to tend to it while Beau started a list of people to talk to. She carried a mug of tea to him, noticing that rain had begun to lash at the windows. Lightning flashed a few miles away, illuminating the deck and barn.

"The storm's here," he commented.

Sam sat in one of the chairs at the table but between her day of physical labor and the soothing tea she couldn't concentrate on reading. A glance at Beau showed him propping his head up with one hand.

"Honey, you're just as tired as I am. C'mon, let's go up."

He didn't argue. While he let the dogs in, she picked up their empty cups and deposited them in the kitchen. Up in the bathroom she massaged one shoulder and then the other. The hot shower had temporarily eased the aches but now they were plaguing her again. She opened her jewelry box to put away the earrings she'd left lying on the counter and when she closed it the wood was already beginning to glow.

Just for a minute, she thought. She cradled the box for maximum exposure to her arms but as it began to warm she set it down again. This was one night she didn't want energy to stay awake for hours. By the time she crawled under the covers, her aches were gone and when Beau snuggled in beside her, she fell asleep to the sound of thunder in the distance and rain on the roof.

The solid sleep didn't last. Wind howled outside, tree branches slapping against the bedroom window, the thunder and lightning moving nearer once more. Sam rolled over, mumbling against the intrusion, reminding herself it was only a storm. The dogs were inside, secure in their crates, and she was safe against Beau.

Light and crash came at the same instant, quaking the house. Sam sat up in bed, staring toward the window. A ghostly woman's figure appeared—slender, wearing a floral print dress, dark hair plastered to her head by the rain. Her arms came up, defending herself as she backed away. She spun and ran into the woods.

"Darlin', darlin' . . . wake up. You're having a doozy of a dream."

Beau's gentle hand on her shoulder woke Sam. She was half-sitting, the quilt twisted around her legs.

"Lightning." Sam felt her heart pound; her breath was coming fast.

"Yeah, there was a strike, really close," he said. "I'm going to walk around and make sure it didn't hit the barn or one of our trees. Could start a fire. You going to be okay?"

She scrubbed her hands across her face. "Yeah. Fine."

With Beau out of the room and the storm continuing to rage around them, there was no way she would fall asleep right away. What was that vision about? Sam would have sworn that the thunder woke her and the frightened woman was standing right here, near the window. But that idea was silly; she'd run off into the woods, clearly not out of a second-story room. It was only a dream. A vivid one. Sam pulled the quilt all the way up to her neck. *Shouldn't have handled the box right before bedtime. Dumb.*

Fifteen minutes dragged by, then Beau came back, batting at the legs of his pajamas. "Whew! I put on my slicker—still got wet."

"Everything all right?"

"Yeah. Couldn't see any damage on our property."

"Property. Hm. I suppose I better go by the Gisner place tomorrow and make sure no tree came crashing through one of those monster plate glass windows or anything."

"You can ride along with me," Beau said as he changed to dry pajamas. "I want to talk to some people in Sembramos and I could take you on up to the house."

Sam almost protested that he needn't drive the extra distance, but in fact it might be interesting to talk with Angela Cayne's grandmother. She nodded and they settled in and turned out the lamps.

* * *

"Our Angie and Molly Gisner, they were quite the pair," Sally Cayne said as she bustled about her small kitchen, brewing tea and offering cookies, apologizing because all she had in the house was store-bought. Beau smiled when she brought out the blue package of Oreos. In a man's opinion, store-bought was perfect.

"Those girls made friends in the first grade." Sally set mugs of tea at each place. "And they were like this," holding up two fingers, pressed together, "always. I can see them in their little tutus when they took ballet classes . . . oh, and that time they showed up for trick-or-treat as princesses." Her faded eyes misted over. "Until that accident tore them apart."

Sam remembered that Molly had died in an accident.

"Angie was busted up in more ways than one. Broken arm, those cuts on her sweet face, but worst of it was losing Molly. Our Angie swore, all the rest of her days, that she'd not had a drink that night. But the cops tested her. Took her license away. I don't know as it mattered. Sixteen years old but she didn't want to drive again for a long time."

"It must have been hard on everyone in town, especially Molly's parents."

"Her father, yes. The man sank into a long bout of drinking—or so I heard. I never knew him all that well. Heather was long gone before the accident. Heather Brooks was her name before she married—she'd grown up here but her own parents had passed. Gisner was a newcomer— showed up to impress us all with his success. He might have impressed some of 'em, I don't know. Not me. But it sure was a shocker, Heather just up and leaving without a word to anyone. He spread the talk that she'd run off with some man, but I knew some of her friends. Nobody had a clue. She'd never said a word, not even to her closest friends, about being interested in anyone else. And she never got in touch with those old friends after she left. I didn't know Heather *that* well, but doesn't that seem odd, a woman cutting all ties like that?"

"I met Linden Gisner," Sam said. "He owns that big white house the other side of town. He said his wife had deserted him and his daughter. Was Molly very young when this happened?"

Sally's eyes traveled toward the ceiling and back. "Not

that young. I'd say the girls were just starting high school. That would make them maybe fourteen or fifteen when she left. I lose track of the years."

Hmm, Sam thought. Gisner had made it sound as if he'd raised his daughter from childhood virtually on his own. A sympathy play? Maybe just part of the bluster he used to hide the pain. From her own observations, she could see why a woman would want to get away from him and not say where she was going. A thought began to form as Beau asked questions about Sally's grandson Matthew. What if Heather Gisner had cut ties so completely that she'd never gotten word about her daughter's death, or Angela's?

She said as much to Beau as they got into his cruiser after Sally had insisted they take some of the early Romaine lettuce from her greenhouse and walked them to the door.

"Maybe Mrs. Gisner knows something about what was going in Angela's life. It's not uncommon for a girl to confide in her best friend's mother."

"Heather left a year before her daughter died in the accident, four or five years before Angela's death," Beau said. "What could she possibly know?"

"Well, at least I think it's worth finding her and asking. We're not even sure if she ever got the news about the girls' deaths. Even her own daughter—no one has mentioned Heather coming back for Molly's funeral or anything. If she didn't come, surely it's because she didn't hear about it." Unless she was scared to death of her ex-husband.

Beau looked over at her as they passed the edge of town. "This idea isn't going away, is it?"

"Well . . . would it be that hard to do a search? We have no idea what her circumstances are now. She deserves to know."

His grin went a little crooked. "Okay. When I get some time in the office, I'll initiate some basic inquiries."

"Try Heather Gisner and Heather Brooks. She could have taken back her maiden name."

"Yes, ma'am."

"Sorry. I don't mean to tell you how to do your job."

He squeezed her fingers. "It's fine. After all, you're my right-hand man."

Sam glowed a little inside. She really had been of help to him in several cases; she only hoped she wasn't wasting his time by checking up on Heather, a woman who quite likely just wanted to stay away. Ahead, the big white house stood bright white on its hill. She pointed out the turn and they followed the long drive to it. The graveled roadway had deeper ruts, signs that last night's rain had run down it in channels. As soon as they stepped inside she could tell that the storm had wreaked havoc with her clean windows too. Her heart sank.

"I wouldn't do them all over again," Beau said as she walked him through the rooms and showed him the spotted glass. "As crazy as our April weather is, they'll just be dirty again in another week."

"I wish you'd said that to me *last* week." She tried to see the lighthearted side of it. At least she wasn't a real estate agent, trying to show off the best aspects of the place. Someone would buy it at the tax auction and expect to do *some* cleanup, surely.

"Linden Gisner told me he'd originally named this house Heathermoor, after his wife. From the bitterness of his tone, I guess he changed that. Still, I wonder when the construction was actually finished."

"Is that another search you want me to do?"

She looked at him and couldn't tell if he was being serious.

"I'm teasing you!" he said. "That is, unless you really need to know."

She gave his arm a tiny jab. "You don't have to take *everything* I say so seriously. Besides, I doubt it's relevant."

"Do you ever get strange feelings in this place, darlin'?" They had stepped into the wine cellar, where she'd pointed out the rows of specially built racks and the bricked walls that made the room feel like an underground vault, even though true cellars and basements were rarely included in New Mexico homes and this wine room was on the ground floor.

"Strange feelings?" The hair on her neck rose a little, just because he'd said it.

"Like a chill. I didn't notice it in the other rooms, but this wine place . . . it's got me wanting my jacket." He shrugged off the feeling. "Probably just because there are no windows, like there are everywhere else."

He led the way out without another word about it and Sam chalked it up to exactly what he'd said. The wine cellar *was* chillier than the rest of the house.

"So, even though I was supposed to log in my visit today, how about if I don't say anything about it to Delbert and just pretend I never saw those dirty windows," she said as they got back into the cruiser.

"Hey, that's the way I'd play it." His grin reassured her that he hadn't truly been spooked inside the house. "Look, if all is quiet in Sembramos this morning, I could get back to the office and start work on those searches we talked about. Want to come along? I could teach you how to do it."

One of these days Sam was going to have to get back

to her bakery business. She trusted her employees implicitly, but she hadn't even put in enough time this week to count the money or get it to the bank. On the other hand, she always loved being included in Beau's work.

"We can put in the preliminary search data and then will need to wait for answers. It doesn't just pop up on the computer screen in five seconds like it does on TV." He smiled at her. "That way, you can get to the bakery with the whole afternoon to do what you need to."

How *did* he read her mind like that? It was probably what made him a great lawman.

Chapter 21

Beau looped through Sembramos, pointing out the Starkey house where the back half of it still lay charred in the sunlight; no sign of cleanup or reconstruction yet. He showed Sam the old Rodarte place and where the Cayne family had once lived, and where Sophie Garcia lived now. Average, small homes, all of them. Everything in the little farming community was modest, middle class. She wondered again at Linden Gisner's decision to build the mansion on the hill outside town. Rather than going to Albuquerque or Dallas or somewhere a house that size might fit in, he obviously preferred to be the big fish in the little pond. It fit with what Sally Cayne had said about him. Sam put the thoughts aside and directed her attention to the passing countryside, where the overnight rain had done wonders already in greening the native grasses.

At the department, things were quiet in the squad room. Beau told her he'd let several deputies take a day off after working the night patrols in Sembramos. With Jessie's funeral past them and Lee's friends and family away in Albuquerque for that service, he hoped things would settle down permanently for the little town and for his men.

Sam watched over Beau's shoulder as he accessed the law enforcement databases and initiated searches for Heather Brooks and Heather Gisner. Some matches to the surname Brooks came up immediately but he explained there was no way to know which of them might be the lady they were looking for, not without further information. He entered the tidbits they did know—prior addresses in New Mexico, the marriage to Linden Gisner, known relatives that included Molly Gisner.

"We'll expand this to include motor vehicle records. We could potentially get hundreds of hits on driver licenses and car registrations, and that makes narrowing it down even more time consuming. We can also try for passport information through the State Department, but then we're talking about needing a stronger official reason for the search."

Sam could see why he'd said they wouldn't be getting quick answers. Her thoughts drifted to the bakery.

"I'll drive you over, if you want," he said.

"That's okay. The walk will do me good." It was only about six blocks and once there she could use her bakery van, which she'd left at the shop so Becky could make deliveries all week.

She hiked the strap of her pack onto her shoulder and set off, following the sidewalk rather than cutting through the plaza and its maze of alleys and narrow side streets.

When she walked in the front door of Sweet's Sweets, Jen looked up in surprise.

"Oh, hey, Sam. I didn't see you drive up."

Sam gave the quick explanation, taking in the sales room with a glance. "Things look good here. No emergencies?"

"All under control," Jen said with a smile. "I've been putting the daily receipts in your desk drawer."

"Thanks." Sam walked into the kitchen, surprising Julio and Becky too, and after a few minutes to catch up on the status of the orders, she sat down at her desk.

Not surprisingly, every question the gang couldn't answer had ended up as a sticky note on the glass of Sam's computer monitor. She pulled them off and sorted them by duties: phone calls to return, cake design questions, and miscellaneous things such as bills to be paid. Surely she hadn't actually thought she could be away for days at a time without accumulating a backlog of sorts. She quickly handled the phone calls and stacked the bills into a pile to deal with later. She'd just reached for the zippered bank bag where Jen had been stashing cash, checks and register tapes when the intercom rang.

"Sam? A lady on line one. She says it's not bakery business."

"Ms. Sweet, hi. I'm a friend of Mary Raintree. She gave me your name and said you had an interesting magical implement. She, um, thought I might be of help in identifying it for you."

It took Sam a moment to make the connection that Mary Raintree must be the witch she'd met at Java Joe's. She stuttered a response to the female voice on the phone.

"What did you say your name was?"

"Oh. I'm Zenda. I'm a friend of Mary Raintree."

Yeah, you said that.

"Anyway, I'd love to take a look at that box."

Sam's inner antennae went on alert. Had she used the word magic with Mary? She was pretty sure she hadn't told the witch about any of the box's powers. And hadn't she asked Mary to call her and pass along names of anyone who might have known Bertha Martinez, not to simply give out her name randomly. So, how had this Zenda found her, if not through Mary?

"I can come by your shop," Zenda said. "I know where it is."

Sam had a flash memory of how easily Kelly had found addresses and locations by using her phone. Another memory, of the chocolatier who'd worked in her shop, the odd man who'd warned her of the box's power and that there could be dark forces in the world, other people who would want to take the box from her. A frisson of fear raced up her spine.

Zenda repeated her offer to come by and the silence while she waited for an answer hung in the air. Something told Sam this wouldn't be a good idea.

"This week isn't good for me," she said. "And I don't have the box with me anyway."

Zenda seemed a little put out. She said she would check back and hung up before Sam could tell her not to bother.

Damn. She should have been firmer, told the woman she wasn't interested in meeting. This Zenda was far too pushy and the whole conversation had left Sam feeling uneasy.

"Becky, do we have any deliveries this afternoon?" Sam asked, stuffing all the receipts and money back into the bank bag.

"Nothing until day after tomorrow," Becky said, not taking her eyes off the flowers she was piping onto a white layer cake for the sales case up front.

"I'm going to take the van then." Suddenly, Sam felt the need to get out of there.

She grabbed her pack and the bank bag, headed out the back door and got into the van. Her eyes wouldn't stay still, glancing behind her and checking her mirrors as she drove down the alley and watched for traffic.

I can come by your shop. I know where it is.

Sam turned right, opting to go out of her way in hopes of spotting someone who might be following her. She merged into the traffic on Paseo del Pueblo Sur, passing the fast food places and the turnoff to the high school, pulling into the Wal-Mart parking lot and circling it before getting out in traffic again, this time northbound toward home. As far as she could tell there wasn't a single car that had made the whole trek with her.

By the time she reached the north end of town and got out into open country she was certain that she wasn't being tailed. She also felt a little foolish for her concerns. This Zenda was probably just an over-eager newbie witch who wanted to get hold of a magical artifact.

But, I swear I never mentioned to Mary that the box had magical properties. She tried to remember the whole conversation with the witch at Java Joe's. She had only described the box to Mary as an artifact and that she was interested in learning about its history—she felt sure of it. Other than telling the woman that she'd heard Bertha Martinez was a *bruja,* she didn't think she'd brought up magic at all. And now this Zenda comes forward, saying she wanted to see the 'magical' box. She didn't get that information from Mary.

Sam parked beside the log house, went inside and immediately locked the door behind her. Upstairs, she picked up the box from the bathroom vanity and carried it to the bedroom, burying it under a pile of sweaters on the closet shelf. It wasn't a secure hiding place but at least the box was out of sight until she got a chance to think of something better.

The chocolatier, Bobul, had warned her, and his words came back now. *Miss Sam, be careful. Bad people will do anything to take box away.*

She stopped abruptly in the middle of the bedroom. If someone wanted this box badly enough, and if they went to the trouble to look up Sam and come for it, they wouldn't be coming here. This house, the phone and all the utilities were listed in Beau's name. She'd only lived here six months. The place they would track Sam would be to her old house, where Kelly lived alone now.

She pulled her cell phone from her pocket and hit her daughter's number. *Okay, don't scare her. Stay calm.*

She managed to make it sound as if she'd received a persistent sales call and was concerned that the woman would come by the house as she warned Kelly to keep her doors locked and her valuables hidden away.

"Mom. Seriously? Don't you think I do that already? I lived in California before I came back home, remember?"

"I know, I know. I just . . . I got a creepy feeling from this caller. Please do your old mom a favor and don't answer the door to anyone you don't know. It'll make me feel better."

Kelly chuckled over the 'old mom' reference but agreed to be watchful. By the time Beau got home, around six, Sam had calmed down by adding up her bakery receipts and putting a chicken casserole in the oven for dinner.

"Got something for you," Beau said, planting a kiss on top of her head as she stood at the kitchen sink, washing vegetables. He held out a slip of paper with a name and phone number on it.

"Althea Brooks?"

"Heather Brooks's sister."

"How'd you get that?"

"Well, while the database searches were returning bunches of names it would take me months to track down, I used the old noodle. Remembered that Heather Brooks grew up in Sembramos, checked through school records. Although she's in her forties now, they actually do keep stuff that far back, at least in this school. I looked up her registration information and came up with the fact that she had a sister, just a couple years older. So, that put me on a search for Althea Brooks. She still lives in New Mexico."

Sure enough, the area code was familiar.

"Farmington. She's been there ever since she left here. Which is part of what made it easier to locate her. If she'd moved around a lot, it could have gotten a whole lot more complicated."

"So, did you call her?"

"Tried to. No answer. That's why I brought this home." He stuck the little yellow tab to the front of a cupboard door and sneaked a carrot out of the bunch Sam was about to chop for the salad.

After dinner, Beau suggested they try Althea Brooks again. Sure enough, this time she answered.

"This is Sheriff Cardwell in Taos County. I wonder if I might take a few minutes to ask you a couple of questions."

To Sam, Althea sounded hesitant over the speaker. "Is this about what I saw on the news earlier in the week? The problems in Sembramos?"

"Indirectly, yes." He gave the quick rundown about why he had reopened the Angela Cayne murder case. "In talking to Sally Cayne she mentioned that your niece, Molly, was Angela's best friend. We're trying to locate your sister to see if we can get some additional background."

"I don't know what I can tell you, Sheriff. Heather's done a good job of hiding. I even hired a private investigator once but he didn't come up with anything."

"Tell me about when she left. What was going on at the time?"

"You need more background before it will make much sense," she said. "Unfortunately, I've got somewhere to be this evening so I need to go."

"Would it be possible for us to meet?" Beau said. "Can you come to Taos?"

There was some hesitation at the other end. "I work all week, teaching special needs kids at a charter school. It would be a day-long trip to drive out there . . ."

Beau and Sam waited, sensing there was more.

Althea seemed to come to a decision. "I have to drive to Dulce tomorrow. We're required to make a home visit to each student's parents, and I've got one whose home is way out there. It's Highway 64 the whole way. I suppose I could drive on over to Taos. I would get there around noon. I really would like to find my sister and you're the first lawman to show much interest in helping."

"I'd really appreciate that, Ms. Brooks." Beau clicked off the call, after repeating his thanks and reiterating the time and place they would meet.

"Since she's already tried to find her sister, years ago, I wonder whether we'll have much luck," Sam said as they settled on the couch with their after-dinner coffees.

"I don't know. But maybe she can fill in some gaps in the time leading up to Angela's death. As she said, there's a lot of background we don't know."

Sam pondered that. "But the big gaps still come down to the night Angela disappeared. Who would have reason to kill a twenty-year-old girl who, by all accounts was pretty popular? And, other than revenge from someone who believed Jessie Starkey and Lee Rodarte were unfairly released from prison, who would have come after *them* all these years later?"

"Revenge fits so well with both men—one shot in the woods, the other struck in the head and kicked. That's anger, pure and simple. One of these days I'll manage to break the alibi of someone in the Starkey clan and probably someone else close to Lee Rodarte, and I think those two deaths will be solved. Somebody up there knows who did it and one day that person will drink a little too much or they'll be unable to keep quiet.

"That still doesn't tell us whether Starkey and Rodarte really were unfairly released, or whether Angela's killer is still running around free. Gut feeling tells me it's the latter."

"So . . . let's take another look at the file." Sam carried their cups to the kitchen for refills and they spent the next two hours reviewing their previous timeline and adding to it from the bits and scraps of interrogation questions.

This time Beau was the one yawning before ten p.m. although Sam was getting tired too. Had they already become old, married people? When he suggested they take a break, Sam agreeably set her lists aside.

Brushing her teeth at the bathroom sink she eyed the empty spot where her jewelry box normally sat. Which brought back her earlier skittishness over the phone call from the unknown Zenda and the probing questions about the box.

"Hon, where's a good spot to hide something in the house? A place where a robber probably wouldn't think to look?"

He finished swishing his mouthwash and spat it out. "Why? You got a big stack of cash you never told me about?"

She laughed. "Fat chance about that. No, it's my jewelry box. I don't want anything to happen to it."

Although she'd told Beau about the odd powers of the box, she'd glossed over the possibility that someone else might want to get it. He wasn't the kind of guy who probed when it came to personal matters and he probably assumed that her simple costume jewelry was worth more than it actually was.

"You can put it in my gun safe," he said.

At her raised eyebrows he paused. "I never showed you the gun safe?"

See, Sam, you aren't the only one in this house with a few secrets. She pulled the box from the upper closet shelf and followed him downstairs. He went straight to the coat closet under the stairs and shoved the coats to one side. Behind them, a small door revealed itself, one Sam had never noticed when she added her own few items to the clothing there. With the wooden panel open, she could see a heavy metal safe, about three feet wide and five feet tall. A black box on the front had a keypad. Below it, a heavy metal handle.

"Combination is our anniversary," he said. "I reprogrammed it when we got married so I could never slip up and forget it. I never told you this?"

"I've never seen this safe. But you might have mentioned having it. Things were pretty crazy last September, if you'll recall."

He pressed the correct series of buttons on the keypad, making sure she watched so she could do it on her own. She knew Beau had a hunting rifle and a smaller one for predator control—every rancher in the West probably did. Shelves above held two cases for handguns—one probably went with his service pistol—and a few boxes of ammunition.

"There's plenty of space here," he said, moving one of the handgun cases to leave a clear shelf. Put anything you want in here."

She handed him the carved wooden box. He showed her the process for locking up, closing the concealment door, and sliding the coats back to their positions. "Just be sure you always close it up like this. No point in having a safe if anybody who walks in the house can get to it."

She certainly hoped that no one with an interest in the wooden box would ever make it that far.

Chapter 22

It felt good, getting back into her bakery routine the next morning. Sam wanted to be in on the interview with Althea Brooks but there wasn't much point in sitting around Beau's office all morning, waiting for the woman to arrive from Farmington. He would call when it was time.

Meanwhile, she tinted a batch of white sugar-paste with enough coloring to turn it delicate pink and began to form the center cones for roses. The cake was to be a bridal shower creation, triple layer, with a smooth white fondant coating and a domed cap of roses and daisies. Small white fondant hearts and piped dots would add a whimsical border.

In the low humidity, the pink cones dried sufficiently for the next step nearly as quickly as Sam could turn them out. She cut petals for the first layering and applied them, set each one to dry, and began to cut the daisy petals and curl them with a bone tool. The work went smoothly, each layer of petals adding majesty to the full-blown roses. Sugar flowers were more labor intensive than piped ones, but they were so beautiful that a lot of brides didn't mind the extra cost.

"Sam?" Jen startled her, so deeply had she become engrossed in forming the flowers. "Um, it's springtime, right? Not even close to Halloween?"

Sam felt her brows pull together. What was she talking about?

"Cause I think there's a witch out front. She's staring at the cakes in the window and I think she's about to—"

Sure enough, the bells on the door tinkled.

"See if you can handle whatever she wants," Sam said with a nod toward the mass of flower petals on the worktable.

Jen walked to the front but returned within a minute. "It's definitely you she wants to see."

Sam had a feeling about this. She washed her hands and went to the sales room, her mind whirling, wondering what to say.

"Ms. Sweet? Hi, I'm Zenda." The apparition wore black, head to toe, starting with a lacy shawl that she pushed back off her black hair, letting it rest on the shoulders of her black dress. The garment's soft fabric hung in a ragged cut nearly to the ankles, which were clad in black stockings. Naturally, black shoes finished the look. Sam guessed the young woman to be in her twenties but the heaviness of her costume added at least ten years to that. In dress and demeanor this Zenda was a complete opposite to Mary—the other witch Sam had met.

"I came to take a look at that, um, item we discussed,"

Zenda began, all smiles and over-familiarity.

"I never said—"

"Well, I just happened to be in the neighborhood." Zenda had a bright, expectant look on her face.

"It's not here." Sam took a breath. "In fact, I don't even own it anymore. I got rid of it."

The bright expression turned downward. "You sold it?"

"I, uh . . . Look, I'm not going to pass along the name of the new owner. You'll just have to accept that it's gone."

Was it disappointment or anger that crossed Zenda's face. She raised a hand, three fingers pointing toward Sam. "That is *not* the answer I wanted." Then she turned and swished out of the shop, the many skirt layers floating behind her.

"Oy!" Jen's eyes were wide. "What the heck was that?"

Sam tore her gaze from the spot where Zenda had rounded the corner at the end of the block and disappeared. "I actually have no idea."

But she did have an idea, and seeing Zenda's persistence and fervor over the box made Sam glad she had hidden it away. She walked back to the kitchen, stewing over the bizarre visit. Botching the next of her sugar roses, she set the petals down.

"I'll be right back," she told Julio as she walked out the back door.

Checking the alley from end to end, she walked over to the back entrance of Puppy Chic, where she was pretty sure Kelly was working a half day.

"Don't let that woman try to befriend you and certainly don't let her into the house," Sam said after describing Zenda. She'd fudged a little about exactly what the witchy girl wanted. "She's very pushy and tries hard to be friendly."

Kelly pulled a little white terrier from one of the wire crates and carried him to the deep sink for his bath.

"Okay, Mom. Whatever."

"Kel, I'm serious. This lady believes she's a witch and she might really know some kind of spell or—" She realized how completely ridiculous this sounded. She rolled her eyes. "I just don't know what to think of her."

"So, did she hex you or something?" Kelly aimed the spray nozzle at the hapless dog.

Sam thought of the creepy little finger motion Zenda had done. Yes. No. "I don't know. She's just weird. If you see her around, go the other direction. And if you don't want to be pestered to death, don't admit to her that you know me."

Kelly gave Sam one of her charmer smiles, the kind Sam recognized from her daughter's teen years whenever she was being humored. She walked back to the bakery, shaking her arms to work out the tension.

The rose petals began to come out perfectly again and Sam had almost put the Zenda incident behind her when Beau called. Althea Brooks had arrived and, since it was lunch time, he suggested they meet and chat with Althea in a less formal setting than his office.

The restaurant he proposed was one of their favorites in the summer months for its outdoor tables under big shade trees, and only a block from his office. However, with the April chill still in the air, they opted this time to take seats indoors. Beau rose when Sam walked in, introducing Althea who looked vaguely familiar. She was near Sam's age, slim, with chestnut hair in a brush-and-go style and smooth skin that didn't require much makeup. She wore jeans and a fitted T-shirt, with a denim jacket. Nothing resembling any teacher from Sam's schooldays but then again, times had radically changed. Maybe fifty really was the new thirty.

"I'm not sure what I can tell you," Althea said, once they'd placed their orders. "As I mentioned on the phone, I haven't heard from my sister in years."

"How long has she been gone?" Beau asked.

"It will be twelve years next month." The speed with which she answered said that she wasn't as unaffected by her sister's leaving as she first portrayed.

"And you tried to track her down?"

"Of course I did. Molly called me to say that her mother had left. The poor kid was pretty upset. I talked with Linden and he did nothing but badmouth his wife for running off with another man. When I didn't hear anything from my sister after a few weeks I called the police but they said she wasn't technically a missing person if she'd gone away on her own volition. I hired a private investigator to look into it, just to let me know where Heather had gone. He came up with nothing and assumed Heather and this man had moved away together, that she'd probably even changed her name. Then ten years ago, when Molly died in the accident, I gave it one more try. I didn't know if Heather had secretly stayed in touch with Molly—it wouldn't have surprised me—but we couldn't find any evidence of it. I thought she should know, in time to come for the funeral. But I had no luck finding an address for her."

"So, as far as you know, Molly was buried without her mother ever knowing?" Sam felt a stab of pain. What if something had happened to Kelly when she lived in California and Sam had never been notified?

Althea shook her head. "It just never made sense. But

then Heather and I had grown apart over the years."

She accepted the iced tea the server brought and they waited a moment until the young man left.

"Heather and I are close in age. I'm two years older, and we shared a bedroom when we were kids, walked to school together every day. In childhood, we had a lot of the same friends but as we got into school each of us bonded with kids our own age. So I guess it was natural that we would drift off in different directions. She met Linden shortly after she graduated—I don't know if he's still around or not. He'd done his military time and was making a name for himself in real estate when they married. Success always attracted Heather." Althea sipped at her tea. "I never seemed to meet the right guy to commit a lifetime to. I found my teaching position in Farmington. Heather settled into being a wife and mother."

"How was Heather's marriage? There were rumors."

Althea sighed. "I honestly don't know. He seemed to treat her well, bought her anything she wanted. He started building that huge house and Heather seemed very excited about having something that large and fancy. I know he doted on Molly."

Her eyes focused somewhere in the distance. Beau glanced toward Sam. About the time Sam started to ask a question, Althea spoke again.

"He doted on Molly so much that, at one point Heather told me Linden had threatened that he would never allow her—Heather—to take his daughter away."

The statement hung in the air while the server approached again, delivering plates of sandwiches and salads.

"So, maybe Heather had planned to leave him?"

"It's possible. She never told me what prompted his comment, only that she knew she could never take Molly away from him. She seemed . . . I guess *resigned* is the best word."

"And she never told you her plans? Ever mention another man, that maybe she would leave with someone?"

Althea picked at the crust of her bread. "We really didn't confide much. You would think, as sisters, we would have remained close, but we just didn't. Our lifestyles were so different and even though we only lived a half-day's drive apart, neither of us made the trip very often at all."

"When Molly called you to say that Heather left— tell me about that," Beau said

"Well, she was crying. I do believe she and Heather were close, although Molly was close to Linden as well. Her dad had informed her that Heather ran off with one of the construction workers. I guess he painted a pretty slutty picture of his wife. Molly was just into puberty right then. I'm sure she didn't even understand all of what he was saying. It was inappropriate for him to talk that way, but by the time I got the news the damage had been done."

"And later? How did Molly handle it after some time went by."

"I tried to stay in touch with her, assure her that I would be there for her until her mom came back. I had no doubt, at least at first, that Heather would get over this little fling of hers and come back to her daughter. Whatever the situation was between husband and wife, I knew Heather loved that girl.

"So, one time I drove over on a Friday evening. I'd managed to get out of school a little earlier than usual, and it was going to be a Monday holiday so I thought I'd just come and do things with Molly, give her a little girl time. I'd called Linden and arranged all this. But when I got to Sembramos, he informed me that Molly was staying the weekend with her friend Angela. I was a little peeved but I drove over to the Cayne's house and offered to take both girls to the movies. They had other plans.

"Both girls were—can I say this?—tarted up with way too much makeup and skirts so short they were embarrassing. They were going to a party with friends. Angela's parents weren't home at the time but I spoke to the girls about being careful and being smart about their behavior. I doubt they caught a word of it. They'd just turned fifteen and gotten their driver's licenses and the world was theirs to do any old thing they pleased.

"I tried not to be judgmental—kids always test the limits. It's how they establish their independence, eventually. I talked some more, realized I might as well have been talking to the walls, decided to get a hotel room in Taos and then I went home the next day."

"Disappointing," Sam said, memories of her own rebellious youth edging at her conscience.

"Well, especially sad because the following summer, a bit over a year later, was when Molly and Angie were in that accident. You can tell them, over and over, but kids don't always get it."

"And you never did hear from Heather again?" Beau asked.

"Not a word. Both the police and the private investigator decided she'd probably done just as Linden said, hooked up with another man and moved away. Maybe she fell so madly in love with him that she's living happily somewhere else; maybe she wasn't happy with him but has been too humiliated to come back. Small towns and the gossip that runs through them can be pretty cruel. Once Molly was gone, Heather really would have no reason to come back here at all."

"Did the two of you have words? Do you think that's why she never contacted you?"

Althea pushed her half-finished sandwich aside. "There was a blow-up between us, after the time she told me about Linden not letting her take Molly away. I told her she should just stand up to him. I'm afraid I said that he was a jerk—maybe words worse than that—and she got pretty defensive. Things were always tense after that and we lost touch, even before she ran off. Contact had dwindled down to birthday and Christmas cards, which is really sad. I hate to think it, but the fact that our last conversation didn't go well, it could be the reason she still won't speak to me. Heather's hard-headed that way."

Beau asked a couple more questions about what happened around the time Angela Cayne was murdered, but Althea couldn't give any information. By that time she'd written off Sembramos and knew nothing about the Cayne murder other than what she'd read in the papers.

They pushed their plates back and Beau walked to the register to pay the check. Sam and Althea stood on the sidewalk in front of the restaurant.

"I brought a little overnight bag and decided to get a room in Taos for the night, visit the galleries, do a little shopping. On my way back, I'd like to stop in Sembramos. Helen Starkey and I were fairly close in our elementary school days. I should pop in and see her," Althea said. She turned to Beau when he joined them. "I doubt I can tell you anything more but if you have any questions, here's my cell number."

She walked to a small red car and got in.

"Very forthcoming," Beau said, as they walked toward Camino de la Placita, where they would each turn toward their respective jobs. "I don't know that we learned anything much about Angela Cayne, other than she went through a wild spell, more so than most anyone else has said."

"Heather Gisner might know, more than anyone else, about what the girls were up to but we sure didn't get any firm leads on finding her."

"Yeah." Beau stared up the street, jingling the change in his pocket. "I was hoping we'd get something useful on that."

"At least you have feelers out. If Althea thinks of anything or can lead us to someone else, I'd bet that she will."

Beau agreed. "Meantime, I think I'll drop in on the deputy who assisted Orlando Padilla on Angela's case, Roy Watson. He retired a few years ago but he may remember something. And I'm trying to get an appointment with one of the defense attorneys. See if they had evidence that wasn't allowed in court or anything like that. I'm sick of feeling like I'm on a dead-end street, everywhere I turn."

Chapter 23

Beau walked into his office to find a message slip. William Gravitz. He didn't recognize the man's name but he knew the firm. Tanner, Gravitz and Ortiz had been the court-appointed firm for Starkey and Rodarte. He carried the message to his office, closed the door and dialed.

"I pulled the case records when you called earlier," Gravitz said. "Our senior partner, Charles Tanner, felt very good about the recent reversal of the verdict. Even with a pro-bono case, you want to do your best for the clients."

Beau had to wonder if he still felt good about it, considering both defendants were now dead.

"I came into this case after the fact," he told the lawyer. "And now that the court has overturned the ruling, it's up to my department to reopen the case and find Angela Cayne's real killer, in addition to finding out who killed Starkey and

Rodarte. I thought I'd see if your office had information that I never got. I'd rather not go through getting subpoenas and warrants, if you know what I mean."

"Being that our clients were cleared of the charges and couldn't be retried, even if they were still alive, I don't see why that would be a problem. I'm sure the families want answers. I'll have to clear it with the partners, of course."

Beau expected that he would need to check back in a few days, but Gravitz simply put him on hold. He came back within five minutes, saying that Beau could stop by their offices. Obviously, the lawyers had already discussed this before Gravitz's call this afternoon. Beau said if it was all right he would run by and get the files now.

"I didn't include the trial transcripts," the young-looking Bill Gravitz said, as he had Beau sign for the four boxes of papers. "That would have been another eight boxes. What we have here is the evidence we obtained in discovery and the confidential interviews with our clients. As I mentioned earlier, you're only getting those because both men are now deceased.

"We took statements from a lot of other witnesses. I also included our private lab report, which showed the murder weapon was not the same piece of rope originally connected with Jessie Starkey. If only that had come in before the conclusion of the trial. It took us six years of persistence to get it admitted and get those men free. Sometimes the politics of the justice system make me want to scream." He rubbed at his close-cut hair, then sighed. "Anyway, it's all here."

Beau picked up the first of the heavy boxes. Thank goodness for small firms who understood that subjecting everyone to months of formal requests for records wouldn't serve anyone at this point. They all knew that Jessie and Lee had protested their innocence all along, and that Jessie's so-called confession had been obtained under duress. The zealous prosecutor in the case had been an unfortunate match for Beau's over-eager boss.

He loaded the boxes into the back of his SUV and decided to take them home where he would have more time to read through them than at the office with phones ringing and deputies in and out all day.

There, he stacked the boxes beside the dining table, which was still spread with the pages of the murder file he and Sam had been going through. Since the law files were technically only on loan from Gravitz, he had to be careful not to intermix the reams of paper. It took only about fifteen minutes of attempting to balance an open file folder on his lap before he decided to dig up an old folding table he knew was stashed around the place somewhere. He rummaged through a storage closet, found it and wiped off several years worth of dust; he was setting up the table when he heard Sam's bakery van in the drive.

"Hey there, handsome Sheriff," she said, dropping her backpack onto an armchair.

Beau looked down and realized he'd forgotten to change clothes, and now his uniform was all dusty.

"I don't mind," she said, coming toward him for a hug. "I'm probably covered in flour and sugar myself."

Sam glanced at the new collection of boxes. "What's all this?"

He explained how he'd taken advantage of the cooperation from the attorneys. "Since we are technically working a cold case, I figured it would be better to keep this out of my office. Plus, this way we can cross-reference their stuff with ours."

"You think there will be discrepancies?"

"There are bound to be. Law enforcement works with the prosecution to catch and put away criminals. Defense lawyers get the defendant's side of the story, usually a very filtered version, but sometimes these guys will spill their guts to their attorney."

"And you can use that?"

"If their client were still alive or if they refused to release it to me, no. But if anybody in the Starkey family raises a fuss, I'm going to point out that we *are* trying to catch their son's killer. I think they will go along with that. Now, as to what can be admitted into court testimony . . . that's something else. We still need evidence."

Sam ran her fingers over the folder tabs in the open boxes. So much paper—where to start? Beau had picked up one that seemed to contain the attorney's initial interviews with Jessie. Sam opted for a folder with Angela's name on it. The sheets inside were photocopies of something handwritten, pages small enough that each sheet of copy paper showed two pages side by side. She began to read.

It only took a few seconds to realize that these were the writings of a teenage girl. By the way they were dated and the casual tone, this was a diary.

"Beau, we didn't come across any of this in the department file, did we?" she asked, holding out the small sheaf of papers. "Could this be Angela's diary?"

He scanned the top page, thinking furiously.

"What would the defense team be doing with this?" Sam asked.

He bit at his lower lip while he put his thoughts together.

"A personal item belonging to the victim could have—would have—been collected by our department, either at the crime scene or perhaps in her home. Anything relevant to the case, that is, if the prosecutor intended to use it in court, has to be passed along to the defense team as well."

"So, Jessie or Lee couldn't have given this to the lawyer?"

"Not likely. The fact that it's a copy, not the diary itself, would indicate that most likely our department collected the diary and then made the copies for the lawyers."

"But you didn't come across the actual diary, right?"

"There are still boxes of stuff back in our evidence room. It should have been passed along to the prosecutor before the trial."

Sam nodded. "Just checking. Can I go ahead and read some of it? See if there's anything that could be a clue?"

"Anything. Definitely."

Sam leafed through the pages and soon discovered that Angela wasn't regular in her journal writings. Dated entries skipped around all over the place, and many of them weren't dated at all. Sam had been the same way, herself, as a teen. She owned a small diary and had usually only turned to it when life became dramatic or heartbreaking. The mundane details of everyday life in high school just weren't that interesting. She began reading the pages in front of her.

I can't think! I don't know what to do!!! They say it's my fault. Molly's gone—it's my fault!!! I should have died—I wish I had!!!!! The writing was shaky, the emotion apparent.

Evidently, a grief counselor had given Angela the book and suggested that she write in order to work through her feelings about the accident. Sam wondered if Althea Brooks had talked with her niece during this time.

Dr. Jones keeps asking me to think back to that night, to remember what Molly and I did. The police asked if we were drinking—no! I told them we don't drink. They don't believe me!! We had Cokes at Molly's house, really sweet ones—I think they had vanilla or something. Her dad was there—he watched us. He can tell them!

A few entries later: *I guess Molly's dad did tell them we weren't drinking. But still, that judge said I have to lose my license for a year. I don't care. I never want to drive again.*

Poor girl. To have her high school world come crashing down, her best friend gone.

Dr. Jones wants me to get out more. I should see my friends again. Molly's dad keeps wanting me to come over and talk. I should be nice to him. He lost his whole family, at least I have mine. When people say things like that I feel worse than ever. I don't want to leave my room. Can't they all just leave me alone?

A dated entry indicated that Angela was still working with the counselor several months later. *Molly wanted to leave with her mom, when we were in ninth grade. I should have let her. Why did I beg her to stay with me? Dr. Jones says it's normal for somebody to want her best friend to always be there. But if I could of let her go. She might be in Kansas now but she'd be alive.*

Kansas. That might be a clue to Heather's plans. Sam noted it, to ask Althea.

Maybe I could even go visit. But now . . . I just want to kill myself.

Uh-oh. Had Angela's counselor known about this? Sam riffled through the pages, seeing that the writing continued. Whatever transpired immediately after the accident, Angela was still alive—until three years later. And when she did die, it wasn't by her own hand. Sam blew out a breath and blinked back tears.

She caught Beau staring at her and told him what she'd just read. "I wonder why this didn't come up in court?"

He gave her a weak smile. "Sad as it was, there was nothing really to connect Angela's trauma of the car accident to her own death, years later."

She nodded. True. But what if, in her later writings, Angela had revealed something? Had she remained depressed all that time? Sam continued reading.

The entries continued in the same vein until one brought Sam up short. *My wrists are healing. When I woke up in the hospital last week I was SO mad!! I really wanted this pain to be over. But my mom . . . the look on her face. Matt said mom cried for three days. I have to stop this, feeling sorry for myself. Dr. Jones has said it—I need to get on with my life. I don't know how. But I'll try.*

Sam had to get up and walk around. She went to the kitchen and made a cup of tea. She'd had her own unhappy moments, growing up in a town where she didn't fit in, eager to get away the minute she could. But never anything like this. And she'd raised a daughter who was basically a happy-go-lucky kid, a little flighty as a young woman but overall well-adjusted. No wonder the Caynes simply had to get out of this area after Angela was murdered. It was one painful trauma after the other for that poor family. She took a sip of the tea and went back to her reading.

A couple of almost-empty pages followed Angela's heartfelt admission that she needed to turn her life around. A few doodles—daisies and puffy-lettered versions of her name—seemed to indicate a brighter mood. When the written entries resumed it was with a more mature hand, and the date indicated that Angela was now nineteen.

He says he loves me!! He wants us to go away together, to be married! I can't believe it!! I don't know . . . he's older. I don't know what my parents would say.

The next entry: *I haven't slept with him yet. It doesn't seem right. He really wants me and I feel special when he buys me things. But I think my parents would freak out if I tell them.*

Sam checked the date. This was getting close. Angela would turn twenty in May. She would be murdered in June.

Chapter 24

Sam dropped the diary pages. A chill passed over her and the lukewarm tea did nothing to dispel it.

"There was a man, Beau. Near the end of Angela's life. Did that ever come up in the investigation or trial?" She folded the stapled pages back so he could read the last one. "Someone older. If it was Jessie Starkey, I can see why she would be worried about telling her parents. The teacher dad and the accountant mom weren't likely to approve of a tattooed rebel with a drug habit."

"Yeah, you're right about that." He read the words on the diary page, then stared off into space. "I don't recall this being brought up during the trial, but someone recently told me that Jessie had his eye on Angela."

He handed the diary pages back to Sam and crossed to the other table, touching pages until he came to the stack that contained the sheriff's interviews with Jessie Starkey.

"Let's see . . ."

"Or Lee Rodarte? Could he have been the older man?" Sam asked.

"He was involved with Sophie Garcia at that time; they had a baby together. But, nothing's impossible. Why don't you grab those sections over there—his interview questions—see if there's anything about a personal relationship with Angela at the same time."

They read silently for several minutes. Sam shook her head over Rodarte's Q&A. The sheriff had asked him very little, aside from denigrating his alibi. Mainly, he'd tried his best to get Lee to corroborate Jessie's confession and implicate himself in the process.

Beau took his time with Jessie Starkey's interrogation, reading every question and every answer. "I don't see where they ever specifically asked if he had a romantic interest in Angela Cayne. They asked if he knew her and he responds, 'yeah, sure, seen her around.' "

"That doesn't exactly sound like a man in love."

"Or one trying to cover up the fact that he's been wanting to get into a younger woman's pants."

"I wish we had a video of that interview. It would tell a lot if Jessie blushed or turned away as he answered the question."

"Yeah, well. We have them now, but the cameras and recorders didn't get purchased for our department until pretty recently."

A crooked lawman's way of giving himself room to twist the truth, at his convenience? Sam had heard way too many Sheriff Padilla stories.

"So, assuming it was Jessie Starkey who was coming on

to Angela, could the interrogators have used his interest in the victim to get him to confess?"

"That, darlin' could be the big question. I'll keep reading. The frustrating thing about transcripts like these is that it's routine to ask the same questions over and over. It could take me awhile to get to that point in the file."

"And if the love interest wasn't Jessie, it could have been anyone," Sam reminded. "The boyfriend might have showed up while her parents were gone. Wouldn't Angela have told him that other family members were home? Maybe she agreed to sneak out and meet him later?"

"Or, maybe he came in, got insistent that things go further. She resisted, he got angry."

Sam nodded, acknowledging that either scenario could have happened.

"The sad thing is that we will probably never know. I just wish Matt Cayne hadn't been wearing his earphones that night." Beau set down the transcript sheets. "I never did get the chance to drop in on Roy Watson today. Maybe that's good. We know a lot more now. I'll plan to go by his place tomorrow."

Sam put the diary pages back into the box where she'd found them.

"Meanwhile, my lady . . ." Beau held his hand out to her. "I have other plans for you and me." The wiggle in his eyebrow said it all.

* * *

Sam awoke the next morning to bright sunlight from the window where she'd forgotten to draw the curtains the night before. Beau's arm was around her, his unshaven face rubbing against her shoulder, a contented sigh coming from him when she rolled over. She stroked his bristly whiskers and kissed him. After too much time in crime files where the worst of human nature came out she'd needed last night's reminder that there were gentle and loving men in this world. He returned her kisses, urgently, and it was another hour before they reluctantly decided it was time to get to work.

"I'll be at the bakery, unless you need me to go along with you," she said giving her lips a swipe of gloss at the bathroom mirror.

"As long as dispatch or the night-duty men don't spring something new on me, I think it'll be business as usual. We've had no trouble in Sembramos for a couple of nights."

"Which is almost scary, isn't it?"

"I just hope things have calmed down there for good."

Sam gave him another lingering kiss, then picked up her bakery jacket and headed out. The sunny spring morning only added to her good mood and she found herself humming as she pulled up to the back of the bakery.

Inside, Julio had already finished trays of muffins, scones and some of the new ultra-cinnamon bear claws that he'd introduced a month ago. A coffee cake sat on the worktable, waiting to be cut into generous pieces, and Becky was piping "Happy Birthday, Isabelle" onto a pink lemonade cake.

Sam took a little teasing from Becky about the rosy look in her cheeks and, out front, Jen commented that married life was certainly agreeing with the boss. Before Sam could think of a comeback, the phone rang and Jen handed it to her.

"Is this Samantha Sweet?" a female voice inquired. "I

got your name from Mary Raintree. She said you have an unusual artifact that may have ties to the Craft."

The moment Sam figured out it wasn't a recommendation for their pastries, she broke in. "I'm sorry, but that item Mary referred to—it's gone. I gave it away already."

This intense interest in the wooden box was becoming too much. When Mary offered to put Sam in touch with someone who might have known Bertha Martinez, Sam hadn't expected calls from all these youngsters. She walked back to her desk and rummaged for the note where she'd written Mary's number.

The explanation again—that she no longer had the box, so never mind about sending any more referrals—and she hung up with only a twinge of second thoughts. She might be cutting off the possibility of reaching one of Bertha's friends who could give her some useful information. And, too, if the witch Mary had the power to detect a lie, she may have seen right through Sam's story.

"How should I approach this job?" Becky asked, pulling Sam's thoughts back to the real world as she held up a sketch Jen had made for a customer who wanted a dozen cupcakes to resemble giant strawberries.

Sam studied the drawing, envisioning the supplies they could put to use. "Bake the cupcakes in red paper liners, for a start. Then I'm thinking red decorating sugar over red icing. They'll really sparkle that way. And edible leaves and stems of—"

Jen stood in the doorway, waving for Sam's attention. She reminded herself that it was good to be needed. "A lady to see you," Jen said. Then, *sotto voce*, "I don't think this one's a nutcase."

"Thanks, Sam," Becky said, turning back to the cupcake order. "I've got enough to get started."

Althea Brooks stood at the display case, glancing up when Sam walked in. "My goodness, you've got a fantastic shop here! If this had been here when I lived nearby . . . Anyway, it occurred to me that I never asked the sheriff if he needed a photo of my sister, for the search. I guess what really reminded me of it was that I had a strange encounter last evening."

Sam felt her eyebrows rise. "What kind of encounter?"

"I walked around the plaza yesterday afternoon after we talked, you know, browsing the shops a little. Found a cute pair of sandals. When I came out of the shop a man on the sidewalk came to an abrupt stop and stared at me. He said, 'Does your old man know you're in town?' I'm afraid I had no clue and I stammered out something about how he'd mistaken me for someone else. Well, then as I walked back to my car I got to thinking, I'll bet he thought I was Heather."

"Really?"

"We look enough alike that I suppose it's possible, especially if it's someone who hasn't seen her in years. That, and the way I've started coloring my hair, just a shade lighter than it used to be."

She pulled a photo out of her wallet. "This is almost fifteen years ago, so you have to take into account that both of us have aged. A little." A chuckle.

Sam gave the photo a quick glance. Heather did look very familiar. The sisters had the same facial structure—high foreheads, prominent chin, straight nose. Heather's hair was nearly the exact shade of Althea's, and even the cut was similar. She imagined present-day Heather would look much as Althea did now.

"The man who saw you, he said something about 'your old man.' I assume he wasn't talking about your father."

"He was about my age. I would assume he's a friend or acquaintance of Linden's. Someone who has known him a long time, if he knew Heather."

That made sense. "Can Beau keep this picture?"

At Althea's hesitation, Sam added that she was sure he could scan it or make a copy and get the original back to her. Althea said that would be fine.

"There's something else I wanted to ask you," Sam said, "something that came up last night."

A customer walked into the shop, so Sam nodded toward the door. Out on the sidewalk they could talk more privately.

"We came across something in the legal paperwork, a mention that Heather might have gone to Kansas. Does that make sense?"

Althea made a little face, her mouth twisting as she thought. "Not really. We have no relatives there, if that's what you mean. Maybe a friend from her school days? I suppose if she was planning to leave Linden she could have put out some feelers about jobs. It was before the days where most applications are done online . . . but she might have mailed out some resumes or something."

"What type of work was she likely to apply for?"

"Well, she wasn't really qualified for much beyond some basic secretarial skills. She'd married so quickly after high school that she never got a degree. And believe me, she'd never have managed as a housekeeper or nanny." She backtracked a little. "Not that she wasn't a great mother . . . but raising someone's else's children wouldn't have appealed to her. She never could understand what I loved so much about teaching."

"I suppose by now she may have gone back to school and become qualified for nearly anything," Sam said, musing aloud.

"But back then? No, I can't think what would have drawn her specifically to Kansas."

Besides this supposed 'other man.' Neither of them said it.

Sam pocketed the photo, promising to take good care of it, and took Althea's card with her mailing address. She watched Althea get into her car before walking back inside, where she found Becky in a mad search for red sugar.

By the time Beau called, near noon, she was ready for a lunch break. Remembering the photo of Heather Gisner in her pocket, she told him she would come by his office and they could go from there to eat.

"Sure, no problem," Beau said when Sam handed him the wallet-sized picture. "We should enlarge it so we have something to send out to other departments as we make inquiries."

He carried the little photo to one of the deputies, with an aside to Sam that this guy was the best in the office with computers.

"We can't go really large without losing clarity," the man said, "but I'll get you the best image I can. Just take a minute or two."

Sam and Beau stood by and watched the computer do its thing, Heather's face coming up a quarter-inch at a time on the screen in front of the deputy. When the full image was displayed, Sam felt a wave of dizziness. She blinked her eyes. No wonder both Althea and Heather looked familiar to her—this was the woman she'd seen in that eerie vision, the night of the lightning storm.

Chapter 25

Lunch went by in a blur, as Beau talked about how he'd been busy all morning in the office and still hadn't gone by to chat with his retired deputy, Roy Watson. Sam's attention kept wandering to the printout of Heather's photo, trying to recall the dream. It wouldn't come to her. Maybe she needed a little time to let the details come back.

"You okay, darlin'?" Beau asked, giving her an intent look.

His plate was empty and she had only nibbled at her sandwich. She nodded in response to his question and took a huge bite. Ten minutes later, she felt better and had eased his concerns.

"Okay, I'm off to see if I can catch Roy Watson at home." He handed cash to the server, and while they waited for change Sam made a quick decision.

"Can I come along?" It wasn't as if she didn't have plenty of other work pulling for her attention but since he'd brought her this far into the case, she might as well learn some of the answers firsthand.

Roy Watson answered the door in his undershirt and an old pair of sweats. White hair, a lined face gone jowly, a large gut and sloping shoulders. When he saw Beau in uniform he stood a little straighter and invited them into his modest adobe home. He muted a game show on the big-screen TV and excused himself, leaving the visitors to find seats on furniture that hadn't exactly been attractive when purchased, at least thirty years ago. Sam perched at the edge of an overstuffed chair that threatened to swallow her if she leaned back.

"Roy was widowed about a year after he retired," Beau said in a low tone.

The layer of dust on the coffee table, the general clutter in the room, plus the two beer cans beside a sagging vinyl recliner pretty well attested to his bachelorhood.

"Well, sorry, Sheriff," Roy said when he returned, wearing a pair of khakis and a fresh shirt, patting at his hair. "If I'd known you were coming by . . ."

"It's okay," Beau said, introducing Sam. "We were in the neighborhood."

They turned down the offer of something to drink and Roy settled back into his well-loved recliner.

"I suppose you've heard about the recent situation up in Sembramos," Beau said. He sat forward on the old couch, his elbows resting on his knees.

"Yep, yep." Watson nodded. "That went back to the Angela Cayne murder, didn't it?"

"It did. New evidence came out and the verdict was overturned. The state freed both men."

"Those two didn't exactly get a warm welcome back home though, did they?"

"It's a mess," Beau admitted. "I'm having to go back and review the Cayne case, in addition to figuring out who's killed Starkey and Rodarte. Three murders in Taos County is a pretty rare thing."

"Well, seems clear that people up there in Sembramos wouldn't have been happy to see those two come back into their midst, doesn't it? Your problem in those two killings will be to narrow it down—there must be dozens of possibilities."

"The town's been up in arms, that's for sure."

Sam wondered when Beau was going to get down to his questions, but figured maybe this was just two lawmen's way of breaking the ice, easing into the subject.

"I have to admit that I was still pretty new with the department when the original murder happened. The sheriff had me assigned to other things. You remember much about it?"

"Oh, yeah. I worked the case. I mean, up to a point."

From what Beau had said in the past, Sam had a feeling he meant up to the point when the news cameras arrived and the grandstanding sheriff moved to the forefront.

"I worked the crime scene. Sad one, that young woman. She would have been real pretty. But out in the woods like that, rope around her neck—it was bad. Out in the weather for a couple days, animals . . . you know. I had to pull back the draping and ask the father to identify the body, there on the gurney. You never forget a thing like that."

"Jessie Starkey eventually confessed and dragged Lee Rodarte in with him," Beau said. "But do you remember what led you to bring them in, in the first place?"

Roy Watson picked up one of the beer cans, started to raise it, discovered it was empty. "Sheriff Padilla said we'd received an anonymous tip. I remember they'd set up a special hotline, wanted information from anybody who knew anything. As usual, there were a lot of callers, not a lot of solid information. The duty officer took that particular call, if I'm remembering this right, passed it on to the sheriff and we picked up Starkey. In the beginning—the part I was there for—that punk didn't want to admit to anything. But then they brought in a length of rope we'd found in his truck. I can still picture it—yellow nylon. They showed him a picture of the girl with the same kind of rope around her neck. He started to get all confused. I got called away for something else, but next thing I knew everybody was pretty happy that Starkey had confessed. When he named an accomplice, it was the icing on the cake."

"The defense attorney told me the rope was the evidence that got the conviction overturned."

Watson shifted in his chair.

"Do you know something about that?"

"Nothing definite. I do remember there being something about chain of custody on the rope. The length of it found in Starkey's truck was supposed to be tested at the lab and matched to the murder rope, but something . . . I don't remember all the details. Something about it didn't quite jell. I felt like we didn't ask enough questions before sending the evidence off to the prosecutor. Remember old Guy Robertson? Prosecutor for a hundred years? He was the one who tried this case. I recollect there being long meetings over it in Padilla's office, the two of them going over the evidence until they were happy with it."

Beau wondered aloud whether Robertson might remember details and share them.

"Nah. He retired right after this case. Guess it was his chance to go out in a blaze of glory or something. Anyway, he retired, moved to Florida to play golf, died a year later. I tell you, golf is hazardous to your health." He chuckled at his own joke.

Beau asked whether there was anything else Watson might remember about the case, anything that would lead them to find Angela's real killer, but the old deputy shook his head.

"Be glad to call you if I come up with something," he said as they stood up.

Sam thought he looked eager to be somehow back in the game, if he could.

Beau thanked him and they walked out to the cruiser parked at the curb. Sam gulped fresh air; the image of Angela Cayne out in the woods had been a little too vivid.

"So, how could the ropes have gotten mixed up?" she asked as they drove away.

"Hard to say. A lot of mess-ups *could* have happened. What actually *did* happen, we'll probably never know. If you have a minute, let's stop by and talk to Bill Gravitz, the lawyer."

Sam glanced at her watch. She could do this and still get back in time to help Becky figure out the strawberry cupcakes if her assistant hadn't worked it out on her own.

The offices of Tanner, Gravitz & Ortiz seemed fairly quiet and the receptionist got Bill Gravitz on the intercom right away.

"Sheriff." He held out his hand when they entered his private office.

Beau did quick introductions and got right to the point. "Just a little follow-up on the evidence you told me about in the Cayne case. One of the deputies who worked that case said there were some issues with custody of the murder rope, and I remembered you saying the rope was the piece of evidence that got the conviction overturned."

"Yeah, it was. I don't know what all happened within the sheriff's department. But the forensic work on that rope was pathetic. Either no one tested both pieces—the one found on the body and the one found in the suspect's vehicle—or somebody covered up the findings. We contended that the ropes might even have been switched."

Sam gave the lawyer a puzzled look and he turned to her.

"The two ropes didn't come from the same source. They weren't even the same brand. I was shocked to learn that. When Guy Robertson held up that hank of yellow rope in court, then showed the photos of the victim with yellow rope around her neck, he deliberately steered the jury into believing that they were the same."

"But—" Beau nearly spluttered.

"Both ropes were in evidence bags, signed and sealed. We didn't question that, but we should have. I firmly believe that someone tampered with those ropes, making the evidence fit the case they wanted to build. I don't know if it happened within the sheriff's department or at the prosecution level."

It was a serious accusation. But the prosecutor was dead now and the former sheriff serving time.

"At least we were able to have our own tests run and we did prove the innocence of our clients. I'm just sad that it took so many years to work it through the system."

So, if evidence had been tampered with and both men likely to have been responsible were out of the picture, who stood to gain by getting rid of Starkey and Rodarte now? Sam let the thought nag at her until they'd left the lawyer's office. Then she posed it to Beau.

"I'm guessing it would be the person who really killed Angela," she said.

"Unless that person did the smart thing and moved far away from here. Then we've just got a regrettable situation where tempers and hotheads took over."

"One person in this whole scenario who did move far away is Heather Gisner, or Heather Brooks, or whatever she might be calling herself. Do you think she could have been involved?"

He debated the possibility as he pulled into his parking slot at the department offices. "I can't think why. She'd moved away to get out of a bad marriage, not because of a beef with any of our victims—that we know of."

"I can't help but think that she might know something about all this." Sam opened her door. "I don't know . . . I can't think of a real reason she would come back to Sembramos, once Molly was gone. It was just a thought."

Her phone rang just then and she gave him a quick kiss before answering it. Beau walked into the building and Sam started toward her van.

"I haven't received your invoice yet, Ms. Sweet," came the voice of Delbert Crow. Damn. She'd intended to do that two days ago. "And be sure to take down the signage, and you can pick up the sign-in sheets. Leave the lockbox. That will be returned to us after the auction."

Okay, okay. She added another trip to the big white house to her crowded mental list of to-dos.

She walked into the bakery, a hundred things whirling through her mind, to find Becky struggling.

"These don't look right at all," her assistant complained. In front of her on the worktable were a half-dozen red blobs that didn't nearly resemble strawberries. They were more like flat-topped billiard balls. "I can't seem to get them to do what I want."

Sam picked one up and examined it.

"And the customer is supposed to be here in thirty minutes." Becky dropped the information with a large dollop of misery in her voice.

Sam touched the frosting on top of the cupcake that was supposed to be sitting in a nice, high mound. "Your icing is way too soft. Let's stiffen it up with more powdered sugar."

She washed her hands and began to scrape red icing out of the piping bag into a stainless steel mixing bowl. "Grab the portable mixer and the color paste. It may turn too pale once it's got more sugar in it."

She turned to the other side of the room. "Julio, would you mind scraping the wilted frosting off these? Gently."

With the three of them on the job, the new frosting began to take shape and held up well on the test-cupcake Sam made.

"Okay, we only needed a dozen, right? Becky frost, Julio roll the tops in the red sugar. I'll stick on the finishing touches." No leaves or calyxes were in sight, so Sam pulled down a tub of green fondant and began rolling out the flexible sugary dough. She'd gotten one cut to a shape that pleased her when Jen walked into the kitchen.

"Sam?" she whispered. "That young woman is back, the one dressed all in black. She insists on seeing *you*."

Oh, goodie. Zenda, the oddball witch of the west. Could the afternoon get any more complicated?

Evidently so. Her phone rang as she was wiping her hands on a towel—her mother.

Chapter 26

Beau looked up from his desk when he became aware of Rico fidgeting in the doorway.

"Sheriff, sorry. There's trouble in Sembramos again. We just got the call."

"Did the caller say what's going on?" This paperwork backlog would never get finished.

"Not specifically. But they report shots fired."

Great. "Okay, you and Withers head up there. *Please* tell me you have your vests on, and grab extra boxes of ammo, just in case. I'm going to put State Police on alert and I'll be right behind you."

Rico patted the bulky plate under his shirt, then turned to leave.

Beau strode to the dispatcher's office. "The trouble in Sembramos—do you still have the caller on the line?"

"No, sir. The name was Sophie Garcia. She said she was inside the bank. Here's her number."

Beau grabbed the message slip and started dialing his phone as he walked to his SUV. "Sophie, it's Sheriff Cardwell. What's going on there?"

"Lee's cousin Bono and his friends. They showed up again." Her voice had a tremor.

"Someone said there were gunshots."

"Yes, I heard two. I'm at work so I didn't actually see anything, but a customer said there's a bunch of people at the park. I think that's where the sounds came from."

"Okay, thanks. Stay indoors and tell anyone you see to do the same."

"Nathan's at school. I'm worried about him. The kids will be getting out any minute now."

"I'll call and order the school to lock down." He wished he'd put his own vest on before he came out. He could be on the road now. "Sophie? Don't worry. We'll get it under control. Just stay inside."

A young mother, worried for her child at the school so close by. What were the odds she would obey the order and not run right over there?

He keyed his radio as he reached into the back of the SUV for his Kevlar vest. "Wanda, get hold of the Sembramos Elementary School. Tell them to go into lockdown. If there are parents waiting outside to pick up their kids, tell the principal to get them inside the building too. There's trouble in the park, and it's only a half-block away. Without putting them in a panic, try to let them know I want everyone off the streets."

The strap on his vest snagged on his shoulder mike and he cursed at the delay.

"Wanda, after the school, contact State Police. I don't know that we'll need them but put them on alert. Any officers already in the area, I'd like them to be around." At this point, probably the more official presence, the better.

He started his cruiser and sighed as he whipped out of the parking slot. This was not how the rest of the day was supposed to go. Hitting the switch for lights and siren, he cleared the town limits in under five minutes. The rest of the normally thirty-minute drive took about half that and he came upon Sembramos to find two state troopers at the edge of town. He gave them a quick wave and headed toward the park at First and Cottonwood.

Rico's cruiser blocked the intersection, preventing anyone from approaching the park from this direction. When Beau angled his own vehicle in, blocking the side entrance to the school, he saw that Deputy Withers's SUV was parked across Cottonwood Lane, near the space between Sophie Garcia's apartment building and the sad little park. At least a dozen people stood out in the open, mostly male, mostly gathered in two camps that, at a glance, looked like bikers versus plaid-shirted locals. A clump of women and small kids huddled under one of the large cottonwood trees. Joe Starkey's battered pickup truck appeared to have knocked over a gleaming motorcycle. Had this been the trigger?

Helen Starkey saw Beau get out of his vehicle and she hurried over, keeping her hands visible, the mane of gray hair waving, her house dress and sweater-jacket flapping in the stiffening breeze.

"Helen, what happened here?" Beau asked, never taking his eyes off the gathering of men.

"We came for a picnic. Some of my Jessie's friends from Albuquerque drove up and we were just going to use up the leftover food people been bringing, get together for awhile and remember him."

Beau saw a plastic tablecloth on one of the concrete tables, a few six-pack-sized foam coolers sitting around.

"And?" he prompted.

"And these men on motorcycles came roaring up. Starting shouting at us."

Would he bet money that Joe and Bobby Starkey had returned the shouts, insult for insult? Probably.

"Someone said shots were fired." He stared into Helen's eyes.

She lowered hers. "Well, I suppose Bobby let off with some bird shot, just to warn 'em off."

Beau bit back a retort. Apparently, taking Joe Starkey's weapons after the hunting incident wasn't the same as disarming the whole clan.

"Then what?"

"One of them bikers, he pulled a knife and then the rest of 'em got their knives and now it looks like a standoff."

Beau raised his chin toward the motorcycle on the ground. "What about that?"

"Well, Joe, he'd gone home for another, um, cooler, and when he come back this lot was here and he musta come up to a stop too fast."

Beau hated this sort of thing. No one was going to back down and no one would come out the winner.

"Sit over there, Helen, and don't move a muscle," he said, indicating a concrete bench beside the school building.

"But my grandk—"

"Let my men handle it, Helen. I'm serious. You stay here."

He kept his eyes on the two clusters of glaring men while

he reached into his SUV for the bullhorn. He caught Rico's eye and the deputy moved toward him. Radioing Withers to have his weapon ready, he switched on the bullhorn and nearly jumped when his own voice came out louder than expected. He adjusted the volume.

"Okay, guys, we don't want any trouble here," he began. Neither side took an eye off the other. "I want the women and kids safe. None of you guys better make a move. Ladies, get your children, walk over to the edge of the park and get behind my deputy there." He tilted his head toward Withers and the patrol car.

Three women moved, two about Helen Starkey's age, the other barely out of her teens. They herded four kids. Two other women stared at Beau and stepped closer to the men. Somebody always had to make an issue out of everything, he thought. He keyed his mike and told Withers to get the little band over to the schoolhouse, beside Helen. While they moved, he addressed the crowd again.

"Bobby Starkey, let me see that gun."

Bobby raised a .30-06 above his head, but he kept both hands on it.

"Bobby, I need you to put the rifle down. Just set it on the ground and step back."

Bobby looked daggers toward the biker group but didn't move. Joe Starkey started to mouth off but Beau couldn't tell what he was saying.

"Rico," Beau said quietly. "Get on the radio. Tell the state troopers that we need everyone on site. Now."

The park had streets on only two sides; the south and west edges of it just drifted away into open meadowland. He indicated with a few hand signals that the additional cars should secure as much of that space as they could. Thirty seconds later three black-and-whites arrived.

A ripple of nervous glances went through the gathering, and Bobby Starkey laid the weapon on the ground.

"Thank you. Now I want—"

He never got the rest of it out. Two of the bikers charged Joe Starkey, and Beau saw a flash of bright steel. Warlike shouts punctuated the air. Beau gave the order and the officers converged, weapons drawn. Rico ran straight for Bobby Starkey, who was about to grab his rifle again, tackling the taller man and bringing him facedown on the grass. Beau abandoned the bullhorn and covered his deputy until he had handcuffs on Starkey.

When he looked up again, he saw that the state officers had the two knife-wielding bikers down. The rest of the group were backing away with their palms raised. Knives lay all over the ground.

"Man, that bastard beat my cousin—killed him! You can't let him get away with it!" shouted the first of the bikers, shaking his fists even though they were bound together.

"We'll talk to everyone, get this all sorted out, down at the station."

Inwardly, he groaned. It could take forever to get everyone's stories. And he had an awful feeling it would boil down to each side's word against the other. Would they end up with any actual proof?

Chapter 27

Forever turned out to be most of the night. With all the Starkeys and the whole extended Rodarte family, Beau's cramped offices couldn't handle the crowd. They put one from each team into their own interrogation rooms, three of the Rodartes into the department's single holding cell, and hauled the rest of them to the county jail a few blocks away.

As stories were taken and warnings issued about not starting fresh trouble, the list of suspects and witnesses dwindled until finally only Joe Starkey and Bono Rodarte, the cousin who'd yelled out about Starkey's guilt, remained in the interrogation rooms. Helen dozed on a bench in the vestibule, waiting to take her husband home.

"What proof do you have?" Beau asked Bono Rodarte for at least the fourth time. The man had remained steadfast in his claim that Joe Starkey had beat Lee to death.

He stole a glance at his watch and saw that it was after two in the morning. His eyeballs felt raw, the lids lined with sandpaper. At some point Sam had called to see what time he would be home, but he'd had no answer for that. He told her to go home and lock things up tight. He still had no idea how far some of these guys would take their lust for revenge.

Bono pulled off his kerchief and wiped his shaved head with it. "I tell you, man. I just know."

" 'I just know' isn't an answer, Bono. You know I can't take that to court. How am I gonna convict him and make him pay for the crime? I need something for the DA."

Bono twisted the kerchief, playing it into a knotted wad. "Okay, here's the thing. You talked to the bartender—Toby? He told me. Said he heard a ruckus out back and saw Joe kicking a man down on the ground. He knows Joe and Bobby Starkey—they buy beer there all the time. Knows what a temper Joe has. He said he just backed away, didn't want Joe turning on him."

"And why wouldn't he have told me that?" Aside from being intimidated by the Starkeys, himself.

"Hell, man, I don't know! Bring him in, ask him again."

Obstruction of justice—more charges. Beau wished it was like on television where the guy confesses and it's all done in an hour. He blew out a breath.

"Okay, I will. I'll get Toby's statement, again. But until then, you're not leaving here."

"*Man*, what'd I do? I got rights!"

"You pulled a knife on Bobby Starkey. That's a deadly weapon."

Bono sputtered some more. Beau could only hold him

forty-eight hours and nearly twelve of that was gone, but it might be enough time. He called Rico in and told him to put the man into the holding cell.

In interrogation room two, Joe Starkey sat back in his chair, one arm draped casually over the back of it, looking for all the world like a guy who thought he was going home in the next five minutes.

"Got it straightened out yet, Sheriff?" he asked when Beau walked in.

"Almost, I think. Just a phone call or two and a little more detective work. Meanwhile, we're sending you over to County for the night. Judging by his attitude, I don't think it would be a good idea to put you in the same cell here with Bono Rodarte."

"What? You ain't serious, Sheriff. You got no proof whatsoever to hold me!" He started to rise and Beau kept a little distance between them.

"Maybe, maybe not."

Starkey's face went red, his fists clenching. Then he seemed to realize that his temper was showing and he dropped back down. "Whatever," he muttered.

"I'll tell your wife she can go on home. She's been waiting. It's late—maybe I better offer her a ride."

Starkey's eyes widened. Not much, but enough that Beau knew he was on the right track. He called Withers in to cuff Joe Starkey and drive him to his bed for the night. Jail would be Joe's home for the next few thousand nights, if this truly was their killer.

Once he'd seen the prisoner safely out the back door and into Withers's cruiser, Beau went back inside. He found Helen Starkey seated crookedly on a bench in the vestibule, snoring softly with her chin nearly touching her chest.

"Come on, Helen. Let me give you a ride home," he said gently.

She rose compliantly, still half asleep. Too sleepy to remember that she'd driven down here in her own car. Beau didn't remind her.

About five miles outside Sembramos, he woke her again and brought up the subject, the real reason for his offer of the ride.

"Helen, was Joe the one who beat Lee Rodarte? We have a witness."

She had started to deny it but at the mention of the witness, her face crumpled. Tears ran down her cheeks as he brought the car to a stop in front of their still-charred home.

"Tell me about it," he said.

Helen sniffed wetly and rubbed the sleeve of her sweater across her face. "He come home real late. Drunk. That's nothin' new. But when he walked into the bedroom and I smelt the blood, I sat up and turned on the light. His shirt had splatters, his Levis and boots were so messy. I like to have had a fit. He was cussin' about some dog that ran out into the road. Said he stopped to pick it up and toss it aside when a police car came along. He was afraid they'd get him for drunk driving. That'd be his last—he's had some already, and next time it's jail. So he jumped into the truck and hightailed it, said he managed to outrun the cop car."

Beau pictured the beat up truck and wondered at Helen's naiveté.

"He told me we better wash the clothes, in case they'd got his plate number and came around. The dog blood would prove it was him behind the wheel. He said he'd talk to everybody the next day, the family, that is. Tell them to stand by his story that he was home. I don't have to tell you that Bobby and some of the boys also have their problems with DWIs so Joe knew they'd all back him up." She wiped at her face again. "I swear, Sheriff, I believed it. I threw all the clothes in the washer and a whole bunch of soap. But then there was his boots. He scrubbed at 'em with a brush but they didn't look a whole lot better. We went to bed and the next morning when he picked out another pair to wear, I stuck the old boots out in the shed."

Beau's interest perked up. Clothing that had been through the wash cycle might not give up enough evidence for their needs—but the boots!

"Are they still there?" he asked, hardly daring to get his hopes up. Especially in light of the fire and the number of people who'd been around the place.

"Might be, unless Bobby's been out there workin' or somethin'."

Beau's heart sank. Joe and Helen had been staying at Bobby's house since the fire. Helen had to be talking about the other Starkey's house, their washer, their shed. That many people with access to the evidence. He started the cruiser and put it in gear.

"I want you to show me where you put them," he said, making the U-turn that would take them to the other house.

Pulling up in front of the darkened house, he realized it was after three a.m. and they could rightfully be shot for prowling around the property.

"I want you to go in, tell JoNell it's you, that you'll be right back and not to worry." At least Bobby was still safely in a cell.

He pulled out the heavy flashlight that was part of

his standard gear and lit the way up the narrow sidewalk, watching Helen go in. This could be the moment she would betray him and half the clan could come out shooting. He keyed his shoulder mike and gave his dispatcher a quick '20' call with the address.

But he heard Helen call out, saying just the words he'd told her. She came back a moment later and led the way around the side of the house. The battered metal storage building—the kind made from a kit, by the look of it at least twenty years ago—had a rusted hasp but no padlock. Helen opened it and the door screamed open in its track. Thank goodness he'd thought to warn the household. This thing was better than an alarm system.

"Get some light in here, Sheriff," Helen said. "I'm afraid I'll step on some old rusty rake or something."

Sure enough, the place was cluttered with tools that hadn't seen the best of care. Beau shined the light around, holding his breath about whether the boots would be there.

Helen walked right to the spot, reaching beneath the edge of a wooden shelf that had been added as a workbench. She pulled out a pair of steel-toed work boots. Even in the dimness of the shed, Beau recognized blood and tissue on them. He pulled out the plastic bag he'd jammed into his hip pocket and snapped it open with a shake.

"Set them in there," he instructed.

She did, another sob wracking her shoulders as she let go of the boot tops.

"You're doing the right thing," he said. "Go on inside and get some sleep."

Asking the impossible, he knew, but he watched Helen trudge toward the back door, a sad shell of the woman who'd hurried to get her grandchildren to safety only twelve hours ago.

* * *

Beau drove past the turnoff to his place, sorely tempted to stop and try to grab a couple hours' sleep before dawn. But he could feel the adrenaline pumping and knew his eyes wouldn't close, and if they did his mind wouldn't slow down. He had to see this thing through.

Lisa, his technician, wouldn't be in until eight but Beau located her test kit and swabbed a bit of the blood from Joe Starkey's boot. He knew enough about the process to confirm that the faint, light purple band on the plastic test meter meant the blood was human. He picked up the plastic bag and told Rico to get Joe Starkey out of his cell, bring him back to the station and to make sure they were recording what was about to happen.

Looking through the small window into the interrogation room where Joe had been questioned half the night, Beau saw the weariness on Starkey's lined, grizzled face. The nonchalant manner from early evening had given way and the suspect now dozed with his head resting on one arm that sprawled across the table. His eyes flickered open at the sound of the doorknob. When Beau set down the bag containing the boots, mere inches from Starkey's nose, the man came fully awake.

"Recognize those?" Beau asked.

Starkey eyed him warily but didn't say a word.

"It's not dog blood."

Joe couldn't take his eyes off the bag. Clearly, he'd

believed the boots were long gone.

Joe's eyes flashed anger. "I told her—"

"Helen didn't do this, Joe. She only tried to help you. You're the one who did the crime."

"Lee Rodarte killed my son!"

"He didn't. We found no evidence of that, and he had an alibi for that Sunday morning."

"But, he—"

"Lee got sent to prison on your son's testimony. That was unfortunate. Neither of them deserved it. But they got out, and that should have been the end of it. Keeping these grudges alive won't solve anything. Don't you see that?" Beau pointed at the boots. "I've got samples on the way to the state crime lab." Fudging the truth just a little. "I imagine that pretty soon now we'll know that it's Lee Rodarte's blood. Won't we?"

Starkey's jaw went tense.

"I'll have to charge Helen as an accessory," Beau said. "Washing your clothes, hiding the boots."

The man's mouth went tight. "She didn't want to. She got real mad at me. Will she go to jail? She loves those grandkids."

"Depends. Joe, you need to tell me what happened."

"After Jessie's funeral, I couldn't stop thinkin' about how Lee was walkin' around, alive and free." The rest of the story came out in a flood, the microphones and camera getting it all.

When Joe was finished talking, Beau handed him a pad of paper and pen and asked him to write out what had happened the night he waited behind the bar for Lee Rodarte to come out. He walked out of the interrogation room an hour after presenting the boots.

Bobby Starkey jumped up from one of the chairs in the waiting area. Beau had hoped County Jail would hold him until morning, delay this confrontation awhile.

Bobby stood less than a foot from Beau. "Helen tells me you're in there forcing a confession from Joe, just like y'all did from Jessie!"

"Did she tell you that Joe killed Lee Rodarte?"

Bobby apparently thought he could bluff his way through with talk of getting a lawyer and swearing he would take his brother home, right this minute. Beau let him rant for a minute before he drew himself up to his full height and put on his no-nonsense face.

"Joe's not leaving custody, not unless a judge says he can, and I just don't see that happening. I'd suggest you calm down and accept the fact that your brother just confessed." He waved the yellow pad. "Bobby, like it or not, Joe did the crime. This time we have evidence and witnesses."

The younger Starkey brother folded. After a couple minutes of pleading, hoping the system would go easy on Joe, Bobby finally did as Beau suggested and left.

Chapter 28

Sam abruptly woke up at five o'clock, startled to discover that Beau wasn't home yet and she'd slept so soundly she didn't know it. A faint sound downstairs, and she heard his footsteps on the stairs. The bedroom door opened.

"Hey, darlin'," he said when she called his name. "I was trying to be quiet."

She rubbed her eyes. "I just woke up. What took you so long?"

He started talking as he pulled off his shirt and went to the bathroom to pick up his toothbrush. "We still don't know who shot Jessie, and I have a feeling the whole Starkey clan won't entirely calm down until we solve that question, but at least our caseload is now 'one down, two to go'. And me, I'm dead on my feet."

He filled her in on the high points of the night, including

Helen's turning over Joe's boots and the taped confession.

She turned down his side of the bed and told him to sleep as long as he wanted.

Downstairs, she debated going to the bakery but she'd left things in good shape there, with instructions to Julio for the cake orders that would need to be addressed first. By now, he would already be there and most likely would have half the daily breakfast items in the oven. She went to the coat closet, pushed the clothing aside and opened the hidden safe. Her wooden jewelry box seemed a little forlorn when she took it out, and she realized she'd missed seeing and using it every day.

When Zenda the witch had shown up a second time yesterday, she'd made Sam a little nervous at first. But the young woman in her over-done magical ensemble had merely been inquisitive with her questions about the 'artifact'. Apparently Mary told her just enough about it to whet her interest but since Mary knew nothing about the box's actual powers, Zenda really didn't either.

"I did some research on the Internet," Zenda had said. "But the box Mary told me about wasn't really described in any of the writings."

Sam merely shrugged. "I don't know what I can tell you, since I don't have it anymore . . ."

Eventually, Zenda had given up and left, Sam hoped once and for all. Despite the weedy black clothing, at least she hadn't done anything hocus-pocus-like. Sam gave the box a little pat but decided it should go back into its hiding place until she was certain the outside interest had gone away.

Now, she moved quietly around the house, feeding the

dogs and donning her warm jacket to go out and give the horses their buckets of oats, a couple of chores that Beau normally did, but he'd looked so tired, poor thing.

Back inside, she spotted her cell phone on the coffee table, the readout showing that her mother had called once again. She gave a sigh and hit the callback button, beginning the call with reassurances that Beau's department had solved the case and all was well once again in Taos County, skipping over the fact that he hadn't actually said as much.

While Nina Rae basically ignored what Sam had just told her, going on and on about how worried they'd been, Sam neatened the stacks from the case file they'd dismantled. They still hadn't made a lot of progress on finding Angela Cayne's killer and hadn't pieced together how it related to the shooting of Jessie Starkey. Beau had briefly mentioned that he was still holding a Rodarte cousin, and it could turn out that one of them had retaliated against Jessie for the original confession and Lee's prison time. They could still be a long way from knowing all the answers. She thought of Althea Brooks again, the woman who'd lost her niece and didn't even have her sister nearby so the two of them could grieve together. The whole situation was sad.

She took the first pause in her mother's narrative as an opportunity say she needed to go, setting the pages back in place before she went to the kitchen. She'd just begun scouting through the pantry and fridge in search of something to eat when she heard sounds upstairs.

"Honey, you didn't even get two hours' sleep," she said when Beau came down.

His face looked a little haggard and he was still in pajamas, but his eyes were alert.

"I think I catnapped but when I rolled over I was wide awake again. Lots to do today. Once we release the Rodarte cousins, I think I'd better be in Sembramos to make sure things stay calm."

"I fed the dogs and horses. Now let me make you a decent breakfast."

He smiled. "I was kind of hoping for that."

She reached into the fridge but it was obvious she'd missed a vital item. "We're out of eggs. Look, you go ahead and shower and get dressed and I'll run out and get some."

There was a small market at their end of town, pricier than the big stores but closer. She gave Beau a little nudge toward the stairs, then went out to her truck. At the market she picked up a dozen eggs and some fresh spinach. Omelets would be nice.

She walked to the checkout stand—one cashier on duty and a line of five people. At least most of them were like herself, grabbing one or two items early in the day. She joined the lineup and recognized the man in front of her. Linden Gisner.

He said hello, with that expression which says 'you look familiar but I have no idea why.' Sam introduced herself, noting that he was buying Excedrin and margarita mix. By the look of him, he needed the headache cure the most.

"I met your ex-wife's sister the other day," she said. The thought struck her that his friend who had greeted Althea as Heather might have said something to Linden. "Did you know she was in town?"

"Althea? No. Haven't heard from her in years."

Sam remembered that there was no love lost between them.

"She's been hoping to hear from Heather all these years. She had the idea that Heather might have gone to Kansas."

He gave a short chuckle as they moved up one space in the queue. "No idea why she would go there. But I guess it's possible."

Sam chafed. Too bad. He might have given them a lead. "Well, I'm nearly done with your house, just going back today for a couple of last-minute things. It's sure a magnificent place, but did you ever notice cold spots? The wine cellar area always felt very chilly to me."

If she was hoping he would say he'd taken care of the taxes, he didn't. Apparently he didn't give a whit about the house that had once represented so many dreams for him. When a guy was rich enough to build all the big houses he wanted, she supposed he could walk away without regret. He thunked the bottle of margarita mix down onto the conveyor and growled something at the cashier.

Okay, Sam thought. *No sense in small-talk before a man's had his headache drugs.* She waited until he'd finished his purchase before she set her items on the belt.

Back at home, Beau looked ready to start the day, shaved and in a fresh uniform.

"How do you do that?" she teased. "If I'd missed a night's sleep I'd be looking like a hag for days."

He laid places at the kitchen table while she beat the eggs and heated the skillet, telling him of her assignment to go out to the big house and pick up her signs.

"I'm glad this job is done," she said as they sat down with their spinach omelets. "The house is faintly creepy and the guy who owns it is just weird—a super-young girlfriend, and I think they start drinking really early in the day." She related the grocery store encounter.

"That's not the strangest thing you've come across with this job."

True. Most empty houses were just that, empty and a little sad, but Sam had come across worse than construction dust and cold breezes in other places where she'd been required to break in.

Beau ate quickly and poured his coffee into a travel mug. "I should—"

"No need. I'll get the dishes and then I'm on my way too." She gathered things and headed to the kitchen.

Fifteen minutes later she walked out to her truck and in another five was northbound on the familiar road. At the big house, everything appeared normal. She parked, pulled up her yard sign and tossed it into the back of the truck. The sign-in sheet she always left on a kitchen counter was still there; she filled it out before deciding that she really should do one final walk-through, just to be sure Delbert Crow wouldn't have any reason to nitpick her work or delay paying her invoice.

The master suite upstairs looked fine and if no one focused on the window glass, even those would probably pass muster. Down in the great room, same thing—a few bits of leaf debris that she'd probably tracked in herself, but she picked those up and stuffed them into her pockets. When she reached the wine cellar she realized that she'd never cleaned this room much at all.

Without electricity, the dim room didn't look too bad but she really should have at least dusted the wine racks and swept the floor. Back to the truck for a broom, dustpan and cloth, along with her big flashlight. She left the door standing open when she entered the chilly room and used her flashlight to get a sense of the amount of dust. The wooden shelves that formed V-shaped racks for wine were thick with it. She started in, resigned to the extra work, hurrying to get it done quickly.

Top to bottom, left to right—she wiped each compartment, moved to the next. At the far right side, about eye-level, her hand hit the edge and she heard a metallic *snick*. The shelf moved imperceptibly.

Oh, great, I've broken something. She dropped her cloth and gripped the edge of the shelf. Instead of a loose board that needed straightening, she found that the entire shelving unit shifted. One more tug and it came outward, leaving a gap of more than a foot from the wall.

Cold air rushed out of the space. Sam backed away.

What the—

She grabbed her flashlight and turned it on again, aimed it at the black space. A set of concrete steps led downward.

To what, Sam wondered as she squeezed through the opening and aimed the light downward. She'd never come across a basement in a home here, and this one certainly wasn't conveniently located to serve as a rec room. Either the house had been designed with a basement in mind from the start, or the wine shelves had been added later as a means of concealing it. Ten concrete steps ended at a landing and a blank wall. She gingerly took her first couple of steps downward.

At the landing, two more steps were revealed and a small concrete-walled room, about ten feet by ten. She aimed the light all around, probing the corners. No furnishings, no storage boxes. Only one thing—leaning against one corner, resting on its stock, stood a rifle. Okay, this was a bit of overkill for a hidden gun safe.

Goosebumps rose on Sam's arms. The cold? Or the discovery that the only item in this entire house was an expensive rifle with a high-power scope?

There could be a logical explanation but Sam wasn't going to stick around to find out. She pulled out her cell phone to call Beau. He could tell her whether she should touch it or not. Surely the taxation department wouldn't be especially happy when the person who bought this house at auction discovered they'd received a gun as part of the deal.

She looked at the lit readout on her phone. No signal. Okay, she was pretty well surrounded by thick walls. She started back up the steps. She'd just cleared the narrow opening back into the wine room when a shadow crossed the doorway.

Out in the foyer stood Linden Gisner.

Chapter 29

"What the *hell* do you think you're doing?!" he shouted.

"I'm cleaning the house," she stammered, slipping the phone behind her back. "Remember, it's my job?"

But his eyes were focused on the wine rack and the opening beyond.

"You went down there, didn't you?" His eyes grew wilder, his face redder, his voice louder. "You snooped in my private room!"

"I—" She felt the phone buttons with her thumb, praying that the signal had come back. "It doesn't matter, Mr. Gisner. It's still your house until the auction."

"You just had to pry around, didn't you?" Although he'd lowered the volume, the quieter tone was scarier. "You *had* to find what's down there."

He kept stepping toward her. The pieces snapped into place.

"Was that the gun that killed Jessie Starkey?" she asked, edging aside, hoping for a chance at the open door.

Gisner's face looked ready to explode, red and puffy. "The justice system failed to keep him. I had to take care of it."

"But why, if he was innocent? The evidence showed that Jessie and Lee didn't kill Angela. Eventually, everyone in town would have accepted that." Her thumb swept across the phone buttons, pressing the one she hoped was the speed-dial for Beau.

"*She deserved it!*" Gisner shouted. "That little whore!!"

What? Angela?

"She killed my baby!"

The car accident. Another step toward the doorway.

"Angela Cayne teased me for years—showing off that little body, flirting, making me want her. Then she gets in the car, drunk, and has that wreck, and it's my Molly who's gone!"

"Wait—Angie said she wasn't drinking that night but she tested positive . . ."

He stepped closer. Sam edged sideways again.

"So what, if I gave her a little something to relax her? She wore that tight shirt that showed off everything, flashed it in front of me all evening. The girl was hot for me, thought she was in love with me! A little booze, she would have come right in the bedroom with me, once Molly went to sleep."

You were coming on to your daughter's sixteen-year-old friend, gave her liquor, and then blamed her? The man was clearly working outside of reality. But then she remembered Angie's diary, the lovesick notes about an older man. The girl had gotten in way over her head.

"But the girls start laughing and carrying on and decide to go out. In Angela's car." His eyes welled up but his snarl was pure anger.

Two more feet to the door. Gisner kept facing Sam as she'd subtly circled the perimeter of the wine room, his back now almost to the basement opening. She edged again toward the light from the foyer.

"Molly was all I had. She always was. Heather was a user. Married me for my money and then stayed home all day. Never did anything useful."

Except raise a wonderful daughter for you.

"Where did Heather go? She must have told you her plans."

"Oh, I know where she went all right. Straight to *hell!*"

"She's dead?" Sam got a sickening feeling that all the searches for Heather Gisner had come way too late. A flash of the face from her dream—the face that looked so much like her older sister.

Gisner didn't answer her question. With wild eyes, he raved about how all women were users who took men for their money and then acted like sluts. When his gaze traveled to the dark opening where the steps led downward, Sam realized that it would only take him one big leap forward to grab her and throw her down there. Had she connected with Beau's phone yet?

She spun and dashed for the foyer.

But he was quick. By the time she'd cleared the doorway, he'd crossed the wine room and grabbed for her arm.

Impossible to get past him and out the front door. She ran across the great room, hoping she could get the wide doors open before he grabbed her. His heavy breathing was too close behind.

She ran the other direction, holding her phone in front of her as she crossed the big room. The little icon showed that it was searching for a signal. Her feet slithered on the tile floor. Signal—*finally*! She hit Beau's speed-dial once again, kept running.

"Beau, help! Up at the big house! Linden Gisner's chasing me!"

She started up the stairs with Gisner no more than ten feet behind her. She kept repeating her shouts for Beau. No time to raise the phone to her ear and find out whether he'd heard her. The master suite, she realized, offered no protection. The bathroom was one of those open to the rest of the room. There was a door on the toilet cubicle, but did it have a lock? Not worth the risk.

Otherwise, the mezzanine. That would be a sure-death drop to the hard floor of the great room nearly twenty feet below.

Gisner was puffing a bit on the stairs, now only a few feet behind her. Sam spun and raised one leg. Her foot caught him in the forehead, sending him crashing back to the landing. But in the process she nearly lost her own balance. She gripped the uppermost end of the banister and pulled herself back.

He got up and bellowed in anger as he started back up the final seven stairs.

The balcony or the bathroom? Sam had no chance to decide. He was nearly upon her.

Chapter 30

She yanked open the French doors where the master bedroom overlooked the great room. On the driveway below she saw flashing lights. The faint sound of a siren drifted up to her.

"The sheriff's here. You'll never get away," she said, trying to calm Gisner down.

But her voice was anything but normal and the shakiness only seemed to make him bolder. He charged at her and she dashed to the balcony.

"Beau! Upstairs!"

Below, she heard the front door hit the wall as if it had been kicked in.

"Sam! Is he armed?" Beau's shout reassured her.

"No! But I'm right at the edge of the balcony."

Beau stepped into sight in the great room below, his gun

drawn. "Gisner! Back away!"

For a moment the crazed man lowered the arms that had been reaching toward Sam's neck as he charged toward her. He glanced down.

"Or what? You shoot at me, I'll jump and I'll pull her down too."

He was still more than six feet away. Not enough to make certain that he couldn't keep that promise. Sam risked a fast glance toward Beau. Two more patrol cars were coming up the drive.

The next ninety seconds crawled. Faint footsteps sounded downstairs; Sam saw Beau make a couple of subtle signals with his head; she caught the sound of careful steps, saw a flash of khaki uniform. She held Gisner's gaze, distracting him as two deputies eased their way up the stairs, weapons drawn.

"Gisner, give it up," Rico said, his service pistol aimed squarely at the killer's head.

This time, the threat to grab Sam and jump never came. Gisner realized it would be hopeless to try. Rico's gun never wavered. As deputy Withers snapped cuffs around his wrists, Gisner started protesting.

"I want a lawyer! I'm not saying a thing." He kept this up until he was in the backseat of Rico's cruiser. The two cars began their descent toward the highway.

Beau let out a shaky sigh and wiped his forehead. He pulled Sam close to his chest and she felt his heartbeat against her cheek.

"You had me pretty scared there," he finally said. "If he had pulled you over that balcony . . ."

From below, she could see that the balcony depth appeared much narrower than it actually was. It would have seemed to Beau that Gisner could reach her with one step.

"I wouldn't have fired at him anyway," Beau was saying. "Not with you right there."

"At least, with three murders to his credit, he won't be out—I hope—ever."

"Three?"

"He admitted to me that he killed Angela Cayne. The reasons will sicken you. And Jessie Starkey. I'm also pretty sure that he killed his wife and that her body was buried in the woods somewhere around here."

Beau gave her an incredulous look. "I'm glad he admitted it to you—but now that he's screaming 'lawyer' we'll have a hard time building a solid case."

"Come with me. There are some facts he can't argue with." She took Beau's hand and led him to the wine room.

Her flashlight lay on the floor, the beam shining uselessly into a corner. If only she'd had the heavy object with her when Gisner faced her on that balcony. She picked it up and aimed the light around the room. Against the base of the shelving that had slid outward, tiny flecks of yellow showed.

"I never swept or dusted this room. I'd actually forgotten, so I started to do it this morning." She bent down and picked up one of the yellow strands. "I think this might be nylon rope. It looks like it."

"Where Gisner cut a length off a bigger roll of it or something— If this matches the piece that was on Angela's body . . ."

"I have something else to show you downstairs," Sam said, leaving the yellow evidence where it lay.

She and the flashlight led the way downstairs and she sent the beam onto the rifle leaning against the wall in the corner. Beau walked over to it and looked down the barrel without touching the weapon.

"Looks like the right caliber for the Starkey killing. Hopefully, we'll get prints from this and be able to ballistically match it to the bullet. This alone should be enough to lock him up for a long time."

So many unanswered questions, even yet. Gisner must have been keeping close track of Jessie Starkey, in order to track him to the woods that fateful Sunday morning. But when she asked Beau about it, he said it was possible they would never know those types of details now that the man was refusing to talk.

He brought bags from his vehicle and while he gathered the evidence, Sam told him what Gisner had said about his attraction to Angela Cayne and his anger over the accident that had killed Molly. "It fits with some of the things Angie said in her diary, about how after Molly's mother went away her dad starting paying the girls more attention. The man is unbalanced, Beau. You should have seen his face—crazy. He was angry with Angela both for rejecting him sexually— even though in his twisted mind he thought she was coming on to him—and for being responsible for the accident that killed his daughter. Remember how Angie described the Cokes the girls drank that evening as tasting really sweet and like vanilla? I think he slipped liquor into hers. Being inexperienced at drinking she probably didn't know what she was getting."

"It looks as if he harbored that grudge quite awhile. Three years later, he probably went to the Cayne house and found Angie unguarded. He either walked in or she may have let him inside since she knew him, but then resisted when he tried to take her away. That accounts for the disarray at their house, but I'm guessing he brought her here—possibly unconscious—and strangled her."

"What kind of a nutcase are we dealing with?"

"One that, I hope, won't even *think* of trying to use an insanity defense. Even though his behavior back then was definitely crazy, he'd have a hard time substantiating that seven years later."

He bagged as many of the small rope fragments as they could find, and took fingerprints from several places along the railing that led to the hidden basemen—just in case Gisner tried to contend that someone else had discovered the secret place and put the murder weapon there. You never knew what angle rich men and their lawyers would try to work.

"So, are you done here?" Beau asked as Sam locked the door on the big white house for the final time.

"I'm done."

She followed his cruiser back to Taos, where a few hours passed as Sam gave her statement, for the record, about the morning's events and the things Gisner told her. Much as she didn't relish it, she agreed to testify to the whole exchange later in court, if it came to that.

"Now, what about his wife?" Beau said. They sat at his desk, eating sandwiches he'd had brought in from somewhere.

Sam first told him about her vision the night of the lightning storm and how she'd felt there was something very familiar about that unknown face, but that she hadn't made the connection with the likeness of Heather Gisner they'd gotten from her sister's wallet photo.

"In the dream, this terrified woman was backing away,

a look of horror on her face. There was a wooded area behind her, deciduous trees, like the ones that grow along riverbanks." She picked scraps off her bread. "I wish I could describe it better. I woke up immediately after I saw her face."

Beau set his sandwich down and picked up the phone, speaking to someone for a few minutes. He ordered special cadaver dogs and a team trained in looking for old burial sites, explaining that the suspected death had happened at least a dozen years earlier.

Sam found that she was no longer hungry.

Chapter 31

It took four days but the team finally located a set of bones less than a half-mile from the white Gisner house, in a wooded area along the stream running by the magnificent house that had never been a home. The post-mortem revealed the bones to be female and of the same height as Heather. Death had come from violent blows to the head. Althea Brooks came forward to give DNA so that a more certain match could be made.

And so it was that Sam and Beau found themselves standing in the cemetery in Taos, where Heather's remains were being laid to rest beside those of Molly.

"It's so sad they didn't get the chance to know each other better," Sam said. Whenever she thought of herself and Kelly and how close they'd become as adults, it brought tears to know this mother and daughter would never have that. It also reminded her to be more appreciative and to savor the times she and Kelly did have.

Althea Brooks, standing a few feet away, must have had the same thoughts. She'd already broken down when, in a conversation with Sam, she lamented the fact that she hadn't done more for Heather, hadn't remained closer in their adult lives. She could have offered sanctuary, or at least encouragement to the sister who might then have been able to stand up to her psychotic husband and find the nerve to get herself and her daughter out while there was time.

As for the Cayne family, the new discoveries might offer a bit more closure. They might also only reopen the old wounds.

"I'm going to Sembramos before I head home," Althea said as they walked away from the graves. "Sally Cayne and I have been in touch since my last visit. We both feel that Angie and Molly would never have wanted to see the town torn apart the way it's been recently. They were sweet girls, the kind who got along with everyone. They would want to see us all getting along now."

Sam nodded. Small towns themselves were a lot like families. When there was strife, everyone felt it.

"So we've planned a 'peace party.' Everyone in town is invited, so long as they come with a desire for peace."

"I think that's a beautiful idea," Sam said.

"You and Beau are invited too," Althea said. "And if Beau wants to be in uniform, that's fine. Peace, with a peace officer to back it up, you might say? But no lawyers—we don't want anyone later finding themselves being sued for admitting to their guilty feelings." She gave a rueful smile. "We'll be at the town park at two o'clock."

When Sam passed the invitation along to Beau he opted

to remain in the Western-style dark suit he'd worn to the memorial service. She knew the jacket was cut well enough to allow a concealed holster under it. She didn't ask whether he was actually wearing it when they left the house.

The small park was crowded when they arrived; many faces were familiar now, others were not. Bright cloths covered the concrete picnic tables and bowls of homemade food were everywhere. Beau spotted Helen Starkey and Sophie Garcia at one of the tables and offered to formally introduce Sam to the residents she'd mainly known through police files and his stories. They walked over to add her contribution of a chocolate sheet cake to the abundance on the table.

"Helen," Beau said. "How are you?"

The gray-haired woman looked up, her lined face more tired than before. "I'm okay. JoNell is helping a lot. And Bobby says he'll get started soon on fixing up my house."

The fact that she talked in the singular tense made it apparent that she knew, down inside, that Joe wouldn't be coming home for a very long time, if ever. He would remain in custody until his trial, and so much would depend upon whether the jury believed that beating Lee Rodarte was a flash of uncontrolled temper or a premeditated event.

"I'm so sad that it has come to this, so sorry about Heather, shocked by that husband of hers," Helen said. "You meet a newcomer, think you're getting to know them. One thing leading to another, all of us torn apart by it."

Sophie Garcia rounded the table and put an arm around Helen's shoulders. "I know. I know."

Helen pulled a tissue from the pocket of her sweater-jacket and quickly wiped at her eyes. "I said I wouldn't do this today. The party is about making friends, getting ourselves over the hurt."

Sally Cayne stepped over in time to hear Helen's words. "Sometimes, friends cry together, Helen. As long as we're not judging each other, then sharing our sorrows will bring us all back together."

Sally set a big bowl of potato salad on the food table, then took Sophie's hand. "I want you to introduce me to Lee's cousin over there."

Only one of the Rodarte cousins had come. It would take awhile for some of the others to become friendly with the people of Sembramos; luckily most of the other cousins didn't live in town but in other parts of the county.

When they were alone again, Beau turned to Helen Starkey. "I'm going to recommend leniency for you when your case comes up. Obstruction of justice is a charge that can go many ways, depending on the amount of involvement. Since you readily admitted your part and you led me to the crucial evidence, I'll tell the court that you helped us tremendously with our case."

Helen nodded, dabbed with the tissue again. When Althea Brooks approached, the tissue got tucked back into the pocket and the two women smiled at each other.

Beau and Sam left them alone, wandering among other clusters of people who were chatting quietly. As they walked up to the group that included Sally Cayne and Sophie Garcia, Sally noticed a group of Starkey men hanging toward the edge of the park, staying to themselves.

"Come on, Sam, let's see if we can get these guys started eating!" She picked up a plate of fried chicken and Sam grabbed some paper napkins.

"There's lots more over there," Sally said to Bobby as he took a drumstick from the platter. "Make yourself a plate, load up on all the goodies."

One by one they filtered toward the table, and Sam saw JoNell's husband talking to Lee Rodarte's cousin as they both piled food on their plates. Maybe this would work out after all. She noticed a woman, middle aged with perfectly coiffed hair, speaking with the two men.

"The mayor, Consuelo Brown," Beau said when she asked. "I don't think she ever thought her job would include near-riot control, like we had that one night. I notice she looks a lot happier today."

Yes, Sam thought, surely being mayor of a tiny town like this more commonly involved socials in the park than the type of strife her small community had endured.

"Now this is more like we used to be," Althea Brooks said, standing beside Sam. "When Heather and I were kids here, there were lots of community events. I remember running around, playing tag, like that bunch of kids over there. The moms would bring food, just like today."

Sam noticed that little Nathan Garcia hung back until Sophie came over and knelt beside him, saying something quietly. Poor kid, Sam thought, he'd barely begun to know his father and now had lost him. No wonder he looked a little stunned. He tagged along behind Sophie until she gave him a chocolate cupcake. Then his smile brightened. He turned to watch the other kids while he ate it. Little steps. He would eventually be fine.

"It's amazing how one man can have such an effect," Althea was saying. "Linden Gisner, coming in here, a newcomer when he married Heather, thinking that he was somehow better than everyone else when he started making all that money with his big real estate deals."

Consuelo Brown had wandered by and joined them.

"It seems like things changed when he began building that mansion. Like he'd had enough of us and didn't want to be part of the town anymore."

"It *was* sort of like drawing a line, wasn't it?" Althea said. "Heather felt it, wanted to leave him."

Everyone thought she had found the fortitude to go, never realizing what had really happened to her. The group got quiet for a long moment.

"Linden Gisner is undergoing psychiatric evaluation now," Beau said. "He has a 'charmer' personality that he uses to bring women into his life, but he can turn on a dime and become abusive in an instant. It's the radical change, from super friendly to wildly psychotic that keeps people off balance. Heather succumbed to it; Angela might have. Unfortunately, the outcome wasn't good for either of them."

Sam thought of the young woman who'd been living with Gisner in recent times, Amber. She had to wonder if reopening Angela Cayne's case and capturing Linden Gisner might have saved Amber's life.

"We're past that now," said Consuelo Brown. "I'm so happy to see everyone moving on. Payback is never as sweet as we might think."

Althea gave a contented nod.

Sam doubted that Althea had come to town with the idea of acting as peacemaker, but it had worked out that way.

Sam glimpsed a familiar face, a woman taking a bite of the chocolate cake from Sweet's Sweets. She walked over to say hello, briefly wondering whether she should say something more about the wooden box. She'd not gotten the hoped-for results in finding more information about it, but for now maybe that was the way things were meant to be.

"Mary, hello. Are you from Sembramos?"

The witch was dressed in a similar manner as at their first meeting—soft pastels, sandals and her long gray hair flowing freely.

"My husband is. He grew up here, and we live just a little way out of town now, between here and Taos." She lifted her paper plate. "This cake is amazing. Such a richness to the chocolate."

Who knew a witch could also be a chocoholic?

"Listen, Sam, I was wondering if I might ask a favor? This thought just came to me."

Sam felt her smile freeze in place. If this was about sending a few more fledgling witches her way . . .

"My neighbor is on a Chamber of Commerce committee that wants to organize a chocolate festival in Taos. She's asked me to help with it but, other than loving to eat it, I know exactly nothing about baking it or shaping it or, really, anything. Would you consider talking to her about the festival idea?"

Without really waiting for an answer, Mary reached into a tiny purse that hung by a long strap across her shoulder. She found a scrap of paper and jotted a number on it, pressing it into Sam's hand.

"I know your reputation for great chocolates, Sam. I know this will be a wonderful match. She's elderly—I have a feeling she would have known your Bertha Martinez. Call her?"

Sam started to ask about Bertha and this neighbor, but Mary had turned away and Sam's attention was diverted by the happy shouts of children who were racing back and forth across the grass, a seemingly boundless source of energy. One day, some scientist would become rich if he could figure out a way to charge batteries or run automobiles from that power.

"Sam?" Althea Brooks was back at her side. "I'm leaving now. It's a long drive. I'm glad everyone seems to be getting along again."

"Thanks to you." Sam gave Althea a hug and watched her walk to her car.

Sometimes, all it took was one person. Big changes come from small acts, Sam realized, and the caring concern of this one woman had helped dissolve years of hurt and resentment and pain. There would still be trials; old hurts could flare again. A sunny afternoon in April wouldn't fix the world . . . but wouldn't it be wonderful if it could.

Books by Connie Shelton

THE CHARLIE PARKER MYSTERY SERIES

Deadly Gamble
Vacations Can Be Murder
Partnerships Can Be Murder
Small Towns Can Be Murder
Memories Can Be Murder
Honeymoons Can Be Murder
Reunions Can Be Murder
Competition Can Be Murder
Balloons Can Be Murder
Obsessions Can Be Murder
Gossip Can Be Murder
Stardom Can Be Murder
Phantoms Can Be Murder
Buried Secrets Can Be Murder

Holidays Can Be Murder - a Christmas novella

THE SAMANTHA SWEET SERIES

Sweet Masterpiece
Sweet's Sweets
Sweet Holidays
Sweet Hearts
Bitter Sweet
Sweets Galore
Sweets Begorra
Sweet Payback

Connie Shelton is the #1 best-selling author of the Charlie Parker mysteries and the Samantha Sweet mysteries. She has won awards for her essays and was a contributor to *Chicken Soup for the Writer's Soul*. She and her husband live in northern New Mexico.

For the latest news on Connie's books, announcements of new releases, and a chance to win great prizes, subscribe to her monthly email newsletter at connieshelton.com

1 — 1
2 — 2
3 — 2
3 — 1.5

27204057R00167

Made in the USA
Charleston, SC
05 March 2014